THE TRUTH SPINNER

THE COMPLETE ADVENTURES OF CASTOR JENKINS

THE TRUTH SPINNER

THE COMPLETE ADVENTURES OF CASTOR JENKINS

BY

RHYS HUGHES

WILDSIDE PRESS

THE TRUTH SPINNER

Published by Wildside Press LLC.
www.wildsidebooks.com

This book
is dedicated to:

All Short and Medium Tellers of Tall Tales

& also to:

Paul Battenbough

CONTENTS

1: THE MÜNCHAUSEN OF PORTHCAWL

The Welsh have a reputation for constantly telling fibs, but in fact they only tell fibs when they speak, never at any other time. So it can be honestly averred that the aforementioned reputation is exaggerated. And if you believe that you'll believe anything. Nonetheless it's true. The worst kind of fib is the true one, especially if it's true only because the teller is unaware of its truth; the second worst kind is the one where both fibber and believer are in collusion. That kind has a name. Fiction.

CASTOR ON TROUBLED WATERS

He's almost fifty years of age, Castor Jenkins is, which for a stereotypical Welshman must be reckoned venerable, if not ancient. Not that he takes kindly to being considered a stereotype. He likes to point out that real Welshmen *don't* live exclusively on a diet of beer and chips, nor do they avoid exercise, work and responsibility every waking minute of the day; the fact he does those things is a mark of his uniqueness and it's just a coincidence that the cliché and his individualism are the same.

But in fact there's some dispute about his true age, and it's possible he might be twice as old as he says, for something incredible happened one day that confused the issue. He was sitting in his favourite pub with his best friends, Paddy Deluxe and Frothing Harris, getting ready to play cards and win heavily, as always, when a disagreement about the integrity of past games threatened to spoil the evening. Paddy started it with a complaint about the physical condition of Castor's cards. His argument ran as follows:

"The state of your deck is abysmal, truly it is, and you might as well be playing with marked cards; for all the different beer stains on the backs, not to mention chip fat drippings, surely form patterns recognisable to you but not to us, and so allow you to know what's coming next."

"In other words, to cheat," added Frothing Harris.

Castor Jenkins announced that he resented the accusation, but his friends continued to grumble and the fuss gained momentum and became an unbreakable refusal to play even a single round unless they used the brand new pack, fresh and unopened, that Paddy had thoughtfully brought with him. And there was talk of reimbursement for previous losses, and hints of compensation on top of that, and finally Castor was forced to back down and agree that the beer and chip stains *might* be considered to be arranged in a suspicious manner.

They played with the new pack and Castor lost every game and he soon found himself owing a sum in the region of £100 to both of them. Unable to settle up on the spot, he offered to go out and find a cash machine and return with the money as quickly as possible. His friends nodded.

"That's a reasonable suggestion," they said.

"I'll be back in ten minutes," Castor declared.

He stood and walked out and they watched him with triumph in their eyes; but it was the sort of triumph that a fish feels when it bites a worm on a hook, and so their eyes glittered sickly, waiting to see what trick was in store, for they couldn't imagine Castor would do exactly what he promised without some effort at regaining the upper hand. Ten minutes passed but he didn't appear. An attempt to contact him on his mobile phone proved futile. Paddy rubbed his nose and Harris scratched his chin, but not in that order.

An hour later Castor returned and he was breathing hard and he staggered around the room before returning to his place at the table and sitting down, still panting and mumbling to himself in a language that was either Spanish or Arabic, Paddy and Harris couldn't agree on that, before shuddering and licking his lips and tugging at his earlobes. They gazed at him in silence and he slowly regained his composure and addressed them directly. He said:

"You won't believe what has just happened to me!"

"Tell us," they replied.

"Very well," he said slowly, "but I need a drink to settle my nerves first. You don't mind if I take a sip of your beer? That's better. And yours as well? Sure, a massive gulp isn't the same as a sip, but listen carefully: I was kidnapped! I know it sounds ridiculous but it's true nonetheless. Shortly after I left you, while walking along the esplanade, I noticed a strange vessel anchored offshore, an old fashioned galleon. Then a boat was lowered from it and began rowing closer and I soon realised there was something unusual about it."

"How unusual?" asked Paddy.

Castor lowered his voice to a whisper. "It was crewed by men dressed like pirates, with black breeches and billowing white shirts, spotted scarves tied around their heads, eye-patches and bristling beards, and many waved cutlasses in the air or carried knives between their teeth; and I imagined that a film was being made, even though I couldn't see a director or any cameras. I wanted to stay and watch, but my first duty was to get your money and so I hurried onwards."

"Very considerate of you," observed Harris.

Castor nodded. "I reached the cash machine, inserted my card, punched in my number and withdrew the crisp notes, but as soon as the money was in my hand I felt myself being lifted up and carried away. A mob of howling ruffians filled the street. They took the cash machine as well, blowing it out of the wall with gunpowder. That explosion disordered my senses, I can tell you! I was so stunned I never properly realised what was going on until it was too late. Everywhere there was chaos, broken bottles on the road, the overpowering smell of rum. When the clouds of smoke cleared I saw that they had bundled me aboard the boat.

"It was at this point I understood that these men were not actors but real pirates. As the history books tell us, pirates don't just attack other ships, they also raid coastal towns, looting and sacking. Porthcawl is a coastal town and ripe for such unwanted attentions. These pirates had obviously decided to make a rapid strike, grabbing what they could and departing before the police arrived. I imagine they were disappointed with their haul, just one cash machine and a single captive, namely myself."

"Not much of a profit there," agreed Paddy and Harris.

"True," sighed Castor, "but perhaps they needed the practice. Anyway I was taken to the galleon and locked inside a narrow cell where I lay in mouldy darkness, my mind filled with thoughts of what pirates traditionally do to prisoners; but after calming down I stopped believing I was destined to walk the plank. If they wanted me dead they would have saved a lot of effort by cutting my throat at the cash machine. So it grew increasingly likely they intended to sell me into slavery. I felt terrible, knowing that you were sitting here waiting for your money, but I had no way of getting a message to you.

"The days passed slowly, and I was sick during a horrid storm, and they gave me nothing to eat and drink but bread and water. When I asked for proper nourishment they laughed in a piratical fashion and treated all my other requests with similar contempt. I began to rot in that prison, but one morning a man more distinguished than the others opened the door and let me out. He was Captain Ribs, he announced, the leader of the pirates, and he had a proposal for me. He led me to his cabin and asked me to sit down and offered the chips and beer I craved. When I was full, he scrutinised me closely and said:

"'We're a man short and to run the ship with maximum efficiency I need to find a replacement. You're the only candidate for the position and so I want to offer you the job. If you don't want it and would prefer the life of a slave in the hellish butter mines of Kowpoo, I'll understand.'

"'I need to think about it. What exactly is the job?'

"'Lookout. Our last lookout fell to his death last night, just like his predecessor, and the lookout before him, not to mention the lookout before *him*, and so on. Without a lookout we don't know where we're going and won't recognise it when we get there, so it's a very important post carrying a great deal of responsibility.'

"I was about to declare that I wanted nothing to do with responsibility of any kind but then it occurred to me that as a member of the ship's crew I stood a better chance of escaping and paying you the money I owed than if I ended up working in the butter mines of Kowpoo. So I accepted. Captain Ribs was delighted and explained my new duties. I had to climb the tallest mast to the crow's nest and call down whenever I saw anything noteworthy. He gave me a comprehensive list of things considered 'noteworthy' and it consisted of the following: land, storms, whirlpools, treasure ships, rival pirates, reefs, cannibals, whales, giant squid, mermaids, lifeboats, seductive cloud formations, alterations in the shape, colour or tensile strength of the horizon line.

"My job began immediately and I climbed the rigging with a queasy stomach. Higher and higher went I, my fingers rubbed raw on the rough cords, my feet slipping, the sweat pouring off my brow in droplets as thick and yellow as chip oil, but determined to reach the top without admitting defeat. I got there safely, in case you're wondering! The crow's nest was hardly bigger or more secure than a large wok with slippery sides and the precariousness of my position generated little or no contentment in my heart. I wondered how long it would be before I too fell to my doom. Fortunately the sea was calm at this particular time and I was able to discharge my duties to a satisfactory degree. Whenever I spied an object on the surface of the ocean I checked the list to see if it merited a shout. 'Large floating log' did not, but 'Large floating log with a man sitting on it' did. And so it went."

Paddy interrupted the story by asking, "How did you sleep?"

"Badly is the honest answer," sighed Castor, "but I was able to curl myself into a ball tight enough to fit the crow's nest. It was cold at night, even in the tropics, maybe because I was so high up. Don't ask how food and drink was delivered to me: if you do that, I'll also have to explain how I relieved myself! While my fellow pirates far below gorged themselves on watermelon and toast spread with butter from Kowpoo, and drank rum and lime juice, I went largely without, but there were occasions when I was allowed to descend. Each time we docked at a port, I had permission to go ashore with the rest of the crew."

"How many ports did you visit?" wondered Harris.

"Too many to remember! We sailed around the world several times and stopped off in Bombay, Rangoon, Surabaya, Shanghai, Osaka, Lima, Montevideo, Luanda and the strange seaside towns that dot the coasts of Lowest Bo, Zing and the Mediocre Utopia, among others. Once we even docked at Tenby in Wales and I saw a chance to jump ship and make my way back to Porthcawl on a bus, with a change at Swansea, but Captain Ribs detained me and so the opportunity was lost. He had something important to say and I had no choice but to let him say it.

"'Look here, Master Jenkins,' he began, 'of all the lookouts I've ever employed you are the best by far. You always shout out at the earliest moment, you never make mistakes and you haven't yet fallen to your death. You are so perfect I wish I could keep you forever! Promise me that if you ever marry and have a son, you'll name him after yourself and bring him up to be exactly like you in every way. That's how highly I regard you. I hope your friends appreciate you?'

"'That they do,' I assured him.

"And so I remained in the service of Captain Ribs and my work got harder rather than easier. He was driven by some unspecified urge, a quest he was unable to articulate even to himself; and I could never work out if his ultimate goal was a distant country, a horde of treasure, international notoriety or some way of forgetting his past. Whatever it was that motivated him also drew us along, in his spiritual wake, as it were, until we became like sacrificial victims who desire our own demise. I recall with a shiver certain adventures in abandoned temples on overgrown islands, engagements with intelligent apes armed with blowpipes, races against ghost ships...

"We committed our fair share of atrocities. We were pirates, never forget that, and I feel terrible shame at some of the things we did. We pillaged the coastal settlements of a dozen nations. Once we discovered the factory where calendars are made, there's only one in the whole world, and sabotaged the delicate machinery by throwing a spanner into the works, a spatula actually. Another time we sailed the wrong way up a river during a charity raft race, scattering the entrants like the smug middle class skittles they were. It was a violent career and I risked a horrid injury every single working day.

"On one occasion we sailed up a narrow channel between two obstacles that struck terror into my heart. The first was a vast iceberg, the second was a smoking volcano newly arisen from the sea. The waters of the channel churned awfully and our vessel swayed from side to side, almost capsizing, and I felt like the weight at the end of a metronome pendulum. As we passed the crater of the volcano, the top of the mast and the crow's nest dipped into the sulphurous flames. Contact lasted only an instant but it was long enough for my clothes to burst into fire. Fortunately the mast then dipped the other way and quenched me on the surface of the iceberg with a gigantic hiss. Such extreme occurrences were quite commonplace!

"This life might have gone on forever, or at least until Captain Ribs led us to our deaths, but one cloudy morning I had an encounter that changed everything. The clouds were thick but very low, practically resting on the surface of the sea, but the top of my mast protruded above them. I was able to look out across a vast fluffy expanse and the effect was very soothing. To my astonishment I noticed a man standing on the clouds far away, but this was just an optical illusion. As he approached it became obvious he was a lookout like me, balanced in a crow's nest at the top of a tall mast. We waved to each other. The situation was very dreamy: we seemed to float like angels, the ships below us completely forgotten, and the serenity of the scene distracted us from performing our duties. Suddenly I realised we were on a collision course!

"It was too late to shout down a warning. The snapping of wood and popping of nails was background music to my prolonged descent into the ocean. I was flung out of my nest far into the mass of clouds and through them into the cold salty water. I thrashed and gasped, my senses reeling, my eyes stinging, and by sheer luck my flailing hands grasped a barrel that had floated free from one of the holds. I hauled myself up, sat astride it and found myself blinking into the face of a beautiful woman. We were the only survivors and she permitted me to share her barrel in return for keeping her company. I entertained her as best as I could by telling her strange but true tales until we were cast ashore on a desert island."

"What tales did you choose?" asked Paddy Deluxe.

Castor Jenkins sniffed. "I can't rightly recall. I think that my encounter with the King of the bicycle-centaurs was one. I mended his puncture in return for my life, as it happened. Anyway, we lived on the desert island, the woman and I, in a sort of paradisal harmony, eating fruit, walking on the beach at night and laughing at the stars. For some reason she found the constellations funny, especially Gemini and Cassiopeia, who knows why? Her name was Charlotte Gallon and she was the captain of the other ship, also a pirate vessel. We became intimate and our first child was born less than a year after our shipwreck. I kept my promise to Captain Ribs and named the boy Castor.

"Sometimes the tide brought useful objects to us. Flotsam and jetsam included tennis rackets, old shoes, waterlogged books, rusty batteries, broken stools and a fondue set. Only one empty bottle was ever washed up on our sands, oddly enough, and only one pencil. I tore one of the blank pages out of one of the books, dried it in the sun and composed a message on it. This was our only chance at contacting the outside world but instead of writing HELP and appealing for rescue I decided to contact my best friends, Paddy Deluxe and Frothing Harris, because I respected them so much; and I did this even though Charlotte told me it was a waste. I hurled the bottle into the sea and watched it bob along."

"What did you write?" cried Frothing Harris.

"I merely repeated what Captain Ribs had said to me. I told my two friends how highly I valued them, went into detail about what superb fellows they were, and urged them to name their own sons after themselves, if they ever had any, and to bring them up to be *exactly* like their fathers. That message seemed more important to me than any request to be picked up by a passing ship and delivered safely back into the comforting lap of civilisation."

"We never received the bottle," said Paddy Deluxe.

"Yes you did," stated Castor.

"I assure you we didn't. No message at all!"

Castor pursed his lips. "The ocean is wide and one might think that messages in bottles just drift around forever, but in fact there's an organised system at work to ensure they reach the persons they are intended for. A secret place exists where every bottle with a message is kept until it can be delivered properly. I learned this from a fellow who interviewed me after I escaped the island; he calls himself the Postmodern Mariner, an investigative journalist who specialises in the mysteries and dramas of the sea. Anyway, to return to the point, my two best friends *did* receive my message, and they acted upon it too, which is how we are able to have this conversation right now.

"Confused, are you? Let me explain that I dwelled with Charlotte and my son on that island for years and years. An oil tanker eventually picked us up. I worked our passage back to the mainland but I never returned to Wales. I married Charlotte and we lived in relative happiness, with only one argument, until I was accidentally killed by a thrown saucepan, which is how that argument ended. After my funeral, my son went on a touching quest. I had already told him everything and he planned to seek out my two dear friends and settle my debts with them. He searched the pubs of Porthcawl for a long time.

"Finally he entered the pub where that card game had taken place all those decades previously. And here I am! Yes, I'm not the first Castor Jenkins but the second, his son, grown to the precise age my father was when he left to use the cash machine. Remember that I was brought up to exactly resemble him in every way!"

"You *are* him!" blurted Paddy.

"You left one hour ago, not fifty years," added Harris.

Castor sadly shook his head. "I have some sad news. Paddy Deluxe and Frothing Harris are dead and buried. They were your fathers and they raised you in the way my message urged them to do, with the same names and identical thought processes. That's the reason for your identity confusion. It was my father who left this pub to obtain money for your fathers, but it is the son who returns to pay the sons. The time difference also explains why you'll find no evidence of a pirate raid when you walk home tonight: that incident happened a generation ago and the damage has long since been repaired. Now to more pressing matters! How much was owed in total?"

"One hundred pounds," answered Paddy and Harris together.

"Would you like that sum in today's money?"

"Of course!" came the roar.

Castor reached into his pocket and withdrew a single coin, a tarnished penny, which he slapped down on the table. "There you go. That penny was in my father's possession during the original card game. Because of inflation over half a century it is worth £100 *in today's money.*"

Paddy Deluxe and Frothing Harris were speechless.

"I'm glad everything is settled," said Castor. "By the way, the machinery in the calendar factory was never fixed and the wrong year has been printed on every calendar since. Curious, don't you think? Don't trust dates from now on, whatever you do. I'm off to the bar for a drink. Then we can toast our ancestors. Come now, my friends, restrain yourselves! Are we not gentlemen? Fighting over a penny is most undignified!"

CANIS RAVER

Do glove puppets ever go travelling on their own? Castor Jenkins is probably the only person able to answer this question convincingly. Nobody else seems to know for sure. Maybe somewhere among the numerous pubs, bars and clubs of the world is another man who can give a straight answer without too looking nervous about it. Maybe not.

But it's no good talking about Kelvin as if he's any old glove puppet. The moment you hear his story you'll know he's different – and even though you have never seen him, you'll still feel certain there will be an instant connection if you ever accidentally meet up.

But anyway… Glove puppets and travel…

Can they do it at all? Real travelling, that is, not merely being carried from one place to another in a bag or a pocket, but setting off with their own bags and pockets and passports and whatever else they need, or prefer, to go with: maybe a toy hand or a book of international gestures or a wad of monopoly money or a bottle of gin for the cold lonely times.

Castor has travelled a fair bit himself but never as far as Kelvin is rumoured to have ventured. Kelvin was sighted all over South East Asia in many different locations – cities, the jungle, on the coast, up mountains, in the ocean. He didn't really have a favourite haunt and was happy to drift along and try anything new, but please don't think he was reckless.

Castor explains his involvement with Kelvin like this:

* * * *

It was Catherine who first tried to convince me that glove puppets are capable of going on adventures without needing an owner. I was staying in her house in Swansea at the time and I spent every day sprawled on her sofa before she came back from work, at which point I usually roused myself enough to engage her in conversation. During the course of my stay, we discussed some pretty profound things and she told me stuff about her adventures with Kelvin in Malaysia. Then she turned to me with a question.

"Have you heard of the writer Flann O'Brien?"

"You gave me his books, I think."

"So I did. Do you remember his theory about how men and bicycles are in danger of exchanging identities?"

"I think I've forgotten," I confessed.

"When a bicycle is ridden down a bumpy road, the vibrations can cause an interchange of molecules between man and machine. The damage is cumulative and in extreme cases the bicycle takes on human characteristics and the human starts adopting the ways of a bicycle. This phenomenon is creating all sort of havoc in Ireland right now."

I was sceptical. "Is that so?"

She brushed her fair hair back over her ears. "Many of the people I met in Kilkenny looked like they needed handlebars growing out of their shoulders to keep them steady."

"But how does this apply to Kelvin?"

"Don't you see? He's a glove puppet and so probably has had lots of hands up him – no crude jokes if you please! – and those hands moved around inside to make it seem he was alive."

"I still don't comprehend what you're getting at."

"If we accept the molecule interchange theory, he must have picked up traces of all the people who ever controlled him, absorbed some of their personalities, mannerisms, even their essential life force!"

"We'd have to track down every one of his previous owners to work out his average personality," I speculated.

Catherine pouted. "Yes and no. Kelvin has his own *sense of self* that is unique and greater than the sum of its parts. I don't accept he's just an amalgam of his operators. Besides I don't know exactly how many people have ever played with him in that way."

"You might be the only one?" I ventured.

She shook her head. "There were others, but I can't specify an exact number. Maybe two or three, maybe a hundred."

"Do you believe he's genuinely alive?"

Catherine shrugged. "I don't know, but he's certainly capable of sentient thought and behaviour. That's why he's so independent and hates being stuck in the house all day."

"Where is he now?" I wondered.

"Travelling again. Who knows where? He's probably taking part in a week long rave on some exotic beach. That's his scene sure enough, mixing it up with the other alternative puppets."

"Surely he's too floppy for that?" I objected.

"I know what you're thinking – my hand played the part of Kelvin's skeleton and he doesn't have a spine of his own or any other supporting bones. That fact never bothered him when he was on his own. Maybe he has a way of stiffening up we can't imagine. Or perhaps he maintains some sort of connection with the shape my hand made when it was up him."

"Like an electromagnetic imprint?"

"Yes and my wrist is aching right now, which suggests he has been dancing for several days already at that rave."

"Do you miss him? Would you like to see him again?"

"Yes, but I can't imagine he'll ever return to Wales of his own free will. It's too grey here, too prosaic. Searching for him would take too long. He could be in Brazil or Goa or Madagascar..."

I pondered this problem deeply. I tried to imagine a glove puppet, any glove puppet, dancing without an operator — handless — around a huge fire on a beach, adorned with tribal jewellery and henna markings, listening to pulsating music under the shimmering stars. It was not an unpleasing image but was it feasible? Personally I think they can do it, perhaps not without difficulties that humans don't have, but with certain advantages too. Humans have to re-hydrate after so many hours. Puppets don't.

I thought I knew a way to entice Kelvin back, but before I could propose my idea, Catherine told me this story:

"I once heard about a glove puppet, a panda, caught trying to smuggle drugs across the border, don't know what drugs, which border or even what type of panda – giant or red – but that's not important. Anyway it was arrested and hauled off to an interrogation room but it wasn't forthcoming with its answers, sitting there in silence almost as if dead. Buckets of cold water and slaps had no effect; it just wouldn't move or talk, so one of the officers insisted on doing a body search. That was a mistake because the moment he thrust his hand inside it to feel around for the contraband, the panda came alive again – which is natural for glove puppets – and it began winking and pointing at the officer as if he was a secret partner in the crime."

"It framed the officer! How cunning!"

Catherine nodded. "Don't trust pandas too much, they're about as reliable as owls. You look distracted, what's up?"

"It has just occurred to me that if we change the character of Swansea – turn it into an exotic place – more exotic than Goa or anywhere else – into *the* most exotic place in the world, then Kelvin might find himself drawn here regardless of the grey skies and drizzle of Wales."

"A good idea, but how can it be implemented?"

"Let's put our heads together," I said.

* * * *

Castor Jenkins will usually pause at this point until someone buys him another drink. Whether he gets it or not, and he mostly does, he'll gaze for a long time out of the window at the Porthcawl seafront, the rocks and the sea. This sea is actually the estuary of the broad River Severn and on the far side, the cliffs of Exmoor loom impressively. To the west are visible the lights of Swansea, that ugly-lovely, beery-leery, sentiment draped town. If cities are female, Swansea likes to rouge its nipples with lipstick.

Unluckily for metaphors, extended or otherwise, cities don't have a gender, that convention is just wishful thinking.

"So what happened?" Frothing Harris will ask.

"Did you come up with a plan?" Paddy Deluxe might add.

Castor Jenkins never wipes his nose on a tissue if he can help it. The sleeve is the way he does it every time.

"Yes, but we had to change everything, every last cultural atom of Swansea, or at least we thought we did. Turned out that once the chain reaction began, it did the job itself. The music, the food, the ambience: all were transformed in a way staggering to behold. We ended up with a place resembling a cross between Havana, Atlantis and Lwachtrop!"

"Where the heck is Lwachtrop?"

"A town on a distant planet... Orange skies... None of us have been there yet, but you'll understand one day. Now I'm getting ahead of myself, a horrid habit! I'll quickly explain what happened... Without Catherine's organisational skills I don't think it could have worked. First we interfered with the local music scene. Have you been to any gigs in Swansea?"

"Never. Oh wait! I went to see the progressive combo King Crimson at the Top Rank on December 6th, 1972."

"We're getting old, my friend... Anyway, the scene is dominated these days by folk duos and soft rock bands, most of them boring beyond belief. There are many good musicians[1], but generally the standard is bland, the tempos are slow, the guitarists tend to noodle, the vocalists often warble in nasal fashion, not the sort of music one might expect to find in an exotic paradise... It was essential to give the scene a mighty kick up the bass drum,

---

1   Huw Rees, Kate Ronconi, Stuart Ross, Monica Konggaard, Neil Woollard, Richard Cowell, Dai Godwin, Nick Moore... The list is endless, not quite endless perhaps, but endless all the same. Not quite the same, agreed, but just enough. And not quite just, unjust in fact. This is called wordplay but it's an obscure example, best avoided.

so Catherine and I hatched a plot that utilised the forces of chaos.

"We got ourselves into an administrative position – I can't recall how – and deliberately double booked, or triple booked, bands. In other words, more than one act would turn up at a given time to play on the same stage. The cacophony that resulted was mostly blisteringly bad, not always, but it sounded like nothing local, nothing Welsh. It sounded *exotic*, like nothing previously known above or below the equator. Then we set off as many fire alarms as we could. The people rushed into the streets while the music kept going (the musicians couldn't hear the alarms above the polyrhythmic din). Swansea suddenly was a city of street parties, of dancing under stars."

"Stars? How do you expect us to believe that?"

"You're right, it was poetic licence. What I really meant was: the low-lying featureless nighttime clouds saturated with oily moisture. But under *those* the inhabitants of Swansea did dance, and the music pulsed, throbbed and squealed and gained a momentum of its own, started to fit together, to become funky and nice, and feet on the pavement slabs moved faster, and hips gyrated in the style known as sensual, and bosoms and groins were thrust back and forth, and it was astounding to behold, incredible to witness, invigorating to describe, and that's how it was, and this was the beginning of the chain reaction I mentioned. Before an hour had passed, Swansea had metamorphosed in a way that not even I might have anticipated. The effect was extreme.

"'If this doesn't summon Kelvin,' I remarked, 'then nothing will.'

"Catherine nodded. 'You know something? I feel he's on his way already. My guess is that tomorrow he'll be back.'

"We joined the fun, drinking and dancing. The process was out of our hands now, beyond our control; the change was unstoppable and that's the way I liked it. I fell asleep just before dawn on the beach, with a dune for a pillow. Sleeping on the beach in Swansea is unheard of – the place is just a venue for empty chip wrappers to blow along, isn't it? I love chips but I loved the change more. When I awoke my head was light. I blinked in disbelief. The path parallel to the beach, where joggers and cyclists like to damage ankles and tyres, was shaded by palm trees. Where had those come from? Surfers rode giant clean waves, shark fins cleaved the blue water further out.

"I found Catherine rocking in a hammock with a *caipirinha* in her hand, her eyes inscrutable behind sunglasses. She sipped her fruity cocktail and smiled in languorous recognition. I noticed that she was wearing a sarong. I seemed to be the only person in Welsh trousers.

"'This event defies logic. It's too magical,' I protested.

"'What's the trouble?' she purred.

"'Palm trees don't spring up overnight, dirty seas don't become clean in less than twelve hours, a whacking great Sugar Loaf mountain isn't upthrust from the seabed quite so readily. I thought we might change the atmosphere of this town, not its actual landscape!"

"'Just accept it for what it is,' she answered.

"I didn't find her attitude helpful, so I left her where she was, swinging in her sheen, and went off to find someone else I knew, anyone less susceptible to alchemy, more constant in behaviour, looks and odour, in short a

Paddy Deluxe or Frothing Harris. But I failed. Everyone wore Hawaiian shirts, everyone had samba hips, there wasn't a single example of Vitamin D deficiency to be found anywhere… I should have just gone with the flow, enjoyed it as a phenomenon, not worried about analysing it.

"But I'm a born worrier I guess and I kept fretting. I found myself a bench in Cwmdonkin Park and I tried to ignore the orchids and hummingbirds, and even the strange insects, until one landed on the back of my right hand and stung me. I swatted it with my left hand and it stung that one too. I don't know what the insect was, nothing native to the temperate climes, that's for sure, but since that moment my hands have occasionally swollen up to gross dimensions. It doesn't happen too often, and they don't stay swollen for more than an hour or so, but when they do swell up I swear I have the second biggest hands in existence. I won't say anything about Prime Time Kenny, the man with *the* biggest hands. He doesn't belong in this story.

"Anyway, I sat there for a long time, while the pseudo-tropical sun started to sink into the west, and then I felt a prickle on the nape of my neck, and I knew Kelvin was back. I looked up and there he was, ambling along the path, maybe twelve inches high with big ears and a bigger grin. He sat next to me and rolled a spliff and just for once I was stuck for words to say. Fortunately he broke the impasse with a simple observation:

"'Rather seasonable weather for the time of year'.

"'Indeed so,' I said, 'and quite contrary to normality. I've never known such a balmy afternoon at this latitude.'

"'Climate is what you make it,' he answered.

"I took issue with this statement. 'No it's not! Climate is the result of several factors outside human control. These factors include altitude, proximity to high mountains, average cloud cover, the thermohaline circulation of the ocean, solar heat absorption due to vegetation…'

"'Climate change is within human control,' he interrupted.

"I snorted in derision. 'What do you know about humans? You're just a toy, a piece of cloth cut and stitched in certain ways, with maybe an electromagnetic imprint of some kind to keep you going. I'm good friends with a former owner of yours, so watch your step!'

"Then I felt bad for having threatened him, but he didn't seem offended and continued airily, 'The human race has been altering the climate since the first outpouring of industrial pollution. A blind process… But I'm Kelvin and know everything about manipulation, what glove puppet doesn't? You can't expect to use us as playthings and keep us ignorant of the mechanics of control. We learn the hard way, with a hands-up approach! Have you any idea what it feels like to be tickled from the inside?'

"'Actually I do, but let's not go into that…'

"Kelvin leaned closer, ignited his spliff and blew the smoke out of the corner of his fabric mouth. 'I'll tell you my secret. None of the changes that upset you so much are real. Don't you get it yet? I've turned the tables on you humans and played a grand joke. The palm trees and breakers, the toucans and jellyfish, the hotter sun and higher mountains… They are all puppets, puppets of my devising! Even the coconuts are puppets!'

"'You mean that the azure sky and sweet zephyr…'

"'Made from cloth... The hammocks and grass skirts, the *cavaquinhos*[2] and *caipirinhas*, the papaya and caramba, the sunburn and heatstroke, the coral and pearls, all of it animated cloth!'

"'What about the horrible sting on my hands?'

"'Even that is a puppet – the pus in your wound is a puppet, the poisoning of your blood is a puppet, everything!'

"'Are you generous or vindictive?' I wondered.

"He blew a pungent smoke ring and explained his intentions. 'Let me tell you something Catherine was never aware of. But before I do, allow me to say how much I dislike sentences that end with the word 'of'. Like that one. And the one before. Anyway, when I was living with her, I moulted a lot, I'm made of cotton and I shed lots of fibres, including from my ears, fibres that became entangled with the fibres of the sofa, knotted to them until they were an integral part of the upholstery, and that's where they remained. In other words, I left a portion of my hearing in Catherine's house. Anything that was said near that sofa, I could hear, wherever in the world I was!'

"'You eavesdropped on us!' I cried.

"He shrugged. 'I could hardly help it. There was no way of *not* listening. And I heard your plan to entice me back and decided to have a little fun of my own. I applied all my expertise at puppetry to trump you, to prove who the real genius is. I'm the one in control, my friend, not you. You got more than you bargained for but that's not necessarily a bad thing. Enjoy it. Why care if the Malibus and dusky maidens are puppets?'

"'Why indeed?' I conceded, but it didn't feel right.

---

2   Little guitars played in tropical lands.

"He gave me a sly wink and I watched him go, flicking ash and humming a reggae tune as he wandered among jewel-eyed serpents and giant flowers. He was headed in the direction of the beach. I imagined him wandering along the shoreline, stopping to examine the big conch shells, waiting for sunset and the throbbing trance parties, rolling another spliff and sending scented smoke in a lazy spiral towards the emerging summer stars. I felt sure he would bump into Catherine in her hammock on the way.

"And talking about summer stars, I know plenty about astronomy and I know the names of many constellations. Some are named after dogs, Canis Major for instance, which means 'the great dog', and Canis Minor, 'the little dog', but I reckon there ought to be a dancing dog too and it should be named after Kelvin. He was definitely a Canis Raver."

* * * *

Castor Jenkins will finish his pint at this point, wipe his lips and gaze longingly at the bar. A newcomer (just like you, dear reader) who wants to hear the rest of the tale will think it's the right time to buy him another drink, but Paddy Deluxe and Frothing Harris will know that to *stop* him telling it, they need to buy him two drinks, one each. That's what they'll do, but he'll tell it anyway, yawning, rolling his eyes and shrugging.

"How long do you think Swansea remained tropical? Kelvin's puppets were good quality, designed to last a lifetime, and in theory there was no reason at all for grey skies and drizzle to return.

"But it did. It always will in Wales.

"Kelvin made one mistake – he misunderstood human psychology. Although the tropical environment was highly desirable, men and women just get bored of puppets after a while. We only put up with them for so long, however realistic and clever they are. And that's what happened. Gradually people stopped going to the beach to surf and dance, the hammocks were left empty and the cocktails undrunk. Desolation set in. There's nothing more desolate than paradise gone to seed, and at some point Kelvin must got disillusioned, packed it all up and left, because one morning I woke to find Swansea back the way it was. Since then it has never been tropical again."

How can Paddy Deluxe and Frothing Harris respond to this ridiculous story? Only with extreme derision.

"Puppets don't come in such unlikely types. People would notice if even the hot sun was made of cloth!"

"Would they? But you haven't noticed your own puppet status."

"What do you mean?"

"Both of you – glove puppets, nothing more or less!"

"Don't be absurd! Prove it!"

"As you wish. Look towards the front door. Who is that coming in? The real Paddy Deluxe and Frothing Harris. Watch what happens when they join me at the table. Then you'll be convinced."

"By all the gods, he's right! They are coming over!"

Castor now smirks and calls, "Good evening, Paddy. Good evening, Harris. I note you are shamefully late."

"Yes, sorry about that, old boy. What's that you've got there, Castor? A pair of deflated puppets in our image!"

"Yes and very nicely made, aren't they?"

"Extremely sinister. But we can't imagine anyone using them. Such a person would need enormous hands."

Castor lays his own hands on the table. "Mine are normal."

And so they are, right now.

THE PLUCKED PLANT

Castor Jenkins has a bad habit of advocating outlandish ideas and even his mildest beliefs are routinely uncommon. If you ask him about the Primeval Soup he'll insist it was leek and potato. He denies the existence of the colour purple, the number seven and the note G#. Once he went to great lengths to prove that mice are related to parsnips. The list is long and disturbing, not quite as long and disturbing as one of his neckties, but sufficient to elicit cries of dismay from the average citizen of the town of Porthcawl.

Given the extreme oddness of his concepts, it was with some relief that his friends greeted his relatively mundane announcement that reincarnation was his afterlife philosophy of choice. With Castor it was more than a question of faith. He knew that reincarnation was the correct theory because he remembered several of his previous lives. He was, so he claimed, an inhabitant of Ancient Greece. When pressed for details, he provided them in exchange for beer. In his slightly slurred words this is the story he told:

"I was a disciple of Pythagoras and I lived in a commune in a garden and it should have been a pleasant existence but I wasn't a particularly nice person. A quick historical lesson might be appropriate here. Pythagoras wasn't just that mathematical chap who devised the theorem about the square of the hypotenuse, he was also the founder of a mystical cult. His followers had to be sober, celibate and vegetarian, and fully committed to the doctrine of the transmigration of souls, which is a fancy term for reincarnation.

"Anyway, I was such a bad person that I wanted to kill myself, because I thought it was the only way to prevent myself doing more damage to the world I lived in. But suicide seemed a terrible sin. I thought about hiring someone else to do the job, a freelance cutthroat or unemployed executioner, but I didn't want to pass off the responsibility. The guilt was mine, the judgment also, and it was only fair that any bad karma in the offing was mine too. I couldn't endanger the souls of any poor assassin with the task."

"Hang about!" protested Frothing Harris. "Did they have the notion of karma in Ancient Greece?"

Castor drained his glass and sighed. "There's evidence that the Pythagoreans were influenced by Buddhism and that's not as unlikely as it sounds. Greece had trading links with India."

"Continue with the tale," said Paddy Deluxe.

"Well then, I was stuck with an insolvable problem. How does one kill oneself *without* committing suicide? I fretted over this question for weeks, months, years; and all that time I continued not being a nice person but hiding it well, so that nobody in the commune ever suspected there was anything malign about me. The answer eventually came to me and it surprised and delighted me because it was so easy. It was a three-stage solution. The first stage involved making no changes to my present character, none at all."

"You remained a bad sort?"

"Thoroughly. I continued to be what I was, a hypocrite, a cheat, a sly and devious manipulator of my fellow human beings. I grew old and my body twisted to match the shape of my mind, but still I felt no remorse. At last I died, asking forgiveness from nobody, for it was important to my plan that I didn't weaken at the final moment. The chill of extinction sprang up in my bones. My flesh decayed, became food for worms and nourishment for roots under the soil.

"My body was gone but my soul soon found a new home. The walls of muscle and nerves that had imprisoned it were now broken and it rose like vapour from a fresh cup of tea and departed my grave. Because I had existed meanly and acquired lots of negative karma my soul was reborn in a lower form of life. I had calculated my nastiness precisely to achieve this aim. The mathematics of evil are complex but I was a Pythagorean and knew exactly what the square of hypocrisy is worth[3].

"I was reborn as a humble plant, a simple herbaceous biennial growing along a riverbank, just one among many other kinds of flora in the region. The sun shone on my lacy triangular leaves, the wind combed spiderwebs out of my little white flowers, clustered in umbels as they were, songs both dire and lovely were sung to me by frogs and birds, other pastoral things occurred involving shepherdesses and pan-pipes. The situation was utopian.

"This was the second stage of my solution. I was a good plant and committed no crime against nature, and so it was clear my karma points would be replenished and that after death I might expect rebirth as a human being. Over a period of centuries transmigration is a jerky process, a soul being knocked down the ladder of evolution, then getting back up, only to be knocked down again, and so on. Progress around the cosmic playing board is rarely smooth."

---

3   It is equal to the sum of the scares on the other two snides.

"You make it sound like a game of backgammon," commented Frothing Harris, "with a soul as the solitary piece that keeps getting captured and sent to the bar until it can re-enter when the roll of dice is favourable."

Castor considered his words. "Sent to the bar," he echoed. Then he nodded and added, "The next time it happens, make mine a double whisky. With a beer on the side. Now where was I? Yes, I was a good plant. I had an earthy odour reminiscent of mice or parsnips, which is what first led me to suspect they are related in some way, and that's also a hint as to what kind of plant I was. Shall I give you another clue? The lower half of my stem was streaked with red or purple. Does that help? Well, I was often mistaken for fennel, parsley or wild carrot. I contained several alkaloids including coniine, conhydrine, pseudoconhydrine and atropine. *Conium maculatum* was my Latin name."

"I'm not a botanist," glumly stated Paddy Deluxe.

"Nor I," admitted Frothing Harris.

"No matter. The day of my death was pleasant and sunny. I had saturated my inside with my favourite drink of rain from a pre-dawn shower and now I was ready for a busy schedule of photosynthesis combined with supporting the weight of resting butterflies and the larvae of the silver-ground carpet moth. But suddenly my existence was cut short by a thumb and five fingers. Yes, I was brutally plucked from the ground by a hairy hand! I later learned what happened to my body but at the time I knew nothing, because my soul was already drifting upwards in search of a new rebirth venue. It found one quickly enough. That's one of the things souls do best.

"My poor body was carried in a sack to a workroom in the cellar of a house. First my leaves were plucked from my stems one at a time and cast into a stone mortar, and then a heavy bronze pestle mashed my remains to pulp. Water was added until I became a solution. I was poured into a glass bottle, sealed with a cork and shaken, and finally balanced on a high shelf in a cool alcove. There I remained for many years while my soul grew and matured in a new body. Because I had been a good plant, accumulating lots of positive karma, I was reborn as a human being. I was back to the man stage!"

"How can a plant be good or bad?" protested Paddy Deluxe.

"They can't steal or cheat or lie," added Frothing Harris.

Castor Jenkins rolled his eyes in mild exasperation. "It's a question of attitude. When I was a plant I had a fine attitude, very diplomatic and easy going, utterly at peace with my environment and neighbouring vegetation, respectful of passing insect life, even well disposed towards worms and fungus. I earned my right to be reincarnated as a human the hard way. And what a magnificent human I became! I started as a promising baby and never looked back! In my youth I was curious about everything, a real sponge for knowledge, but I was disturbed by the way the world kept changing. I wondered how I might trust a universe that simply wasn't stable. So I looked for certainty in mathematics and logic and other abstract systems of thought.

"In other words I turned into a philosopher, a rationalist, a teacher of the young people in the city where I dwelled. And while I lived in this fashion, debating in the public squares, going to symposia, that bottle full of the juice of my previous body stood patiently on its shelf, waiting for the moment when it would serve another purpose, a purpose devised by that evil Pythagorean so many years earlier. I was oblivious to this fact, unaware of the schemes of my former self, but I doubt that knowing would have made a difference; I was too committed to wisdom for its own sake and I continued teaching.

"Athens was a glorious city at that time but constantly threatened by external powers and internal dissent. The last thing its rulers wanted was a maverick wise man, a radical sage, agitating the people and opening up their minds. I was arrested and condemned to death for impiety. The year was 399 BC. An executioner was chosen to descend into the cellar of a particular house and fetch a bottle from a shelf. Yes, it's true. In Ancient Athens condemned prisoners were compelled to drink *hemlock*. That was the species of plant I had once been! I was plucked by the herbalist who was employed to make poisons for the authorities and in the official judicial repository I had lingered."

"You were Socrates!" exclaimed Paddy Deluxe.

Castor inclined his head. "I don't like to brag, it's a very inelegant thing to do, but you're right, I once was Socrates, the wisest philosopher of olden times. I'll tell you about my final moments, if you like, but first allow me to point out that I was wise only in the sense that I *knew* I knew nothing. That's what I always claimed, but paradoxes like that annoyed the prominent Athenians and turned them against me. I was also suspected of being a potential traitor. It's true I opposed democracy and saw much to admire in the tougher Spartan system, but my loyalty to Athens was unwavering. The trial was a farce but I accepted my fate philosophically. As a philosopher, what else could I do?

"Trials in Ancient Athens were different from what they are in modern Wales. There were no judges: the jury was supreme. To ensure fairness, juries were huge, 501 men were present to decide my case. After I made a speech in my defence and the prosecutor, a chap named Meletus, made a speech against me, the jury voted on my guilt. This didn't go in my favour, 280-221 was the outcome. Oh dear! But what would the sentence be? Our custom was for defendant and prosecutor to each suggest a penalty. I proposed a fine of 30 minae (about £1886 in today's money[4]) and Meletus proposed death. Another vote was taken and the result was 360-141 in favour of death. Charming!

"But the truth is that I contributed to my own martyrdom every step of the way. I could have resigned from philosophy and avoided the trial. Even in prison I had a chance to escape: my friends bribed the guards but I refused to go. I did everything in my power to ensure my execution. My followers assumed this was because of my superior moral courage, my desire to live within the rule of law, my disdain for earthly experience. Even I was unaware that I was really paying for other crimes, crimes not mentioned at my trial, crimes in my past, that were committed in my previous life as a wicked Pythagorean, and that the death sentence was *his* justice rather than the justice of the state."

"Did drinking the hemlock hurt?" asked Frothing Harris.

"It wasn't a comforting beverage," said Castor in a quiet voice, "unlike beer or whisky, but I can't say there was unbearable pain. I drank the bowl dry and then

---

4   At the words "in today's money" both Paddy and Harris clenched their teeth and growled.

walked around a bit. Plato was there, a close friend, a bit humourless but not a bad sort, and when I felt suddenly weak he helped me to lie down on a pallet. Then the executioner came and pinched my foot, asking me if I could feel anything. 'No,' I answered. He pinched my legs at regular intervals up to my thighs. 'Still nothing,' I remarked. He nodded and said, 'When the numbness reaches your heart, you'll be gone.' And that's exactly what happened. I died and my soul left my body again and went elsewhere, but I don't know where. Of all my numerous incarnations I only remember those three, and it's an amazing coincidence that they all happened in sequence in the same country."

Paddy and Harris conferred together. Finally they said:

"We believe your story because we both read about the death of Socrates in a book and it was exactly as you described. If you weren't Socrates there's no way you could have got the details right."

"Glad you're not naïve in any way," commented Castor.

"What will you be reincarnated as next time?"

This was a question Castor didn't like. "I might make a reasonable guess, based on a tally of my sins against a tally of my virtues, but it would require lots of work and take the mystery out of the process. Reincarnation is an enigmatic business and shouldn't be controlled too much. I've already meddled more than enough with it. Look at what I managed to do with those three sequential lives! I planned my own murder in the first, ended my second as a bottled poison, consumed that poison in the third. It enabled me to kill myself without committing suicide. What else lets us get away with such blatant paradoxes?

"Buy me a drink, I'm feeling generous," he concluded.

WHEN WALES PLAYED ASGÅRD

The glory days of Welsh rugby were in the 1970s, everyone knows that, and the general feeling is that such heights of sporting excellence can never be equalled. Castor Jenkins knows better. Not only were they equalled recently, but actually bettered, and he was the man who made the miracle happen. At least that's what he says, but there's no evidence to back up his claim, because the bravest game Wales ever played was an away match and took place not on Earth but in the supernatural realm of the Old Norse Gods. Only a return match in Cardiff against the same side will provide conclusive proof.

Castor explains the entire sequence of events in the following manner: "It was just after a crushing defeat against the All Blacks in the Millennium Stadium and I was waiting in the station for a bus back to Porthcawl, feeling rather low, cursing myself for wasting my money on a ticket, when I fell into conversation with a man also waiting in the queue. There was something unusual about him but I couldn't put my finger on it. Maybe it was the horned helmet, bearskin coat and broadsword slung at his belt, maybe not. Plenty of people use match days as an excuse to dress up in unconventional clothing.

"We boarded the bus and because the vehicle was crowded we ended up sitting next to each other. At first we talked about the game in a half-hearted manner, in the same way one might talk about a broken washing machine or bicycle puncture, but then I forgot the rules of discretion and bewailed the fact I wasn't responsible for picking the Welsh side. I felt sure I could select a winning team if I was given a chance to do so. The main difficulty, I admitted, was that my ideal team consisted of players already dead. 'That isn't necessarily a problem,' replied my companion, and I arched my eyebrows at that.

"He lowered his voice to a whisper and went on to explain that he wasn't really a mortal man but Ullr, the god of skill, hunts and duels from Norse mythology, and that he had powerful contacts in Asgård, the Viking version of heaven. I knew in my heart he was telling the truth; there was something compelling about his whole demeanour, and I felt proud to be sitting next to him. I think he was pleased by my easy acceptance, and he grimly grinned in a reassuring way, if I might be permitted a paradox. Then he closed his eyes and recited, 'Hann er ok fagr álitum ok hefir hermanns atgervi. Á hann er ok gott at heita í einvígi...' and though I understood not a word, I nodded in agreement.

"'That verse is about me,' he said, 'and comes from the *Gylfaginning* of Snorri Sturluson. It's very flattering."

"'I bet it is,' I responded, 'but I've never read any Viking poetry.'

"'Don't worry. Sturluson isn't like so many other poets, obsessed with his own ego, he's a good sort and won't give a damn whether you've read him or not if you ever bump into him in Asgård.'

"'Am I going there?' I spluttered.

"'Sure. I'm in a position to give you what you want. You've convinced me that you can put together a Welsh side greater than the present one, and I think it's a grand idea, really I do, and I know that Thor, Odin, Loki, Tyr, Baldr and the rest will agree with me. Asgård has its own rugby team, you see, and we're good, better than the All Blacks in their prime.'

"'So why watch rugby in Cardiff?' I asked.

"'I often come down to Midgard – that's the world inhabited by men – to check out the sport. I've supported Wales for almost one hundred years. All the Norse deities do the same. In fact I noticed Freyja, the ravishing goddess of fertility, in the crowd, rooting for the other side.'

"'The blonde in the cloak of robin feathers? I noticed her too!'

"'Listen to me. If I help you, it's not an act of charity, it's purely selfish, Odin's boys need some decent competition.'

"'Is the Asgård team really so mighty?' I asked.

"'We've won the Six Million Nations' Cup six million times in a row... Our last game was against the Microscopic Giants of Microgigans, supreme champions of Happenstance, and we thrashed them 6,567-3. Naturally we had to perform the 'Rite of the Blood Eagle' on their manager after the match, but we always do that to the managers of every losing side.'

"'Is that a pleasant rite?' I asked gingerly.

"Ullr leered at me. 'No.'

"I have to be honest here and report that I felt suddenly nervous, but behind the fear was a stronger emotion, a patriotic desire to see Wales beat the best that Odin could throw at us, and I decided to accept the challenge. We formally shook hands on it and then Ullr explained to me how we were going to get to Asgård. Instead of staying on the bus all the way to Porthcawl, we would get off at Bridgend and he would summon suitable transport from there. I had read some Norse mythology when I was younger, not much but enough to remember it featured a ship named *Naglfar* that was made entirely from the uncut fingernails of dead men. I confided in my new companion that I didn't care to travel on such a vessel as I feared my itches might be over-scratched.

"He roared with laughter. 'Even the Norse gods move with the times! We'll get to Asgård on a bus like this one!'

"I joined in with his laughter but my mouth drooped sourly when we arrived at Bridgend bus station. Ullr raised a ram's horn to his lips, blew a vibrant note and suddenly a new bus trundled into view – a bus made from fingernails! I boarded with a sigh, chose a seat without any grime, toe-jam or bum-fluff under it, and gazed indifferently out of the window. The passing landscape rapidly grew strange, the familiar Welsh grey skies became blood red, fiery and full of flying shapes, some of them winged women in armour.

"I formed the distinct impression we crossed a rainbow bridge made of solid light, and drove up the trunk of a monstrous tree, quite against the laws of gravity and sanity, before suddenly appearing at the borders of Asgård, the realm of the Gods. Without pausing for a toilet break, we approached the walls that surrounded this paranormal kingdom and passed through a gate of blood-rusted iron. The road twisted between towering cliffs and finally emerged on the Plain of Idavoll at the very centre of Asgård. A part of this plain was a zone known as Gladsheim where the hall of Valhalla was located.

"Ullr had been silent during the journey but now he asked. 'Have you had much experience at organizing sporting events?'

"'Yes, I once arranged a special kind of steeplechase for a local fete. It involved a selection of vicars, sextons, vergers and deacons chasing after the steeple of their church while I ran off with it.'

"'Ridiculous. How could a mortal man carry a steeple?'

"'Sometimes I have big hands,' I said.

"'I think you are a liar,' he cried, 'rather like Loki, the god of mischief, who you might be unlucky enough to meet; but I find you entertaining nonetheless. Tell me something else highly unlikely.'

"'I once posted myself in a box. Does that count?'

"He was gravely disappointed. 'No.' But then he saw that we had nearly reached the hall of Valhalla. 'Here you will find all the dead Welsh rugby players from the past. You may select any you like.'

"This prospect pleased me and I have to admit that I was feeling confident. Let me describe Valhalla as I remember it. For a start it was large, smoky, dark, smelly and noisy. The floor was awash with spilled mead and ale. I went inside and found myself thrust into a chaos of shouting and fighting. It was just like Wind Street in Swansea on Friday night. There were long dead Viking warriors hitting each other with axes, good practice for Ragnarok, the end of the universe, or so Ullr informed me. I wandered rather nervously among the benches, plates of food and the severed limbs. Red beards and red-rimmed eyes formed an ocean of northern ire into which I wallowed like a punctured coracle.

"Despite the mass of people I felt horribly alone, and then abruptly I recognized a shape in the flicker of a brazier.

"'Gwyn Nicholls!' I cried in amazement. 'You were captain of the side that won the Triple Crown in 1902.'

"'That's right, boyo. But who are you?'

"I recognized another shape. 'Watcyn Thomas! In 1931 you played 70 minutes with a broken collarbone and scored a try.'

"'That's right. Against Scotland.'

"Ullr peered over my shoulder. 'Do you choose these two?'

"I nodded and Ullr prodded them along with the point of his sword. And that is how it went for the next few hours, with me wandering through the dimness and bumping into great dead Welsh players, and Ullr confirming whether I wanted to add them to my team or not. Eventually I had fifteen players and we left Valhalla and plodded along to a training ground where the god left me with a wink and a shake of the hand. I nursed my bruised fingers and pondered. From what Ullr told me just before he left, I had only one week to get my side in shape before the big match that would take place in the new stadium on the far side of the Well of Urd, beneath Yggdrasil, the World Tree.

"I confided my worries to my team. 'It's not much time!'

"'Don't be daft, boyo!' cried Dewi Bebb, winner of thirty four caps between 1959 and 1967. 'We're all fit and keen.'

"'That's right,' added Ray Cale, hero of the 1950 Grand Slam and notorious for his robust play. 'We're ready for anything!'

"I accepted their reassurances and we started training. My main problem was that I didn't know the opposition, I hadn't seen the Asgård team play and thus I couldn't devise any effective strategies against them. I had to settle for making guesses based on what I remembered about Norse mythology. Then it occurred to me I could ask my players to fill in the details I didn't know. They regularly went to watch Odin's boys thrash all other teams in existence. The news wasn't good and I began to regret ever boasting to Ullr on that bus out of Cardiff. For a start, ordinary rugby balls weren't used up here but the severed head of a frost giant with quite different bouncing qualities.

"I also learned precisely what the Rite of the Blood Eagle involved. The victim is tied facing a post and his ribs are cut from his spine and his lungs pulled out through his back, so that they resemble wings, inflating and deflating as slowly and agonizingly his life drains away.

"The days passed and my confidence began to drain away also. I realized I had made a bad mistake. Allow me to explain my mistake as best I can… It's natural for human beings to feel the past is better than the present, that the players of olden times were faster and stronger than those of today. And maybe they were. But the point is this: they weren't *that* much better, a little bit better maybe, but twenty or thirty times better? No! And that's what would be required to beat Asgård, players twenty or thirty times better than the modern Welsh side. I just didn't have players of that calibre. We were going to be slaughtered, and in my case I was going to be sacrificed in a particularly nasty way.

"The week was already over and Ullr sent a bus to pick us up. I said nothing to my players about my fears. They were in good spirits and I didn't want to lose the only strength at our disposal – mighty ignorance. The bus took us towards the Well of Urd and the new stadium and we pushed through the crowds on their way to the same place. In the changing room I gave a last inspirational speech and then I went to take some air. The atmosphere inside the stadium was incredible, overpowering, apocalyptic. To settle my nerves I smoked a cigarette and this seemed to attract the rage of a certain section of the crowd who made insulting dragon faces at me until I stubbed it out with a twist of my heel.

"To my amazement I recognized the referee, a fellow who called himself the Postmodern Mariner. We had met shortly after my career as a pirate with Captain Ribs and my island idyll with Charlotte Gallon. He was a reporter who wandered around looking for strange stories connected to the sea. I managed to get close to him and ask what he was doing up here. He shrugged and said he originally came looking for information on Jörmungandr, the serpent that circles the world at the bottom of the sea, but somehow he'd ended up as a forced volunteer in this match. Nobody ever wanted to referee an Asgård game. The abuse from the dead Vikings in the crowd was just too much.

"We didn't have time for a longer conversation than that. The match was about to start. I paced the touchline as my players walked out of the tunnel to a chorus of insults and threats from the rows of the packed stadium. Every voice in the place was raised against us. The sweat on my skin, already cool, turned to ice when the home side emerged. Fifteen Norse gods in full armour, Thor in the lead, swinging his hammer and shouting with the force of a small volcano. I glanced up at the red sky expecting rain, but it was just Thor's mocking laughter sounding like thunder. Then the coin was tossed, a coin with only one side – Odin's mythical disc – and the game began. I covered my eyes.

"The referee used a miniature ram's horn instead of a whistle to blow off. The stampede of feet was like a land-slide. I heard the pitiful shrieks of Arthur Gould, captain of Wales no fewer than eighteen times between 1885 and 1897, but I still couldn't bring myself to look. Then there was a roar and I knew that Asgård had scored their first try. Finally I had to peer between my fingers. I watched the god Hœnir convert easily for another two points. He celebrated in modest fashion, for he was the silent god and considered something of a ditherer by Odin. I groped for another cigarette, thought better of it and ran my fingers over my ribs. The Rite of the Blood Eagle awaited me...

"Many tries followed in quick succession. All the gods scored at least one, and some of them – including Dagr, Höðr, Njörðr, Váli and Kvasir scored a thousand or more. I have to be honest and admit that I didn't recognize all the players on the Asgård side. One of their flankers looked like Tommy David, the Welshman who defected to Rugby League in 1974, but that couldn't be so; my Norse mythology was probably just rusty. I didn't know whether I wanted half time to come quickly or not, it might be a relief to have a pause in the carnage but it would also mean the moment of my doom was closer. I was in no mood to encourage my players for the second half but I did my best.

"I considered various methods of cheating. I wondered if I might hide myself in the ball and control its movements from within, a trick I had learned from a dwarf surrealist boxer named Engelbrecht[5], but I was too bulky, plus there wasn't a ball in play, just a severed

5   Consult *The Exploits of Engelbrecht* by Maurice Richardson, recently reprinted by Savoy Books.

head, and I didn't fancy hiding inside that even if I fitted. I wondered if I might cause a diversion of some kind, maybe give the gods the idea that Ragnarok had started, and that they needed to be off to fight Surtr and the fire giants, while the universe collapsed around them. This way the match would have to be abandoned. It seemed a good plan and I briefly considered what I needed to do to create the right impression.

"It has been told that certain events will signify the imminence of Ragnarok. If I could duplicate these convincingly everything would be fine. One of these events was the death of the god Baldr by the trickery of the villainous Loki, who slew him with a spear made of mistletoe. Another was the onset of the *Fimbulwinter*, three successive winters without a summer between them, a time of chaos and fratricide. Yet another was the eating of sun and moon by the wolf brothers, Skoll and Hati. There would also be a series of earthquakes that would snap every bond and fetter in existence, allowing the monstrous Fenrir to escape and wreak havoc, plus the rainbow would crack and fall.

"After a few moments of careful thought, I decided I couldn't replicate any of these events except in a most amateurish fashion. So I hastily devised a substitute plan, clutching my groin as if I needed to relieve myself, leaving the stadium and looking left and right as if for a place to answer this call of nature. Nobody noticed my departure. They were too intent on enjoying the scrum and the tearing apart of Wilfred Wooller, who helped Wales defeat the All Blacks in 1935 and was a fine cricketer too. His head was ripped clean off and booted into touch. I believe it was Odin himself who did the deed. I looked back and saw a one-eyed man with a long white beard and wide brimmed hat.

"I never discovered what the final score was. It was 3,765,987 to nil when I left, with twenty minutes still to go, so four million to nothing is a reasonable guess. I found the bus made of fingernails in the car park and climbed into the driver's seat, then I started the engine and off I went with a squeal of tyres. I put my foot down and got back to Bridgend in record time. I didn't have to wait long for a connecting bus to Porthcawl. I came straight here to the pub where I was mighty pleased to see my friends, Frothing Harris and Paddy Deluxe, sitting at the same table as always, without a care in the world, and I looked so shaken and pale they bought me a few drinks to calm my fraught nerves.

"I'll never complain about the Welsh squad ever again, even if they lose to the All Blacks on a regular basis. I've seen a Welsh side get hammered for real and it wasn't pleasant. I don't go out in thunderstorms anymore, and I avoid all the props of Norse mythology as much as possible – horned helmets, trolls, runes, longships, the board game called *hnefatafl*, – with the exception of mead. They don't serve mead in this pub, but I'll have an ordinary lager if you're buying. Did I tell you about the time I fell through a hole in the fabric of spacetime and ended up back in the Iron Age? It was called the Iron Age because people there ate a lot of spinach. Yes, that's right, a lager please."

INTERSTELLAR DOMESTIC

Nobody outside Porthcawl, and hardly anyone inside it, can remember that Wales once had a space program that enjoyed greater success than the combined efforts of the Americans, Russians and Chinese. Only one mission was ever launched but it was responsible for several important 'firsts', including the discovery of alien life and the triggering of a cosmic war. What's more, it was done on the cheap, without even the need to build a spaceship.

There are those who doubt that men ever walked on the moon, but proof of the Welsh mission can be found at the far end of Porthcawl pier, especially on stormy nights. An object stands there that resembles the monolith in Arthur C. Clarke's *2001: a Space Odyssey* except that it's a different colour, shape, texture and size, and serves an entirely different function. Porthcawl proof is not like other kinds of proof. That's what makes it special.

Castor Jenkins is proud of the fact that he was the man who made the mission happen, but he's bitter that he hasn't received greater recognition for his amazing achievement. When he's in a bitter mood, the only way to cheer him up is to buy him a beer. The same is true when he's in a lager mood. If you mention the word 'proof' he'll think you're offering him whisky. But sometimes he'll soften and tell the entire story in a sober fashion.

And when he does tell it, this is how it goes:

* * * *

It started in the pub while Castor was lecturing his friends on philosophy, history, semiotics, chemistry, ballistics, phenomenology, geography, cybernetics, geology, psychology, algebra, apiology, sociology, epistemology, oneirology, needlework and physics, among other topics.

Somehow the subject of the speed of light had come up. Castor declared that it wasn't so difficult a barrier to break and that he knew exactly how to do it.

"The speed of light is an absolute limit!" protested Paddy Deluxe.

"A theoretical maximum," confirmed Frothing Harris.

"Not so!" cried Castor. "Listen carefully, because last night I discovered a way of travelling even faster. I was lying in bed awake, I couldn't sleep because of the fog outside my window. Some people don't like cats howling, others despise noisy neighbours, a few detest the opening of fridge doors downstairs during searches for early hours cheese. I'm not like them. What stops me from getting to sleep is fog. I regard its clamminess as a personal insult, its tendrils as a form of bullying and its dispersal patterns as mean and uncouth.

"In the distance a fog horn roared like the mating cry of a plesiosaurus (such a cliché but so accurate!) and I began pondering the methods used throughout history to warn passing ships away from rocks. Foghorn is one technique; lighthouse is another. So then I started thinking about revolving lamps and giant lenses and it occurred to me that the secret to faster than light travel might have something to do with the sweep of lighthouse beams."

"Which travel at the speed of light," frowned Paddy Deluxe.

"No more, no less," added Frothing Harris.

"Not the actual beams," cried Castor, "but their *sweep*. I want you to imagine a lighthouse with an extremely powerful lamp. This lamp turns on its axis, throwing out light in the process. Imagine that it completes one revolution every ten seconds. At a distance of one mile, the beam draws a circle 6.28 miles in circumference, and thus the speed of the sweep is approximately 2260 miles per hour. At a distance of one hundred miles, the circle has a circumference of 628 miles and the speed of the sweep has increased to almost a quarter of a million miles per hour. At a distance of a million miles, the circumference is 6,283,180 miles and the speed of the sweep is no less than 2,261,944,800 mph."

"And the velocity of light is?" queried Frothing Harris.

Paddy Deluxe answered, "186,282 miles per second."

"Which is equal to 670,615,200 mph," smiled Castor, "or more than three times slower than the sweep of a million mile long beam. And one million miles isn't so far. The moon lies at a distance of 238,854 miles from Earth. The other planets of the solar system, to say nothing of the stars and galaxies, are considerably further. If you were hanging on the end of a million mile long beam, you'd be whizzing through space faster than a photon."

Paddy and Harris exchanged a look of astonishment.

Castor took full advantage. "That's right. At that point, the sweep has exceeded the speed of light. I know what you're going to say. A sweep is not a real *thing*, it's an optical illusion, a psychological connection, an observer's convention that bears no relation to the movement of actual photons. That might be true, but I don't see why even an illusory principle can't be used as the motive force for an interstellar vessel of some description. I believe that the dawn of a radical new era in space exploration is within our grasp."

"The practicalities will surely be daunting!" cried Paddy.

"And the expenses crippling!" blurted Harris.

At this moment, the man sitting on the next table turned his head and lifted the brim of his hat so that his face became visible. He had been sitting there quietly all along, unobtrusive and meek, but with twitching muscles in the fingers of his long hands. Now he made himself known in a forthright manner. He licked his lips and fixed Castor with a stare so wide and arid that his yellow eyes resembled the beds of evaporated seas. Then he said:

"Pardon me for interrupting, but I couldn't help overhearing your conversation. I'm a stranger to this town and my home is a distant city with customs that might seem eccentric to you. Therefore forgive me if I say anything that seems rude or odd or viciously grandiose. I am one of the cleverest and most resourceful men you are ever likely to meet, a devious manipulator of objects and people, a cunning and ruthless schemer, a twisted egotist of inordinate wealth and malice. May I join you at your own table for a minute?"

"He seems a reasonable fellow," remarked Castor to his friends, and turning to the stranger cried, "Why not?"

The man pulled up a chair. "I am infatuated with the moon, I love anything to do with her, she is the finest thing in the sky! Her highly comminuted and impact gardened surficial layer is charming, her occasional outgassing of radon, potassium and polonium is divine, and her lack of a bipolar magnetic field, with all magnetic activity centred in the crust, is sweet and innocent to a degree rarely encountered anywhere else in this modern age!"

"Her dimples are nice," conceded Castor.

"I prefer the moon and moony things," continued the stranger, "to everything else in existence, even to the taste of Forgetfulness Honey. As the moon's biggest fan, I have dedicated my fortune and intellect to creating a shrine to her; and in fact the city where I come from was founded by myself, and is ruled by myself, for the sole purpose of allowing me to spend my time mooning around beneath the moon. I am actually a sort of mad dictator."

"What does Forgetfulness Honey taste like?" asked Castor.

"I don't rightly remember," was the reply, "but it's very nice. Anyway, not only am I a dictator, I'm also an inventor, and the majority of my inventions are utterly ridiculous, for instance the living plates and bowls complete with arms and legs that I manufactured last year. But despite my genius and wealth I've never been able to create a vehicle capable of taking me to the moon, which is my dearest wish. If I heard you correctly, you have a plan for a new kind of propulsion unit based on lighthouse beams. You also mentioned the moon. I am the man who can fund your scheme. Look no further!"

Paddy and Harris waited for Castor's reaction.

Castor smirked and said, "That's a kind offer, but I think you underestimate my ambitions. The moon is far too close for what I have in mind. My faster than light drive is worthy of a proper mission, a voyage to one of the zodiac constellations! I must decline your help with apologies."

The stranger stood in a sudden fury, turned on his heel and stamped towards the door, looking back over his shoulder with a grotesque leer. "Buffoon! You'll regret obstructing my lunar machinations!"

Then he stormed out, slamming the door as he went.

"What a dreadful man," sniffed Paddy.

"The world is full of crazed despots!" lamented Harris.

Castor gave an airy wave. "We don't need a sponsor. It is within our means to build a spaceship by adapting existing technology at very low cost. Consider this conundrum: if lighthouse beams hold the secret to breaking the light speed barrier why don't lighthouses go flying into space? Why doesn't the lighthouse at the end of Porthcawl pier shoot off towards the furthest reaches of the universe? The drive unit is in place; there is sufficient fuel for a mission. Something else is missing, perhaps one very simple element."

"A navigation system?" suggested Paddy.

"Life support?" chimed in Harris.

Castor shook his head. "Simpler than those. A timetable. That's what I believe is missing. After all, I doubt something as complex as an interstellar craft would be anything other than automatic. We won't be required to pilot the thing, merely act as passengers, so it's just a question of knowing when the next flight is due to take place, and the only way to be absolutely sure is to take matters into our own hands. I require a sheet of paper and a pencil."

These items were provided and Castor scribbled the words *Earth to Gemini Express, Departing 18:30* on the paper. He studied it carefully and glanced at the clock on the wall over the bar. "The next flight is in ten minutes. We'd better hurry. Leave your drinks and follow me!"

"Are we really going into space?" cried Harris.

"Yes indeed." Castor led the way outside and along the esplanade. The sea was rough and the tide was high and big waves broke over the railings, while the wind flung beer coloured globules of spray at the white bulk of the Grand Pavilion. They managed to reach the pier without getting too wet. Then they picked their way to the lighthouse at the end. Castor circled the edifice searching for a means of entry. There appeared to be none. Beating the sides with his fists achieved nothing but bruises. He stood back and pondered.

"A spacecraft is an advanced piece of technology. It surely wouldn't be entered through a normal door. Maybe there's a voice-operated portal of some kind? That's more in keeping with what I know about futuristic devices. Let me try. I command you to open and let us inside!"

A previously invisible hatch in the side of the lighthouse slid back silently and Castor stepped through without hesitation, gingerly followed by his less confident friends. The hatch instantly closed behind them and the three explorers of the void stood pressed tightly together in the narrow space. There was hardly enough room to breathe or shift weight from one foot to another. Frothing Harris discovered that his mouth was muffled by Paddy's left armpit, but he still managed to question the standards of these travelling arrangements.

"Isn't it supposed to be bigger on the inside than the outside?"

"You're confusing reality with fantasy," explained Castor. "This is an authentic interstellar spaceship, not a science fiction prop. It seems to be fully automatic, just as I imagined, without a single control for us to play with, so I guess we just stand here and wait to reach our destination."

"Why Gemini?" wondered Paddy.

"The two main stars of that constellation are Castor and Pollux. Naturally I'd like to visit a star that shares my name. Who wouldn't? But there's another reason. I have a twin brother called Pollux, so my family connection with Gemini is deeper than you might suspect. My brother looks like me, he's a perfect double, but he's the exact opposite in character."

"You mean he always tells the truth?" quipped Harris.

Castor ignored this remark and attempted to scratch his nose. The air inside the lighthouse began to grow stale. "Shame there aren't any portholes. Wouldn't it be marvellous to view the passing parsecs of infinite space outside our window! All those glorious nebulae and pulsars!"

"When will we be setting off?" complained Paddy.

"We're already on our way," answered Castor. "Don't expect any feelings of acceleration. This isn't a motorbike but a sophisticated star-cruiser and it doesn't obey the laws of provincial motion."

"Rather too high-falutin' for me," grumbled Harris. "How long will the journey take? What if we asphyxiate first?"

"We're already there!" announced Castor. "We crossed a distance of fifty light years in the blink of an eye. Imagine!"

"But what sort of eye?" whispered Paddy. "Anything at all might be waiting for us outside. I don't care to be eaten; I haven't had my own supper yet. I wish I never allowed you to talk me into this."

"Are we on the surface of a planet?" asked Harris.

"One way to find out!" Castor declared.

He ordered the invisible hatch to open. Smoothly it did so. With a whistle of appreciation, he stepped out slowly on the alien ground and stretched his cramped limbs. "I'm the first human being to stand on a world orbiting a distant star. I deserve eternal fame for this act!"

Then he grew suddenly morose and snorted, "But they won't give it to me."

"Who won't?" asked Paddy and Harris.

"The newspapers and television stations back home, the Welsh establishment, the Taffia[6], you know who I mean!"

"Is the atmosphere breathable?"

Castor inhaled deeply. "Eminently so! Come and join me."

"The place is inhabited!"

"Yes, isn't it wonderful?" Castor strode off towards a collection of buildings that fronted an agitated sea.

"It looks a lot like Porthcawl," grumbled Paddy.

Harris squinted and pointed. "Doesn't that building over there bear a curious resemblance to the Grand Pavilion?"

"And the esplanade is identical!"

"I don't think we've actually gone anywhere," said Harris.

Castor stopped in his tracks. Then he turned a fierce glare on his two friends, shook his head in melodramatic despair, clutched the railings tightly and looked out over the waves while chewing his lower lip. "Tell me, if you please," he said coldly, "what colour is the sea?"

There was a long silence before Paddy answered meekly, "Orange."

"And the colour of the sky?"

"Also orange," mumbled Harris, "with an unusual sun in it, four suns in fact. Is Castor a quadruple star system?"

"It is. Now take a look at the building you describe as bearing a resemblance to the Grand Pavilion. Would you

---

6   Taffia = Welsh Mafia.

please give me an estimate of its height. An error margin of 10% is acceptable."

"Between three and four thousand feet..."

"And a description of the material from which it has been constructed?"

"Green crystal! A single giant emerald!"

Castor nodded and set off once again. Paddy and Harris struggled to keep up with him. There was no doubt in their minds now that they really were on another planet, but the pseudo-familiarity of their surroundings was still troubling them. It was Paddy who blurted out:

"The coincidence seems too implausible!"

Castor had softened. He slowed his pace and spoke with a smile, "Maybe not. It might be that the *basic* design of Porthcawl is a fundamental constant throughout the universe. For example, nitrogen exists on Earth and in fact makes up 78% of our atmosphere and is found in amino acids and all living tissues. Nitrogen also exists on Mars, albeit in much smaller quantities. Does that mean that Earth and Mars are the same place? No! It's simply that nitrogen is an element common to both, a shared possession. And so it might be with our hometown. The Grand Pavilion could be an inevitable structure."

"We accept that. We have no other choice."

Castor said, "Why don't we go and get some chips? I can smell the delicious aroma of potatoes and frying fat!"

"Is that wise? Alien food might be toxic."

"Call yourselves pioneers, adventurers?" mocked Castor. "Bah! I should have gone to the moon with that mad despot, at least he had vision and courage! What will the historians say about this? That Paddy Deluxe and Frothing Harris were like trembling kittens in the shadow of the great Castor Jenkins? Is that what you really want? Be men just for once!"

"I suppose I could do with some chips," muttered Paddy.

"Just a small packet," sighed Harris.

They found a chip shop not very far away and Castor stroked his chin. "Maybe it'll be best if I go in alone. The inhabitants might be hostile. I can also learn some of the local customs for later."

Paddy and Harris stood outside and watched the proceedings through the grimy window. Castor was communicating with the man behind the counter by means of a flurry of hand signals, none of which Paddy or Harris understood. Within a few minutes Castor emerged with three packets of chips. They were surprised that he had paid for all of them, but he winked and revealed that on this planet the standard currency was earwax.

"I've had rank deposits building up in both my ears for years, so now I can be considered a rich man," he said.

They devoured the chips, which were just as soggy and cool as the Welsh kind, and then stood aimlessly while a frown deepened on Castor's forehead. He glanced in the direction of the lighthouse.

"I think we should go now," he urged.

"So soon?" cried Paddy. "What's the trouble?"

"Well the timetable I created didn't specify a return time. What if the spacecraft leaves without us? Do you want to be stranded here? What's the point of becoming martyrs to the cause of the Welsh Space Program? Life is too important to throw away in such a careless fashion. Who cares what the historians say? We can always return tomorrow or next week!"

Something in Castor's tone made Paddy and Harris feel a tinge of panic. They hurried back along the esplanade, and now the suns had set and it was twilight and the constellations were becoming visible.

Castor pointed at a faint star, "More proof, if any doubts linger. That is Polaris, the North Star, but it's in the south!"

Paddy and Harris said nothing. Working out the positions of stars while orbiting a star that wasn't the sun was too complex. Easier to take his word instead. When they reached the lighthouse, they slid open the hatch with a voice command and squeezed into the stuffy darkness.

"Not a moment too soon!" announced Castor.

"Are we off?" blabbered Harris.

"Yes indeed. In fact we're already back. The real Porthcawl lies outside. Before we step out and return to our old way of life, let me confess something that has made me feel a bit sad. This voyage of ours has changed everything. We'll never be able to talk in quite the same way as before, the experience was too futuristic. Even language will have to alter to help us assimilate the adventure and that's a change I have mixed feelings about.

"Consider what it means now for us to 'turn on our left sides' or 'fly out of the kitchen'. Before the voyage, the first phrase meant we were shifting position in bed; the second meant we had to leave the kitchen in a hurry. Now the first means we've just flipped a row of switches on the left sides of our bodies; and the second means that we are mounted on hover-scooters. The *domestic* no longer exists as it once did. It has become interstellar!"

"That worry is too obscure for us," said his friends.

"Well here's one less obscure – the inhabitants of that other planet are probably offended that we left without saying goodbye. Suppose they declare hostilities against Earth, to teach us a lesson? I believe we've just triggered a cosmic war. If we're lucky, they haven't invented interstellar travel yet and will find it impossible to actually launch an invasion."

"What shall we do?" cried Paddy and Harris.

"It's too risky ever to go back. If our craft is captured, the secret of the faster than light drive will be exposed!"

They left the lighthouse and walked to the pub. The storm had died down and the sea was relatively calm. When they passed through the door of their favourite haunt the decrepit barman said:

"That chap with you earlier – the one with the hat and moon obsession – came back when you weren't here. I think he wanted immediate revenge. When he saw you had gone he left a message."

"What was it?" asked Castor.

The barman consulted his memory. "Well, he said that without the moon there would be no tides, no ebb and flow, no howling dogs, no total solar eclipses, no wax and wane, no werewolves, no moonbows, moonrakers or mooncalves. Then he added that you, Castor Jenkins, had done the moon an injustice and would pay dearly one way or another!"

Castor was disappointed. "Was that all?"

The barman nodded. "I'm afraid so. What can I get you?"

"Beer. One pint of," said Castor.

"Aren't you going to buy a round for your friends?"

"Good point," admitted Castor, "but they haven't finished their old drinks yet. They left them on the table, where I note they still are. I abhor waste. They should finish those before they get new ones."

"I'm surprisingly in agreement with you," said the barman.

"Drink up!" cried Castor as he returned to the table. Paddy and Harris sipped their stale pints with expressions of disgust. While they did so, Castor threw back his head and stared at the ceiling, as if he could peer through the plaster and tiles at the stars beyond. All the while he muttered to himself in vinegary awe, "We ate chips on another world!"

* * * *

That's the story as he relates it, with all its essential details intact. The first time he told it to Paddy Deluxe and Frothing Harris they regarded him with disappointment and disapproval and said:

"You've told us a great number of tall tales, but you've always been careful to ensure we can't disprove them, leaving open the question of whether you are a dreadful liar or just possibly telling the truth; but on this occasion you've made a simple and drastic error. You included us in the story! But we know for a fact that we never went to Gemini with you."

"Of course you went there," chuckled Castor.

"No we didn't. We would remember such an amazing thing."

Castor shook his head. "I'm sorry to break the news to you this way, but the madman who loved the moon *did* take his revenge when he returned to the pub. He spiked your beers with Forgetfulness Honey. That's why you don't remember. I guess he wanted to steal away our memories as punishment, hoping to deprive us of some wonderful past experiences. A clever and devious trick! I was lucky, I had already drained my pint and so ordered a fresh one on my return. You should never have drunk those stale beers."

"How can you be sure Forgetfulness Honey was in our drinks?"

"I'm a minor expert on bees and their products. Didn't I treat you to a lecture on apiology, among other topics, just before our voyage? Stale beer is a vile substance anyway. In future you must always buy fresh pints. Why not practice now and get one for me at the same time?"

THE CREAM-JEST OF UNSET CUSTARD

Three times Castor Jenkins dreamed of the marvellous trifle, and three times was it snatched away while still he paused with raised spoon above it. All delectable and wobbly it was, with layers of sponge soaked in brandy and thick whipped cream, to say nothing of the yellow custard, not quite set, like the sweat of the primordial sun that once oozed over swamps wherein things that ought to crawl were learning to walk, badly. And so, unhindered by this overblown prose and the prosaic concerns of everyday, he decided to seek the trifle in his waking life and taste it on his fleshy tongue, no matter what the consequences might be.

But where to look, and who to ask for directions if he got lost, were puzzles of no easy solution, and the enormity of the quest threatened to overwhelm him and cast him into a stupor, in much the same manner that greyish clouds overwhelm the caravan parks and holiday chalets along the Cambrian coast. But let us talk not of weather and turn instead to the questions of whether and whither – *whether* mortal man has any right to seek an object glimpsed only in his night visions, and *whither* such a searcher should go to obtain life insurance at a reasonable rate, for it is no trifle to hunt and devour a dream trifle.

The obvious place to negotiate for directions, insurance and advice was the dark enchanted wood that stood between Porthcawl and the village of Nottage. Smaller than in days of yore, it nonetheless remained the sylvan abode of zoogs, gnoles and other intertextual beings as cruel and brutal as any surprise ending needed them to be. Castor pulled on his hiking boots and selected a stout staff. But he paused at his front door as a better idea struck him, and he realised there was no need to disturb the unpredictable zoogs and gnoles among the whispering leaves and twisting roots of the wood that never will have a name.

Instead he turned to the resource that all modern seekers after secrets, both good and bad, consult as their primary oracle, namely the unfathomable Internet on the glowing mystic monitor. In his bedroom on a desk stood his ebon computer and for many hours Castor sat in his hiking boots with curved spine before the glowing screen, clicking and scrolling and tapping keys like some insectoid supplicant of a half-remembered formic creed. His investigations were thorough and astute but at first yielded no intelligible result, and not even the most blasphemous pages that mutate in the darkest gibbering corners of Wikipedia could aid him in his quest, but at last he found what he wanted on Facebook, a few moments after the dread stroke of midnight chimed dismal.

He learned – and long would the foul knowledge blight the nethermosts of his sanity – that the most evil man in Porthcawl was a certain Mr Hugo Bloat, and furthermore that this depraved individual held the dream trifle in his possession and planned to broach it before dawn. Despite the convoluted syntax in which he was trapped, Castor wasted no time in visionary speculation, but changed his boots for sensible shoes, and his staff for a simple cane, and hurried out into the sombre crepuscularity of the moon-saturated town.

The streets were deserted, slick with freshly fallen rain, and the pounding of the distant surf was a rumble of chthonic and goetic hunger in his conchophobic ears, while the few remaining clouds – those black argosies of moisture – in the inverted abyss of the sky were like ludicrous and tessellated but highly mobile similes that awfully flee an overwrought sentence beyond the restraint horizon. Yes they were. Anyway, with a shake of his head (and a shrugging of the parentheses) he lurched down the abandoned ways in the direction of that residence he had never dared to pass, even when emboldened by beer.

For it has been rightly remarked[7] that in the tallest and thinnest houses dwell the grimmest and sickest souls, and long had it been whispered among the gloomy fishermen down by the misty harbour that the narrow high gabled abode of Hugo Bloat was a place to be avoided at all times. Old Gutsy Conker swore he saw a face in the highest window once that was the exact shape of a set of wind chimes, a face that moved in a horribly sensual manner like the hips of an arcane dancing priestess and tinkled as it did so. And because Old Gutsy was known never to lie, unless paid specifically for that purpose, no person had dared walk that way since. His elbows smelled of fish but not his hands. A bit odd, that.

Castor was no fool and had taken precautions before setting forth into the loneliness of this unnaturally quiet paragraph. From a chest bound with iron hoops in a corner of his bedroom had he retrieved a fetish thing found by him long ago when he sailed the seas with the pirate Captain Ribs. Once on a mysterious island in the heart of a lost overgrown city, while fighting off a tribe of intelligent and sinister monkeys equipped with blowpipes, he plunged through a hidden trapdoor into a secret catacomb, and here had he discovered, by the light of a flaring flambeau, the mummified priest-king of an unknown antediluvian civilisation. Robed was the mummy

---

7   Just now.

in garments that powered to dust at the merest breath or touch, and also adorned with a mask of onyx and gold and materials unknown even to pseudoscience.

So scary was this mask that Castor never shaved himself while wearing it nor did anything else that might require him to gaze into a mirror. But now he fitted it over his face and relished the confidence it gave him. Under the house of his friend Frothing Harris went he, and also near the house of his other friend, Paddy Deluxe, and both gentlemen stumbled out of bed and looked down as he stalked past, roused by some morphogenic twaddle resonance and goaded into attitudes of gaping ghastliness until the masked figure was gone, and then they went back to bed but could not sleep a wink, for they were simple horror story background characters and took everything too seriously.

As for Castor, his heart beating a rhythm scarcely heard since the ancient jungle gods danced to the drums of their reptilian followers when the archaeopteryx filled the sulphurous skies with croaks, he reached the gate of Hugo Bloat's thin mansion and walked up the path with quivering knees. At the black door he rapped the knocker, a knocker shaped like a hideous toad swollen from a diet of poisonous ants, a toad from the same jungle as the drums mentioned in the previous sentence, and stood back and waited with the sweats of dread pouring in oily and almost sentient streams down his face behind the mask. Itchy nose! Involuntarily he glanced up and his heart figuratively turned to basalt, the most inhuman and demonic of all igneous rocks, as he perceived nothing less than a set of wind chimes that resembled a human face! Hideous, hideous, oh!

His first instinct was to turn and flee, but it was too late, as a bolt slid back and the door swung open and the pale visage of Hugo Bloat, most evil man in Porthcawl – has that been mentioned already? – loomed out of the musty shadows, and thin lips curled back over milky but pointy teeth, and anaemic gums shone unhealthily, and filmy pale blue eyes sparkled not with ordinary human glints, and a thin hand protruding from a voluminous sleeve stretched forth and beckoned Castor to cross the threshold and the candle that Mr Bloat held aloft in his other hand spilled hot wax like the ichor of a ghoul over the curiously stained floor, and then the voice issued forth like the rustling of desiccated worms in a sieve:

"Come in, come in, old boy! You're the last to arrive. The party's about to start. There's lots of grub and drink!"

Into the hall went Castor, following the wavering light of the sickening wick, and Hugo Bloat kept up a constant dismal chatter as he led his guest to a flight of stairs that went down, not up, into a vast cellar far below the sane ground, and together they lurched down the steps, deeper and deeper into a hellish region of metamorphic devils and vintage clarets, finally emerging in a large room that contained a table around which sat men and women who wore masks of different kinds, all hideous. And then with a shock that almost caused him to implode, in some bizarre biological incident, Castor realised that not *all* the guests wore masks. Some of them really had faces like that. Cripes! Before he could die of fright, Hugo Bloat addressed the gathering, and Castor was forced to nod and smile.

"Our last guest is here!" cried Mr Bloat, "and I must admit that I'm pleased, because when I sent out the telepathic invitations I wasn't sure everyone got one on time.

You know how these things are. Anyway, without further ado, let's celebrate Cthulhu's birthday!"

"C-c-c-c-c-cthulhu?" stammered Castor.

"Yes, the great priest of the Great Old Ones, the green sticky spawn of the stars, the awful squid-head with writhing feelers, the rubbery amalgam of octopus and dragon, the thing that cannot be described (even though I just did), mighty Cthulhu himself! And today is his birthday! And we're going to have a party, with games and food!"

Castor asked timidly, "Will there be trifle?"

"Absolutely. The greatest trifle ever created, for Cthulhu is one billion years old today! Now please take a seat."

Castor did so, feeling he was locked inside a fever dream in the same way that the end of a snapped key is locked inside a lock. A bit like that anyway. He sat at the last remaining spare place at the table, at the opposite end from Cthulhu himself, or itself, if we're going to be pedantic, which we are, well I am at least, you can be whatever you like. The lights were dim and all Castor could see was a scaly, winged, flabbily clawed, amorphous, bubbling, grotesque, slimy, evil and very very very very very dubious metaphor for sexual repression. He scanned the table and noticed his dream trifle standing in the shadows. Yum! He licked his lips.

A cake was brought for Cthulhu but it didn't have a billion candles on it, for Hugo Bloat explained aloud that such a number would be excessive as well as impossible. No, it had one hundred candles instead, each flame representing ten million years, and the guests encouraged the monster to blow them all out in one go. Cthulhu managed to blow out ninety-three with his first wheezingly liquidy rasp and had to take a second puff to deal with the remaining seven. Then the singing began, a chanting as vile and arcane as Castor had ever heard in his most toxic nightmares. And yet he was forced to join in for the sake of good manners.

Happy birthday to you!
Happy birthday to you!
Happy birthday, dear Cthulhu!
Happy birthday to you!

Three cheers! Hip, hip, hurrah!
Hip, hip, hurrah! Hip, hip, hurraaaay'ai'ng'ngah h'lee-
l'geb f'ai trhodog uaaaaah aaaaaiiiiiieeeeeeeeeeeee
eeeeeee!

For he's a jelly gross fellow,
for he's a jelly gross fellow,
for he's a jelly gross fellow,
Ph'nglui mglw'nafh Cthulhu R'lyeh wgah'nagl fhtagn!

There was a wild round of applause and then the guests began tucking in to the meal. The trifle was broached, bowls of the stuff were passed around and Castor tasted the most cosmic flavours imaginable. He asked for seconds and was granted his heart's desire. Pays to be assertive! Finally satisfied, he was able to take time to inspect the gathering more closely. It seemed to be composed of monsters and humans in roughly equal measure. Apart from Cthulhu, the monsters included Azathoth, Nyarlathotep Yog-Sothoth, Ithaqua, Aphoom-Zhar, Dagon, Zoth-Ommog, Tsathoggua, Yig, Shub-Niggurath, Derleth, Ghatanothoa, and Hastur the Unspeakable, about whom there is not a lot to say.

After the meal there were games. Castor took part in 'blobbing apples', 'musical scares' and a weird hybrid of mysticism and funkiness called 'pinning the grail on the honky'. More games were about to follow, Castor was ready for them, and so were all the guests, when suddenly another figure entered the room from a trapdoor under the table. Plates and uneaten jelly flew everywhere. The table toppled over and smashed into pieces. This new arrival was Nagoob, the androgynous mother of Cthulhu. Nagoob grimaced and shook a tentacle-finger and said, "It's getting late. You've had your fun. Time for bed!"

Cthulhu kicked up a fuss but in vain. Off he went with Nagoob, dragged by the lobe of one his ears, and the other monsters drifted away one by one, making various excuses. Without the birthday abomination present, the party quickly deflated. The human guests stood aimlessly and some of them departed too. Castor thought about leaving but he went up the wrong flight of steps and emerged in a room with a cool sound system. A beautiful girl from Macedonia by the name of Brankica Bozinovska was also there. They selected some great music and danced until morning, like adults, like people without psychological problems.

THE DAY THE TOWN OF PORTHCAWL WAS ACCIDENTALLY TWINNED WITH THE CAPITAL OF THE CHEESE AND BISCUITS EMPIRE

When Castor Jenkins wanted to give up smoking, he realised that the further he had to walk to obtain cigarettes the less often he would buy them. Shortly after this revelation he required a fresh packet, so he left his house and proceeded down the street, but instead of pausing at the corner shop he kept going. He also passed the supermarket and several newsagents. Soon the town was behind him and he was in open country with night drawing on.

It was creepy, very creepy. Owls hooted in the trees. Ghosts mounted on bony stallions jousted with skeletons mounted on spectral mares. Stuff like that. Castor kept walking under the enormous moon without altering his stride until one of the moonbeams slapped him in the face and it became apparent that the yellow globe above was actually a balloon with a rope ladder dangling from it. On impulse he climbed up into the wicker basket.

There were no other occupants: the balloon was adrift on the aerial currents and heading east. Castor gripped the side of the basket and peered down at the gloomy landscape. On the very tops of the trees, where they thought they couldn't be seen, the owls played backgammon. The hooting was just an act. Feeling he would never trust an owl again, he settled back to enjoy the ride. Far below, stunted hills rushed past like grounded clouds on castors.

Fatigued by that strained simile, he slept soundly and when he awoke he was over a choppy sea with the end of the rope ladder trailing through the tops of the waves.

He looked down and saw a triton, a male mermaid, with a trident slung over its back, climbing the hemp rungs with intentions that were obviously not friendly. Castor cut the ladder with his penknife and the triton plunged back into the deeps from whence it came.

The balloon soared higher, the sea gave way to land, mountains thrust up their peaks like free jazz triangles, and the low pressure began to give Castor the same sort of headache as cheap red wine, but without the fuss of uncorking. Many of these mountains were crowned with crumbling castles, malign gothic confections fused to the rock, and figures in hooded cloaks roamed the battlements, pointing at the balloon in surprise and dismay.

Once a strange flapping machine that seemed a combination of vulture and bee spiralled up from a tower and flew alongside Castor. Then it turned and punctured his canopy with a great artificial sting, pumping yellow venom through clear tubes before disengaging and plummeting to the ground with folded wings, littering an icy valley with splinters of wood and scraps of fabric. Castor felt no sympathy. His main concern was for his own survival.

The balloon began to lose height and there was no ballast in the basket to toss over the side. Down it drifted, closer to the serrated peaks, closer to the impossibly decadent castles, and Castor felt his time was up at last. But then he passed over a particularly sharp ridge and noticed the crater below, a crater filled with a lake. On the shores of this lake stood a circular city, a collection of narrow houses with tall chimneys. All was not yet lost!

The basket touched down in the cold waters of the lake and the deflated canopy settled next to it. Castor used his penknife to cut the cords binding the basket to the now useless mass of silk, hard work indeed, and when it was finally free he leaned over the side and paddled to dry land with his bare hands. He approached a rotting wooden jetty, snatched hold of a dangling knotted rope, pulled the basket against a thick mooring pole and climbed up.

There was nobody in sight. Castor called out a general greeting but received no reply. He shrugged and went to explore the bizarre city. He passed a kiosk that sold cigarettes but did not spend any of his money there, preferring to continue up a cobbled street to a public square where some sort of ceremony was taking place. Men and women stood in a ring around a black vertical structure that he eventually identified as a large water clock.

He asked the nearest person, "What's going on?"

The reply was sorrowful. "We're waiting for rain. Our clock has been empty for almost a year and until it fills up again we can't tell what hour it is. Time has stopped in our city, I'm sorry to say, and we are helpless to do anything about it, and in fact we can't even move."

Castor said, "Why don't you fetch a bucket of water from the lake to fill the clock? Surely any liquid will do?"

"How can any of us walk to the lake? Time has stopped and thus all motion is impossible. Don't you know anything about physics? Without time there is no movement: in fact TIME is nothing more than MOVEMENT. Without movement, there is no going anywhere!"

"I'll fetch water for you," offered Castor.

"Nonsense! If lying wasn't impossible without time I'd call you a liar and slap your lying cheeks, you monster!"

"But you are moving right now, your lips anyway."

"No I'm not. Stuff like that is an illusion. The thing that depresses me is that we're going to have to wait for all eternity because rain can't fall in a place where there's no time. What a dilemma!"

"I'll resolve it for you," announced Castor.

Since leaving Porthcawl, he hadn't relieved himself once and now his bladder was painfully full. He pushed through the immobile crowd, reached the side of the water clock and regarded the service ladder pegged to the side. Climbing this, he straddled the opening at the top of the device, unbuttoned his trousers and ensured that the reservoir was no longer dry. There was a sudden shifting of gears, a grind of wheels, jerk of a minute hand.

The crowd gasped. "Time has been restarted!"

Castor climbed down amid cheers. Strong hands patted him on the back and a portly man in bursting clothes thrust his red face at him. "How may we ever repay you? I'm the unofficial ruler and thus in a position to give you the freedom of the city, and so I hereby do, with all the traditional benefits, such as free use of public transport, pickles and concubines."

"I accept the honour," announced Castor.

"Let us repair to the nearest tavern at once and joyfully slide many beers in your direction, not forgetting a chip supper!"

"Sir, you are an astute judge of character!" declared Castor. "But I must point out that the amount of fluid I contributed to the clock will allow it to run for a few hours at most. I base this judgement on complex mental calculations of volume and pressure that I made during the act."

"In those situations I usually just whistle," returned the ruler. "You truly are a prodigy. But the solution is obvious!"

He shouted out a few instructions and the crowd formed an orderly queue. One by one they climbed the clock and followed Castor's example, filling the device to the brim with highly pressurised kidney juice. Now the clock was guaranteed to keep going for many months, if not years. The ruler led Castor out of the square along an alley and through an archway into a courtyard. At the end of the courtyard stood a venerable, shadowy tavern.

Castor entered and took a seat in the common room. Perching opposite him, the ruler ordered beer and chips. The tavern was almost deserted. A musician sat on a stool in the corner, discordantly plucking at an enormous lute with twenty strings. Before the ruler could make any remarks, a buxom serving girl hurried up with two enormous jugs. Castor accepted the beer and took a deep gulp gratefully. A big bowl of chips followed shortly.

"Your first time in Chaud-Mellé?" asked the ruler.

"Is that the name of this city? I've never heard of it. Are we still in Europe? I arrived by free balloon and don't have my passport. But to answer your question properly, yes I'm a newcomer, and before you wonder if my purpose is business or pleasure, I left Wales to buy cigarettes."

"We are not quite in the Europe you know," explained the ruler, "but occupy a buffer zone between Earth and Happenstance, a planet that recently collided with our world and got stuck to it. Don't look so distraught! The impact was very mild and nobody noticed who didn't see it occur. But there were other effects. Weather patterns were seriously disrupted."

"Is that why you don't get much rain these days?"

"Exactly. When our water clock went dry, we literally ran out of time. So you came along at the right moment!"

"Why not invest in mechanical timepieces?"

The ruler grimaced. "The situation is tragic. Chaud-Mellé was once famed for its clock towers, hundreds and hundreds of them, and the precisely timed gothic excesses and tabulated debaucheries they made possible. But now we are left with just one *clepsydra* (the correct term for a water clock) and are no superior to any ordinary Alpine settlement full of yodellers and sausages! This has nothing to do with the collision but was our own fault."

"What happened?" wondered Castor.

"We decided to relocate the city on a whim. It was already surrounded by tall mountains, but they weren't quite high enough for our sense of the melodramatic, so we contacted the Carnacki Moving Company to transport our buildings, bridges and roads a hundred or so miles north, into the heart of a more impressive range, but most of the structures went missing during the actual move and then the firm went bust and we lost our right to compensation. We were left with maybe 10% of our original city and what remained was all jumbled up and scratched. We truly were treated in a shoddy fashion!"

Castor nodded and finished his beer. The ruler was attentive and ordered him another. "Moving is always a stressful experience," said Castor, "and ranks with marital breakup and toothache."

The ruler was bitter. "In a warehouse somewhere, our buildings are gathering dust: the opera house, the university, the prison, the hothouses where we harvested Forgetfulness Honey, not to mention the public parks and squares with fountains, all covered by tarpaulin and un-loved!"

"How did you harvest Forgetfulness Honey?" asked Castor.

"I don't rightly recall. All I remember are those strange giant bees that look like gliders... Anyway, there's no point crying over the past: it has never cried over me, at least not to my present knowledge!"

"Why are you the *unofficial* ruler of Chaude-Mellé?"

"Because I'm the head of the most secret society in the city – so secret I'm not sure who the other members are – or even if there are any – and my proper title is the Impotentate of the Platinum Dawn. But you can address me by my real name, Jubjub Loos, like one of my close friends."

"Will I get to be on such familiar terms with you?"

"That depends how long you stay."

"I was just passing through," said Castor, "but I'll be glad to break my trip for a couple of luxurious months here."

"Good man," said Jubjub, and he called for more beer.

Castor drank himself into a stupor and woke, blink-ing, in morning sunlight in a nicely furnished room on the second floor of the tavern. A little bell stood on a low table next to his comfortable bed and almost by instinct he reached out and rang it. Breakfast was instantly brought to him by a semi-naked maiden who also soothed his hungover brow. After another short sleep and a hot bath he dressed in the fine clothes that had been left for him.

He descended into the street and was applauded by a large crowd of people but his progress wasn't hampered in any way. Wherever he went people saluted him, called out compliments or offered him their bodies for sexual purposes. Wandering into the market he emerged with bags of free fruit that had been thrust upon him. In a small restaurant he ordered coffee and a light snack and was given wine and a big complicated meal instead, for free.

He waddled out of the restaurant, burping all the way, and decided to look for a quiet place, maybe a leafy park, where he might digest his food in peace. Keeping to the less obvious alleyways he managed to avoid too much attention until he was compelled to cross the Rubellas-trasse, one of the main arteries of the city. A sedan chair that was approaching suddenly stopped, its door opened and Jubjub himself jumped out with a very low bow.

"My vehicle is at your service. I will walk!"

"I don't need it, thanks," said Castor, but felt he had no choice. He climbed into the box and allowed the runners who carried it to take him on a circuit around the city until they were exhausted. Then he disembarked at a sweet shop and filled his pockets with lollipops and toffees.

Feeling bloated beyond belief, he entered a sauna and had his stomach cramps massaged away by three women, a redhead, blonde and brunette. He remembered that his main objective was to buy cigarettes, but he decided to complete that task some other day. It was too relaxing here. Relaxing and strangely stimulating... One of those wonderful paradoxes again!

Castor remained in Chaud-Mellé for almost six weeks before things began to go wrong. People around him became less accommodating, waiters and concubines grew surly and muttered about payment, the sedan chair runners made excuses for not carrying him, citing sprained ankles and blisters. At last he decided to lodge a complaint with the Impotentate. He walked to the Temple of the Platinum Dawn and knocked loudly on the door.

Jubjub answered in person. He appeared to have no office staff. He regarded Castor with a mixture of regret and rage.

"I thought I had the freedom of the city!" snapped Castor.

"You did, I mean you do," replied Jubjub, "but there has been a small problem, a change, an unforeseen consequence. In short, you are no longer as welcome here as once you were. Oh, we continue to honour you – it's our duty – but do so without any love, in fact we have only malice in our hearts now. Life has been comfortable enough for you, I dare say, in the past six weeks. But for the rest of us things have gone rather badly. There has been a severe economic downturn, the stock market has crashed, and the crime rate is soaring."

"None of that is my fault!" protested Castor.

"I assure you that it is. When you urinated into the water clock, and thereby set an example that we all followed, you contaminated the actual *seconds*, *minutes* and *hours* by which this city lives. Life in Chaud-Mellé recently has (for want of a less vulgar word) been pretty pissy."

"But this is weird! Liquid is liquid, surely?"

Jubjub shook his head. "That's not the case here. Thanks to you, we have been using smelly yellow time instead of the clean blue kind. Our businesses are failing as a result. Everything has got worse."

Castor Jenkins chewed his lower lip. "It's probably best if I depart Chaud-Mellé and resume my original quest. I'll bid you farewell and leave you alone. But can you give me any advice about the lands that lie to the east?"

Jubjub pulled at his chin. "My knowledge is vague. Why don't you head west and return home instead?"

"I want to buy cigarettes," said Castor, "and I can't go back empty handed. But I would like to have some idea of what awaits me beyond the mountains."

"Very well. Before you enter Happenstance proper, you must cross the Cheese and Biscuits Empire, a vast realm north of the Grape Lands. I know nothing about its government or people. There is a precarious path that will take you from Chaud-Mellé as far as the Sorbet Glacier. Then you must brave the ice and yodelling until you reach the first Gouda Gate. That's all I know."

Castor smiled. "Good enough. Now I will equip myself for the voyage and leave you in peace."

He took final advantage of his status and obtained new hiking boots, a rucksack, warm clothing and food from the appropriate shops without spending a single coin. But no maps were available anywhere and it was clear that few people, if any at all, had ventured east from the city. Castor set off with a confident stride. He passed through the thin outskirts of Chaud-Mellé, climbed the steep side of the crater and located the start of the narrow path.

The weather remained good and the sun set in a display of rich orange and purple behind him, slopping colour over the snowy peaks on all sides, so that he stopped to turn and watch. Then he continued in the fading light but storm clouds took advantage of the dusk to sneak up. Rain and more rain! He sheltered under an overhang, wrapped himself tight in his heavy coat and slumbered fitfully. In the morning he was cramped and sore. Onwards he went in dampened spirits.

And so his journey grew less enjoyable with each passing day. Finally he topped a rise and peered down at an immense wedge of lemon ice. The Sorbet Glacier! Stumbling down the path, he reached the smooth surface just as a figure stepped onto it from the other direction. This figure approached rapidly, a man carrying a case on a strap over his shoulder, and Castor shouted an amazed greeting. He recognised the stranger, a man called the Postmodern Mariner, having met him on two separate occasions in the past.

They paused in the middle of the glacier and shook hands. "Where are you going?" they asked each other.

The Postmodern Mariner answered first, "My destination is Wales, the town of Porthcawl in fact. There's a rumour that the mating cry of a plesiosaurus was recently heard on a night with poor visibility. I want to investigate and maybe write a short article about it."

"Permit me to save you the effort," Castor said.

And he explained that the cry of the plesiosaurus was nothing more than the lonely sound of a foghorn. The Postmodern Mariner reached into his pocket for a pencil and notebook, squinted at a list and ticked off the top item with a sigh. "In that case, I'm going to Chaud-Mellé for some vegetables, bread, chocolate, coffee and toothpaste." He struggled to read his own handwriting. "And a packet of lentils. What does that say?"

Castor peered at the list. "Paprika, I think, or kraken…"

"I sometimes doubt that supernatural sea creatures exist at all! My job is a very dispiriting one!"

Castor was sympathetic. "I had an encounter with a triton a few months ago. Please don't give up yet!"

"Where are you headed?" the Postmodern Mariner asked.

"To the Cheese and Biscuits Empire. I know nothing about it and can't even be sure if it's a kingdom or a republic."

The Postmodern Mariner pursed his lips. "A long and difficult journey by foot, over many glaciers much worse than this one, between mountains infested with brigands, through forests full of creatures that even the gnoles have nightmares about, and over swamps that smell like the armpits of an octopus. Do you have some other form of transportation you might use? A helicopter for example?"

"I don't," Castor admitted.

"How about a motorbike fitted with Gatling guns?"

"I'm afraid not."

"A mechanical riding spider with tungsten knees?"

"Just my own legs."

The Postmodern Mariner blinked and puffed out his cheeks. Then he said, "In that case, why not take the Sea Train?"

"What's that?" asked Castor.

"A vehicle originally invented in Brazil to carry mermaids between different subaquatic carnivals."

"But we're inland," protested Castor.

"You don't understand. The Sea Train doesn't just run under the sea, it can go anywhere. The name refers to how it's constructed. It's made from solidified sea water."

"How bizarre," commented Castor.

"The nearest Sea Train station is at the far end of this glacier. The next express is due twenty minutes from now. That will take you directly to Rysnap, the capital of the

Cheese and Biscuits Empire, skirting all the perils on the way. It's free to ride, but once you arrive in Rysnap you'll have to offer the Gross Fondoo something in return."

"Is the Gross Fondoo the melted – I mean elected – ruler?"

"Yes, he's the big cheese. But ruling is only one of his hobbies. He does other things as well and when he gets angry his brow throbs with smelly blue veins. He likes to spread himself around."

"What gives him the right to run an empire?" cried Castor.

"He's very runny, that's what!"

"I'll offer him one of my stories in exchange for the train ride. Everybody likes to hear the tales of Castor Jenkins, the Münchausen of Porthcawl. Maybe I'll entertain him with an account of how I once swallowed an apple pip and for many years had a tree instead of a skeleton."

"You define yourself as a Münchausen?"

"No, no, I always tell the truth. That was a slip of the tongue! Anyway, I have many stories the Gross Fondoo will like to hear, I'm sure. Thanks for the help and good luck with the shopping."

"Be careful. The Gross Fondoo is a difficult man to please…"

"Yes, yes, thanks again! Goodbye!"

Castor hastened to the end of the Sorbet Glacier where he found the little platform and a wooden bench on which he could rest. Punctual and strange, the Sea Train emerged from a tunnel carved into the side of a mountain. It slid to a halt and Castor entered one of the carriages. It was unlike any train he had known. The sides were made of brine that was somehow fixed in place without being frozen and the floor of the carriage was littered with the lost bangles and necklaces of mermaids.

The train pulled out of the station. Half expecting an urchin or jellyfish to suddenly appear and demand to inspect his ticket, Castor found it hard to relax and enjoy the journey. It was impossible to see anything through the windows: they were speckled with ancient trapped moonlight. Whenever the train lurched around a bend, the windows swirled and reset in new patterns of luminosity. Castor imagined that bizarre and monstrous scenes were taking place outside the train, but he never got to know for sure.

He was on the train for almost twelve hours before it finally pulled to a halt in Rysnap's main station. Castor disembarked and marvelled at his surroundings. The city was vast, modern and intimidating, far beyond his expectations. Nobody spoke to him or even noticed his presence. He wandered around, realised he was penniless and found a quiet park where he could devour what remained of his hiking supplies. He didn't care to sleep rough in such an unfamiliar metropolis, so he decided to seek out the Gross Fondoo and ask for employment as a raconteur.

Having just made this resolution, he was approached by two uniformed guards who pounced on him with shackles and carried him to a motor cart. Roaring down the boulevards, Castor had a free sightseeing tour of Rysnap. Mighty towers, massive public sculptures, cheese and cracker restaurants... This city had it all. At last the motor cart stopped in front of a palace and Castor was unloaded and hefted into the presence of the Gross Fondoo, who regarded him with eyebrows like poppy seeds sprinkled above his eyes. His voice was sickeningly sibilant.

"So this is the fellow who tried to avoid paying the fare!"

"I'm willing to pay it now, plus a fine!" blurted Castor. "Allow me to pay by telling a remarkably tall story; it is more of a conjecture than a factual account. It's about the backgammon tournaments of the owls..."

"Bah!" groaned the Gross Fondoo. "I don't need another tale teller. I already have an excellent one."

And he clapped his hands and roared: "Pollux!"

Into the room bounded Castor's identical twin brother. Castor protested in alarm, "But he's the exact spiritual opposite of me! Surely you don't enjoy his anecdotes and narratives?"

"The exact opposite, is he?" crooned the Gross Fondoo. "Does that mean you are a pathological liar?" Then he clicked his fingers and cried, "Pollux! A tale!"

Pollux Jenkins rolled his eyes, pulled his nose, shifted his weight from one foot to another and began, "Once I was swallowed by an ant, not a giant ant but an ordinary one, smaller than average in fact, and it was a tight fit, especially as I was a hippopotamus at the time..."

"Enough!" commanded the Gross Fondoo. He turned to Castor. "That short demonstration must convince you that we don't need another raconteur. You must offer something else!"

Castor had no possessions and realised he was in a tricky situation. As if by accident he was struck with inspiration. "Why don't I offer you the town of Porthcawl? I don't mean as a physical gift, in the sense that the town of Obidos in Portugal was given to the king's bride on her wedding night. I mean in a symbolic sense.

Have you heard of the custom of twinning towns around the world? Rysnap and Porthcawl could be twinned. You would be able to send your young people there for an education, take part in cultural exchanges of all kinds, woo our women…"

"Very well, I accept this offering," said the Gross Fondoo. He clapped his hands again. "For the first cultural exchange, I command 10,000 of my fiercest warriors to march on Porthcawl immediately!" He turned to grin at Castor. "I hope Porthcawl is good enough to be twinned with the beautiful and powerful city of Rysnap. If it isn't, you'll be in trouble for trying to trick me. Tell me about the charms of your town."

Castor took a deep breath. He thought about Porthcawl and its many attractions: the surrounding dunes and golf courses, the enormous caravan park to the east, the rotting funfair, the annual pantomime at the Grand Pavilion (a building with a seating capacity of 643), the grey limestone headlands, the greasy pubs and chip shops, the rain, the rain, the rain, the retired people, the evil seagulls and dogs, the yeasty beer.

"I've got something else to offer you!" he babbled.

The Gross Fondoo raised one of his peculiar eyebrows. "It's too late to recall my warriors, but if you want to give me a second gift, I won't complain. What is it?"

"Extra salt for your crackers."

The Gross Fondoo looked left and right. "Oh yes? Where is this salt?"

"The Sea Train… If you break it into tiny pieces with hammers, you can sprinkle it over your crackers. The train is made of brine, you see, and it has been proven that sea salt is healthier than rock salt."

"Good idea! I accept that suggestion as a formal gift. Well done! In fact it's such a fine idea that I feel I owe you some change. What can I get you? A packet of cigarettes, perhaps?"

"I've just quit," replied Castor Jenkins.

2: TRIBULATIONS OF THE HUMAN BEAN

Castor has seemingly been everything in his time; he worked in a circus and was an ornithologist once; and his knowledge of mythical creatures is second to none. The following pages fill in some of the gaps about all that, and also describe the first time he became friendly with Paddy and Harris during a strange silky and silly adventure in their company. The literary agent who sold this book also has a turn telling a personal story in which Castor just happens to be one of the characters.

THE MONKEY'S PAWPAW

The seaside town of Porthcawl sparkled like the fake jewels on the cheap necklace of a bad actress. But Castor Jenkins and his friends didn't notice the effect because they were inside it.

They sat in their usual pub near the broad window that looked over the rocky shoreline; and Castor finished the bowl of crisps that stood in front of him, washed the barbed crumbs down his throat with a greedy gulp of beer and wiped his lips with his sleeve.

"This is all very peculiar," he said thoughtfully.

"What is?" chorused his friends.

"There hasn't been a storm for a week. It hasn't even rained for three days. But we are living in Wales! It always rains in Wales. Can you see that strange yellow ball in the sky?"

His friends squinted as they followed his finger. "Do you mean the one that hurts the eyes to look at?"

"That's called the sun, that is," explained Castor, "and it's something they get a lot in foreign countries, even in England; but Wales, Ireland and Scotland aren't generally allowed to have it. Occasionally, as a treat, it comes to visit; but it never *stays*."

His friends nodded wisely, then Paddy Deluxe said, "I might as well confess that I'm to blame for this. I found a magic charm, you see, on the beach, and I used it to make a wish."

And he reached into his pocket and pulled out a battered shoe with a few limpets clinging to the heel. Castor frowned and inspected it, stroking it with gentle fingers and humming.

"Impressive. It appears to have been designed for a left foot. But how do you know it's magic? It might just be an ordinary item of footwear lost by a sailor after evil mermaids tricked him into undressing. Such objects do circulate with the ocean currents."

Paddy smirked. "Turn the shoe over. What do you see? It's the official mark of some ancient water demon."

Castor answered, "Yes, you're quite right. That is certainly the symbol of an ocean-based demigod. Although much eroded his name seems to be CLARKS. I ought to check my grimoires and other books of sorcery later to learn what his attributes might be."

"Anyway," resumed Paddy, "I used this shoe to ensure the endless rain of Wales went away. That's why there haven't been any storms or drizzles lately. So I'm the one to be thanked."

Castor was just about to congratulate him, with appropriate zeal, when the other friend interrupted. Frothing Harris reached into his own pocket and drew out his own battered shoe.

"Not so fast!" he objected, as he flung it on the table. "For it seems I'm about to be cheated of my rightful allowance of praise. This is the magic charm I found last week; and I used it to make exactly the same wish that Paddy did. So who is to say who is truly responsible for driving away the bad weather? It might well be me!"

Castor picked up the second shoe and examined the sole. "It was made for a right foot, but it doesn't form a pair with the other one, for shape and texture are different; but it does have a magic symbol carved into it, also much eroded, and the name of a rival oceanic demigod, MARTEN. If only I had my reference books to hand!"

"Or to foot," wryly commented Paddy.

Harris asked, "How can we determine which of us was responsible for making the dreadful rain stay away?"

Castor said, "I don't use the word *blame* lightly, but you must share it equally, for when the same wish is made independently on two charms of similar design, the force is multiplied."

"Doubled, you mean?" asked Paddy.

"At the very least," acknowledged Castor. Then he sighed and finished his beer and seemed much dejected. Eventually, after considerable urging from his anxious friends, he added, "I fear it will never rain again and that Porthcawl will wilt in the grip of an eternal drought and we will be forced to brew our beer from sea water or else perish. By wishing away the rain twice you have banished it forever."

Harris frowned. "Are you sure about that? The prognosis is an extreme one and I would like to know what reasons you have for making it. Until I am convinced of my guilt I refuse to feel remorse. I acted in good faith at every stage of the wishing process."

"Me too," said Paddy, waving his shoe.

"Very well," said Castor suddenly. "I will tell you a tale about another case of double wishing and you may draw your own analogies. But first I require further lubrication. Buy me a pint and be quick about it! For soon beer will be too briny to stomach except in small doses. Now let me relate the tragedy of a cyclops on a roof..."

* * * *

It wasn't a normal cyclops (said Castor) but a particularly horrid variation properly known as a *spolcyc* that is more rare and perhaps more evil than the basic kind. In the past century only a dozen have been reported; and the

Reverend Richards had the misfortune to be lumbered with a stubborn one that wouldn't leave him alone.

I'll tell you a secret about the Reverend. He never stopped regretting his move to Porthcawl, but it wasn't his decision in the first place. His bishop had ordered him to come here. At first he rather liked the seaside town; its relative quietness and the sea views appealed to him; and his church seemed a venerable edifice.

And yes, it is visually a charming structure, that's for certain, but it had a tendency to attract spooks and monsters. Maybe some former priest was of a sorcerous bent and opened an astral gateway without shutting it later. Let that be a lesson to you! Always close astral gateways securely when you set off exploring spirit worlds.

And pick up your psychic litter! And don't light fires!

Whatever the truth of the matter, Reverend Richards was plagued with more than his share of grims. He had demons popping up behind the pews and even getting stuck in organ pipes; and his bell made a moaning sound instead of a metallic clang, and when he went to check he discovered that the clapper was an inverted skeleton.

Do you know what a *nogrog* is? It's like a gorgon but not quite. In fact it has mongooses for hair and it preys on gorgons. It's a sort of backwards gorgon. I mention this because every type of monster is supposed to have its own negative version, and the *nogrog* is the best known of this bizarre subset of mythical beings. Anyway...

One night during a thunderstorm, the Reverend was roused from sleep by a knocking on his door. He dressed quickly and went down and found himself confronting a group of drenched parishioners who cried, "On the roof. It's up on the roof. A monster!"

"The roof of my house?" babbled the Reverend.

"No, no, the roof of the church!"

The Reverend was sick of demons and other frights; he wanted only to return to bed, but if he turned his back on his parishioners and they wrote to the bishop to complain of his negligence, as doubtlessly they would, he would be in for a severe reprimand.

So he snatched up an umbrella and followed the agitated group to the building. The umbrella blew inside out instantly and was snatched away by the wind and sent flapping over the town, ending up in a hidden valley to the west where all lost umbrellas are busy evolving into a new species of crow. But that's a different story.

By the time he reached the cursed church he was sodden, bedraggled and alone, for his parishioners had melted away to their own homes one by one, having fulfilled their duty simply by notifying him of the trouble. He sneezed and blinked at the roof.

It was too dark to make out much, but a black shambling silhouette of indeterminate size was definitely perched on the summit of the tower. It clung there precariously, wobbling.

A sudden flash of lightning illuminated the scene!

It was a being unlike any he had ever seen. It was almost spherical and seemed to be made entirely of eyes.

Yes, it was a *spolcyc*, the negative or reciprocal of a cyclops. As we all know, the cyclops is a visually challenged horror, possessing one eye; the *spolcyc* has its own weaknesses, despite its greater observational abilities, being unable to pass through thorny thickets or roll over broken glass. It's an endangered being for that reason.

The Reverend repressed his instinct to flee.

He stood in the lashing rain and wondered what action to take, but the only solution that occurred to him was to fetch a ladder and climb to the roof; he had a vague notion he might be able to talk the *spolcyc* down. All the same, he wasn't confident it would listen to him. Perhaps it was stuck fast up there. But how it had managed to get to the top of the tower in the first place? He would be sure to ask.

There was a ladder in the little shed that sagged its rotting planks in a corner of the overgrown graveyard. This was where the sexton kept most of the tools of his trade; he needed a ladder to climb out of graves once he had dug them. The Reverend picked his way through the damp grass and was relieved to discover that the shed was unlocked. He opened the door and groped around in dusty darkness.

Finally he extracted what he required, an extendable ladder that at full reach was sufficiently long to take him to the roof of the church. Leaning it against the most dependable gargoyle, the Reverend scaled it rapidly to the guttering and pulled himself over.

He stood on the sloping roof and gingerly made his way across the wet slates to the base of the tower. The *spolcyc* leaned over from its perch and watched his approach; being made of eyes it could scarcely do otherwise. With a shudder, the Reverend returned the stare, in an attenuated fashion, with his single hazel pair of peepers.

"Now look here, my good thing—" he began saying.

Suddenly there was a mighty flash and a deafening boom and with his ears whistling, the Reverend fell backwards, sliding over the slates almost to the very edge of the roof. He shook his head numbly. A lightning bolt had scored a direct hit on the church!

The *spolcyc* was shivering like a supersonic jelly, for want of a better simile, and the pupils of all its eyes were grossly dilated; and to his horror the Reverend saw that his own image was reflected in every black pool of unholy perception. Then he shrieked.

He shrieked with pity for his own tarnished soul!

We all know how a bright light can create an afterimage and how it's not unknown for such afterimages to last for many hours. So intense had been the lightning flash that an afterimage of the Reverend had appeared in every single one of the *spolcyc's* innumerable eyes, an afterimage that was so deeply burned it was permanent.

The Reverend realised this as he lay sprawled on the slates. For long minutes he absorbed the implications, then he regained his willpower and dragged himself over the roof to the point where the ladder connected the guttering to the ground, and he descended, rung by careful rung, back to ground level, the *spolcyc* high above.

This was a dreadful outcome, the very worst!

Wherever it looked, the *spolcyc* would see the Reverend superimposed on any background; he would be perpetually in the monster's sights. That was truly an unholy and unwholesome fate for his image, and more to the point, his parishioners wouldn't like it.

They would associate him, the Reverend, with it, the beast; they would deduce in their narrow-minded way that there's no smoke without fire, no eyelash without an eyelid, no afterimage without collusion. He would be tarred, thickly, with the unnatural brush.

The bishop would be furious too…

Besides which, he didn't care himself to be constantly observed, even in the confines of an optical illusion, by a *spolcyc*; it felt blasphemous and icky. He had to find a way of wiping the afterimage away! But how could such a tricky remedy be implemented?

There were two doctors he knew vaguely, deadly rivals but experts in all manner of medical techniques. He would ask them individually to help and he felt better once his resolution had been made. Returning the ladder to the shed, he squelched slowly home.

The following morning, he paid his first visit to Dr Vaughan, who was happy to listen to his problem; the medical savant expressed confidence that he could devise an effective antidote to the afterimage. It would take a day and cost a few thousand pounds.

"And that's a real bargain, believe me!" he declared, before adding in a low tone, "The main thing is that you asked me and not that idiotic quack, Dr Frazer, who would be sure to cheat you and leave you in a worse mess than you are already in. Pah! I spit on that cretin! Whatever you do, don't go anywhere near the poxy charlatan."

The Reverend sighed and felt duty bound to confess that he intended a visit to Dr Frazer immediately after this consultation was over. He wanted to give the task to both doctors simultaneously to increase the chance of success, for competition was likely to make both strive harder; the bishop would expect no less. Yet he was sorry.

"Humph!" groaned Dr Vaughan. "I have no intention of swallowing a feeble apology appended to such an insult, and I regard your procedure in this matter to be cynical and unworthy, and yet I can't turn down a chance to humiliate my rival. So yes, I do accept your commission! I will nullify the afterimage completely while that fool gropes and clatters in the murk of his incompetence. Just wait and see!"

Wincing slightly at the triumphant use of the last word in that speech, the Reverend thanked Dr Vaughan and left his consultation room with a lump in his throat. Already he had some bad premonitions. He found Dr Frazer to be in an equally waspish mood.

"You mean to tell me that you went to visit that pompous fake before coming here! Well, I am mortally offended by that news. Doubtless he filled your head with lies and slanders about me. In your favour is the fact you evidently didn't believe them, for now you are here; and your strange little problem does give me the opportunity to degrade that buffoon. In other words, I accept your commission!!

The Reverend went away, satisfied and appalled in equal measure. He planned to avoid his church for the day. But as it happened, that decision wasn't his to make. As we'll soon learn…

Dr Vaughan refused to treat any more patients until he had solved this odd case. He said to himself, "I imagine that Dr Frazer will utilise modern scientific methods to wipe away the afterimage; but I have something that is far more potent. True monkey magic!"

And he took a little key and opened a secret cabinet concealed behind a portrait of himself and he reached inside and withdrew a papaya. It was mummified and odourless but a magnificent example of the tropical fruit nonetheless. He held it up to a dusty green sunbeam that slanted through his tinted window and smiled thinly.

"The sacred papaya of Spanko the monkey god!"

He had acquired it while travelling through the land of Gabon when he was an intrepid medical student, many decades previously. It could grant a single wish and he had been saving it for a special occasion. The special occasion had arrived at last! He caressed the fruit lovingly. He had found it in the temple of a ruined city in the jungle. Sweeping all his papers and equipment off his desk with a vigorous forearm, he gently placed the fruit at the centre of the expanse of teak.

In the meantime, Dr Frazer was also refusing to examine new patients. He said slyly to himself, "I imagine that Dr Vaughan will utilise modern scientific methods to wipe away the afterimage; but I have something that is far more potent. True monkey magic!"

And he took a little key and opened a secret cabinet concealed behind a portrait of himself and he reached inside and withdrew a papaya. It was mummified and odourless but a magnificent example of the tropical fruit nonetheless. He held it up to a dusty purple sunbeam that slanted through his tinted window and smiled thinly.

"The divine papaya of Basha the monkey god!"

He had acquired it while travelling through the land of Congo when he was an intrepid medical student, many decades previously. It could grant a single wish and he had been saving it for a special occasion. The special occasion had arrived at last! He caressed the fruit lovingly. He had found it in the chamber of a lost pyramid in the jungle. Sweeping his papers and equipment off his desk with a violent forearm, he softly placed the fruit at the centre of the expanse of mahogany.

The old name for papaya is pawpaw, by the way. I'm sure you already knew that. So let's just state the play:

Two monkey gods, two pawpaws, two wishes…

Anyone who is familiar with the primate deities of Africa will want to protest at this point and cry, "But isn't Zumboo the only god of monkeys? Didn't he conquer all others and ferry them in a banana canoe to the land of unreason where they disintegrated?"

The answer to that is no, it's just a myth. There are still many monkey gods. Thomp is another, for example. True, Zumboo's the most powerful, but so what? The point is that Spanko and Basha both exist and are equals in terms of magical force. Which explains the following. Both the wishes acted simultaneously, you see, and amplified each other. Exactly like the same unwise wish on the magic shoes.

The wish uttered by Dr Vaughan and Dr Frazer was as follows: "Let it henceforth be impossible for the *spolcyc* to see the Reverend Richards. In the pungent name of all simian fruit..."

When praying to monkey gods, one must always say 'apemen' instead of 'amen'. It's a crucial point. Neither doctor neglected this formality; thus the wishes were granted, or rather one wish was granted twice. And never again did the monster see the Reverend.

Unfortunately, nor did anyone else see him from that moment, at least not in his customary form. Had only one doctor made the wish, doubtless the afterimage would have been cleansed from the *spolcyc's* multitude of eyes; but a double wish produces a far stronger effect. And so it happened that the Reverend ended up in the one place in the universe where a beast made of eyes could never glimpse him.

Yes, he vanished into the creature! More accurately, he was absorbed by the *spolcyc* so that he became its body, with all the eyes studded over him, looking outward. Even if he stared into a mirror he wouldn't be able to see himself, because the eyes covered him completely. However hard he searched, he would never find the image of himself ever again. That's how the reinforced wish was fulfilled!

He came down from the roof eventually, after the bishop arrived with a catapult and peppered him with sand grains. He was chased through the streets of Porthcawl until he shook off his pursuers. Some witnesses later said they saw the *spolcyc* submerge itself in the sea; but I happen to know for a fact that's not true. A creature made of eyes simply isn't safe where there are swordfish to cause punctures.

In fact there are very few locations where it might feel at home, where it is unlikely to be harassed by angry citizens of sundry rank; there's only one logical course of action and that's to adopt a disguise. The Reverend who was also a monster did just that. Somehow he acquired clothes and a mask and continued to inhabit Porthcawl without risk of being wiped dry, which is the doom a *spolcyc* fears most.

* * * *

Castor finished the story and drained his glass to the dregs. Paddy Deluxe and Frothing Harris squirmed on their chairs. The awkward silence lasted another five minutes and then the friends cleared their throats, twiddled a few thumbs and finally broke the news.

"Your tale is very wrong in terms of veracity; and you are perhaps not the smartest teller of it," sniffed Paddy.

Castor slowly raised his eyebrows. "What do you mean?"

"It is easily disproved," Paddy said.

Harris added, "We know for certain that Reverend Richards remained in human form, in his *own* form, and that eyes and disguises have nothing to do with his subsequent life. The facts are mundane. The bishop felt that he wasn't the right man for the job and thus expelled him from the church. Thoroughly defrocked, he looked for another career and found one as the barman of a pub, of *this* pub in truth."

And he jerked a thumb at the figure in question, who stood behind the bar with his elbows splayed on the counter. Castor looked and nodded as he observed the peculiar stiffness of the barman, his badly proportioned frame and fixed features. Certainly it was the Reverend Richards there in the shadows, waiting to pour the beer.

"Yes, of course," said Castor with a small smile.

Then he reached into an inner pocket of his jacket and drew out a tiny violin and an equally small bow; and he began playing a sad song, just as modest in dimensions as the instrument itself but profoundly deep, almost bottomless, in emotional impact. Not to weep at this wrenching melody was impossible, despite the numerous mistakes in the playing. Paddy and Harris both shed tears, and Castor too.

As for the barman, he started shaking all over, and his clothes abruptly became wet, but his face remained dry. Then his inflexible fingers undid buttons, untied knots and unhooked hooks; and in a paroxysm of vigorous melancholy he burst out of himself like a dragonfly escaping its chrysalis. But with more eyes. Many more eyes.

For an instant he stood there like an optical fountain, shining and salty and unbelievable; he had more pupils than an underfunded school teacher and each iris was a different colour, which is the detail that most intrigued Paddy and Harris; and then he took fright and shambled down some back passage where customers can't follow.

"There's no more cunning disguise than to dress as yourself," declared Castor with a sagacious sigh. He returned the miniature violin to his inner pocket and blinked at his friends. Paddy and Harris glanced at each other, shook their heads, and one of them said:

"The moment he was rumbled, he squelched."

"Yes," answered Castor, holding his empty glass to the light, "and now you have driven away the rain with your shoes, we must seize any chance to collect every drop of available liquid."

"You don't intend to drink his tears, do you?"

Castor shrugged. "Not straight. But I might start brewing my own beer at home. Call him back, will you? Just rattle your money on the counter if that doesn't work. And get me a pint of ale while you're at it. No, make it two. This weather is unseasonably dry."

HOME SUIT HOME

It began in the village of Lladloh. Empty houses vanished overnight and nobody knew how or why, and when the owners returned in the morning there was nowhere for them to live, but whether the cause was natural or criminal none of them dared to guess. Only if a building was occupied at all times did it remain in place, so people stopped going out, a safeguard that precipitated a minor famine.

The mayor made a token attempt to tackle the problem by encouraging his citizens to fill rooms with mannequins or the cardboard silhouettes of real people, but it didn't work. Whatever evil force was taking the houses wasn't so easily fooled. I believe that Phil the Liver was the mayor at that time, but I might be mistaken. The politics of that cursed village are truly intricate and fretful to say the least.

Not for long did Lladloh remain the only affected settlement. Rapidly the phenomenon spread to other parts of Wales, to north, south, east and west, not forgetting Monmouth, where the market imps did a brisk trade selling voluminous tents to the homeless; nor even Swansea, whose hairy inhabitants dwell in burrows and so were mostly unaffected. No domicile in the stunted nation was exempt.

Even the offshore islands suffered. The lighthouse of Caldey vanished one keeperless night. And finally the epidemic reached the isolated town of Porthcawl, where the collective will vowed to get to the bottom of the mystery, or at least halfway down it.

"The collective will shan't be denied!" cried Collective Will, his name a perfect coincidence in the context of his utterance. Determined to put a stop to the property thefts, he called a meeting of the most eminent local citizens. During this meeting, while the attendees were absent from their homes, their abodes disappeared.

"An inevitable consequence," declared Billy Belay.

"Indeed so," agreed Collective Will at the next meeting, the following day. The eminent citizens had moved into a large seafront hotel where at least one person was permanently on the premises, usually the manager or a badly paid staff member, but it was decided to convene for the talks in a nearby pub, before it too vanished.

"What is a likely way forward?" asked Paddy Deluxe.

Collective Will sighed and rubbed his chin. "Our combined funds are meagre and should be reserved for the purchase of beer and chips, for are we not Welsh? No professional detectives are affordable, nor any amateur sleuths available, so Karl Mondaugen must be given the task. Surely you know to whom I refer? The mad inventor originally from Munich. He has devised all kinds of novel wonders."

"Hardly a time for reading!" objected Billy Belay.

"By 'novel' I meant original or unique," explained Collective Will with the faintest grimace. "There are no inventors quite like Mondaugen. Even his eccentric façade is a prototype."

Frothing Harris confirmed this. "And once he made a soap trombone. I saw the result with my own eyes and the eyes of others. The lather of the low notes was especially scouring."

"Impressive," nodded Paddy Deluxe, "but will he agree to work for us for nothing? And if he does, how can we know what his true motives are? How may we even be confident that his motives haven't been patented! It might cost us more in the long run."

"But gentlemen, what other choice do we have!"

"Who said that?" cried Paddy.

"I did. Yes, I'm one of your eminent citizens and therefore an attendee at this series of meetings. Already I have an idea for a contraption to trap the force or being that is committing these thefts. In my laboratory I'll be able to fabricate this contraption in a few weeks. Unluckily my laboratory was part of my house, and my house was stolen yesterday, and so first I'll have to invent a new laboratory."

Most of those present merely gawped at Karl Mondaugen, who sat on a black sofa that was possibly a giant pumpernickel, his long green boots swinging over the side like gherkins so mutated they resembled footwear and his lederhosen glistening. But Collective Will collected enough of his wits for the following exchange:

"Why not invent one then?"

Mondaugen pouted. "I'll need a laboratory to do so."

"Can't you pretend this pub is one?"

"Only with great difficulty."

"Don't you have any great difficulty on you? I suppose you'll have to invent that in a laboratory too?"

"Actually no. I invented some earlier and put it in my pocket. Let me reach in… Here it is, a pure gram of great difficulty, enough to permit the pretence you desire. Now I raise it to my nostrils and snort it like *so*. My head spins, my pupils dilate."

"Are we your pupils?" wondered Billy Belay.

Mondaugen made a dismissive gesture. "I can't abide students, so you are merely neutral observers."

"We look forward to seeing your laboratory when it's ready," declared Collective Will, "and even more forward to seeing what inventions come out of it, especially if they remedy the plague of the disappearing houses. You can rely on our support."

"My laboratory is already finished!" cried Mondaugen. "It is this pub, as you suggested it ought to be, so technically you are trespassing, but I'm a gentle soul and won't prosecute. As for my aforementioned contraption, I'll notify you when it's done."

"We can't afford to pay you, remember."

"The ecstasy of creation is remuneration enough! I am an amateur and therefore spit on money, not in the metaphorical sense but with a patented spitting machine that can eject thin streams of saliva with sufficient force to punch a hole of perfect smoothness right through a noteworthy stack of the largest denomination coins."

"The committee is very pleased to hear that," said Collective Will, but the spare change in his pockets jangled despondently, so he called an end to the meeting and the eminent citizens slowly finished their pints of beer and wandered back to the hotel.

Karl Mondaugen watched them leave.

And then he threw himself into his work, not stirring from the pub for three weeks, living on peanuts and pear cider and constantly utilising the implausible and impossible tools he carried everywhere in jacket pockets often rumoured to be bigger on the inside than the outside, pockets oddly created with the aid of those tools.

But he didn't shun the more conventional implements of his trade and could be located in his corner banging with a hammer and joining wires with a soldering iron at most hours of the day and night, to the annoyance of the landlord and his customers. But no complaints were lodged against Mondaugen, for it was rightly feared he might design and deploy a horrid and innovative retaliation on anyone or anything that dared interrupt him. He had been known to do that before.

Finally he sent a message to the seafront hotel that his contraption was complete. He requested that the committee of eminent citizens meet him not in the pub, but on the esplanade in front of the Grand Pavilion. When they arrived and gathered around him, he displayed a box no larger than a brick and pointed proudly at it.

"What exactly is this?" asked Collective Will.

"A robotic cottage," answered Mondaugen, "that has limited reasoning powers and can walk on retractable legs. If we leave it unattended in this spot, the force that is making vacant abodes vanish won't be able to resist the bait and will steal it like other empty houses, but my cottage has been programmed to return to this precise location and will hasten back to it. A magnetic compass and pedometer are embedded in its brain, which can be consulted to pinpoint the coordinates of the hideout of any abductor. Then a raiding party can be sent out..."

Collective Will cleared his throat and said, "Ah, a cottage. Yes, I can discern the windows and door."

"Rather small, isn't it?" ventured Frothing Harris.

"Unconvincing," sniffed Billy Belay.

"Pathetic," sneered Paddy Deluxe, who was perhaps the least cautious of all the eminent citizens. But these negative judgments failed to hugely infuriate Mondaugen, who merely rolled mildly exasperated eyes at the idiocy of lesser mortals and said:

"At the moment it is compressed. Do you believe I would create a full sized cottage inside a pub? Are you insane? See how I reach forward to press this tiny switch on the side."

He did so and the box rapidly expanded, pushing the eminent citizens out of the way until they found themselves standing around a true cottage that suddenly stood incongruously in the spray from the sea. Blocking the esplanade like this wouldn't endear any of them to the orthodox citizens of the town, so it was essential that Mondaugen's plan worked. Collective Will murmured nervously to himself.

"Are you murmuring?" demanded the mad inventor.

"Yes, but appreciatively. Honest."

"What are we required to do next?" asked Frothing Harris.

"Nothing at all," replied Mondaugen. "The cottage is sentient and will take care of itself, so I suggest you retire and entertain yourselves in your customary fashion. Tomorrow morning, if you wish, you may reconvene here to witness that my invention has gone, but don't expect answers until it returns, and I can't say how long that will be, for it entirely depends on the distance to which it is taken."

"Can't you offer a rough estimate?" asked Billy Belay.

"No. For if the hypothetical abductors are based in Cardiff or Tenby, then one or two days will suffice to bring the cottage back, but if they are based in Japan then many years may pass. And if the abductor is a natural force existing at the centre of the Earth or in outer space the return will be considerably longer, I'm afraid."

"Longer? Don't you mean *eternal*, bearing in mind that legs can't walk on magma or vacuum!" cried Billy.

Mondaugen smiled. "The legs I invent can tread on anything. But it is time for me to depart and concern myself with other projects. I intend to crystallise the feeling of déjà vu next and use the crystals in a new type of repeating laser. If I'm successful it won't be the first time I've done such a thing! So farewell, gentlemen!"

And he left with long eccentric strides.

"He's too crazy to be a mad inventor," said Paddy Deluxe.

Collective Will nodded sadly. "But he's the best we've got, so we must keep him sweet at all costs. All costs except money, but that goes without saying, even though I said it."

At this point an eminent citizen spoke up who had remained silent in all the meetings to date. He was dressed in silk like a dandy, with a blue silk shirt, green silk trousers, a yellow silk waistcoat and a purple silk hat, a costume adopted especially for this occasion, nobody could guess why. He was none other than Castor Jenkins, notorious trickster and the most genuine fraud this side of the Irish Sea. Standing with his thumbs in his belt loops, he drawled cynically:

"The robotic cottage will never work!"

He was eyed suspiciously by the others, none of whom cared to reply to that statement. Castor frequently said things that weren't true. And yet he often confounded his critics by being absolutely right about incredible matters, so nobody knew quite how to regard him and his utterances. The lack of reaction didn't dismay him and he smiled as he walked around the cottage, peering through the windows at the empty interior. The legs were evidently coiled up somewhere under the building and would appear only when walking became necessary.

By the time Castor completed his circuit of the cottage the others had drifted away. He therefore spoke to himself when he cried, "I'm the only one able to solve the enigma!"

Then he chuckled and rubbed his hands at the departing backs. "Wait and see!" he called. Like the other eminent citizens, he had lost his own house during the first meeting of the committee, but he believed he knew exactly what had happened to it and he was simply biding his time before publicising his theory. Maximum renown was the factor Castor was most interested in, so he didn't want to compete with Karl Mondaugen until the inventor had obviously failed.

Which happened abruptly the following day.

Collective Will and Hugo Bloat were first on the scene, at the crack of noon, for neither were early risers, shortly followed by Izaac Spoilchild, Frothing Harris and Harold the Barrel. After lunch, Paddy Deluxe came along too and he was no less astonished than the rest of them. The worst thing had happened. The cottage was still there! How could this be? Why hadn't it vanished into thin air?

An answer was soon provided. The cottage was no longer empty, for during the night squatters had moved into it, breaking down the door and installing new locks of their own. Now they were redecorating the interior rooms. It was as simple as that. Smoke rose from the chimney and steam issued from picturesque cracks in the walls, but this didn't mean the robot was powering itself up. On the contrary, those were cooking vapours. The odour of boiled lentils competed and combined with the tang of salt air, a tasty clash. Faces at the windows grinned out. Paddy Deluxe glared back and pulled his hair in frustration.

"Can't we evict them?" he spluttered.

"Not without a protracted legal battle," said Collective Will. "After all, we don't own the property either."

"But surely it's blocking a public right of way?"

Hugo Bloat seized the initiative. He rapped on the front door until his knuckles were sore and bellowed, "You can't stay here. How can decent people stroll up and down the esplanade with this thing to obstruct them? You must move it immediately!"

Then he turned to chuckle at his colleagues. "When they discover they can't do that, they'll have no choice but to evacuate the cottage. I'm rather a crafty old fox, don't you think?"

His rhetorical question was greeted with nods.

But the squatters soon proved he wasn't. They were more resourceful than anyone gave them credit for. They located the override console that permitted the cottage's electronic systems to be controlled manually and suddenly the house rose up on two spindly but strong legs with reversed knees like those of an angry ostrich. Then it began slowly striding inland. It didn't lurch very far, however.

The eminent citizens watched in dismay as it mounted the steps of the Grand Pavilion, passed through the big entrance into the echoing interior without even scraping its sides. Good driving certainly! There came forth a rumbling sound. Then the cottage was seen again, high up. Somehow it had climbed onto the roof, where it settled down gently, clearly in a place where no pedestrians ever passed.

By this time all the other eminent citizens had also turned up and they groaned in chorus at the sight.

"I told you so," said a cool voice.

It was Castor Jenkins, of course, and he was still sheathed in silk from head to toe, but now he carried a rucksack slung over his shoulders and in his right hand he held a gigantic magnifying glass on a pole that was both a device of detection and a stout walking staff. He was clearly prepared to embark on a long overland journey.

"Are you going somewhere?" asked Paddy.

"Indeed so. I plan to put an end to the disappearances and reclaim my own living place. Why don't you come with me? This is the best way of getting your house back intact."

"I won't come," snorted Collective Will.

Billy Belay, Izaac Spoilchild, Hugo Bloat, Harold the Barrel, Captain Dangleglum, Sunstew Mynci, Hywel Price, Tin Dylan, Aluminium Dewi and Huw Rees also declined the offer.

Only Paddy Deluxe and Frothing Harris decided to accompany Castor, which is how they first become close comrades with the trickster, forging a friendship that would result in the loss of much cash and patience over a period of several strange decades.

"Will you tell us what you think?" asked Paddy.

"About what?" blinked Castor.

"The mysterious disappearances, of course!"

"Certainly. I think that trolls are responsible for all of them."

"Why on earth do you think that?"

"Because every eye-witness who has ever been properly questioned on the matter has attested that trolls are always seen in the vicinity of a house that later vanishes.

But that's not all. High definition surveillance cameras mounted at strategic points around the town have never failed to detect at least one troll loitering in the vicinity at those instants when the houses do disappear. Trolls are the culprits!"

Paddy Deluxe shook his head and laughed.

"It must be a coincidence. Why would a troll require a human house? We all know that trolls live only under bridges. Plus trolls are accredited members of decent society. They never cause trouble and are deemed to be the most trustworthy companions for men and women who can't afford human friends, certainly superior to the dogs and cats they have replaced, in the history of urban loneliness!"

"Those histories need to be rewritten," remarked Castor.

"I don't understand why you are slandering trolls!" blurted Paddy.

"There's a clue in my clothes," said Castor.

Paddy and Frothing Harris stared closely at him for a full minute, but at the end of that period they felt themselves no wiser in determining why he seemed to have evolved a loathing of those gentle stony giants that are so polite and pleasant at all times.

Castor's attitude towards trolls was an obvious symptom of insanity, a dangerous paranoia, but neither Paddy nor Harris decided to change their minds about travelling with him, for the simple reason that such paranoia is sometimes the same as insight…

As it happened, they set off together later that day.

It was near the end of the afternoon, an odd time to begin a journey on foot, and the sun was sinking behind them, for they were headed east, and their long shadows hurried ahead impatiently over the dunes that undulate between Porthcawl and the Ogmore River. Avalanches of sand trickled at their feet and gnats tickled their ears.

"I've just realised that we haven't asked you where we're going. Is it as far as Caerphilly?" asked Paddy.

"Much further than that!" said Castor.

Frothing Harris recoiled in horror. "You mean Bristol or Bath?"

"Further," replied Castor.

"Surely not Brighton or Dover?" stammered Paddy.

"Venice," smirked Castor.

His companions fell silent at this, but they didn't slacken their pace, so anyone observing them would assume they hadn't properly heard Castor's answer. Slowly the landscape changed. They were still among dunes and the sun had set, but they could see perfectly clearly. Dark sand pulsed red, like friendly radioactive blood.

"Venice," repeated Castor suddenly.

"In Italy, you mean," replied Frothing Harris dourly.

"A long way," said Paddy Deluxe.

"Yes," nodded Castor. "More than eight hundred and fifty miles along the realistic route, but we're going to use a short cut that partly exists in a parallel dimension and partly doesn't. In fact we have already crossed the invisible border into a magic realm."

"Does that explain why the dunes are usefully glowing with their own inner light?" enquired Frothing Harris.

"It does indeed," confirmed Castor.

"How much time will this route save us?"

"Most, if not all. But you can't really save time the same way you can save money or marmalade, I'm sorry to say. It will spend itself eventually whether you want it to or not."

"Are there any dangers to worry about?"

Castor frowned deeply. "Apart from the bicycle-centaurs, no. At least I'm unaware of other kinds of monster inhabiting the region. Having said that, I don't regularly come this way, but I carefully studied a map of our route, so I don't think we're lost. As you can see, the sandy path ends here and an asphalt road takes over."

"Will we have to walk all night?" asked Harris.

"Yes, we will. Be strong."

Much to everyone's surprise, the sun abruptly rose.

"That was quick!" cried Paddy.

"Different dimensions, different conventions," blandly replied Castor, but he cast apprehensive eyes in every direction and clutched the pole of his magnifying glass more firmly.

"Now I understand the purpose of that thing," said Paddy Deluxe. "It's to concentrate the sun's rays and melt the tarmac on this road to impede the onslaught of the bicycle-centaurs, isn't it? That's the real reason you brought it. Nothing to do with being the fashion accessory of a detective. It's a tool of defensive warfare!"

"Not exactly," said Castor with a blush.

"What's it for then?" asked Paddy.

"For making the Glass Towers of Glimpse feel less lonely."

"What does that mean?"

"You'll find out soon enough. In fact you'll find out now, as we seem to be already there. Clearly the short cut has contracted since I obtained the map of it. I won't complain!"

They entered a ruined city with shattered walls.

"This is Glimpse?" asked Paddy.

Castor nodded. "And those are the Glass Towers!"

"What are you talking about?" blinked Frothing Harris. "Those things are just flat circles of glass, enormous round windows that someone has placed down on the ground."

"Like hard lakes," added Paddy Deluxe.

"Shall we step around them? Or walk over them? We can hardly wade through them," pointed out Harris.

Castor frowned. "Please show more respect. These were formerly the tallest structures in this particular cosmos, the most glorious products of the engineering genius of a civilisation that died out a billion years ago. Legends still describe how the Glass Towers thrust into the stratosphere like astounding godlike test tubes."

"What happened? Did they melt?" asked Paddy.

Castor shook his head. "Not exactly. Unlikely as it may seem, glass is not a solid but a super-stiff liquid. It flows like all liquids, but so slowly the motion can't be seen. Have you ever examined old church windows? They are thicker at the base than the top because over centuries the glass has flowed down enough to create a discernible difference. Eventually all glass objects become flat pools."

"That's amazing," conceded Frothing Harris.

Castor Jenkins now did something strange. Most of the things he does are strange, but this one was especially so. First he extended his pole until he clutched it only in one hand at its very extremity, then he gently rested the magnifying glass on the ground, so that its lens resembled a miniature version of the flattened Glass Towers. He stood in silence for ten minutes with bowed head and shut eyes.

Then he withdrew the magnifying glass and nodded to himself as the Glass Towers seemed to hum in pleasure or gratitude, surely an acoustic illusion caused by a light breeze.

"Let's go," he said. And set off.

Paddy followed. "What was all that about?"

"They sometimes get broody," Castor replied, glancing back over his shoulder at the devastated city.

"Who do?" frowned Paddy Deluxe.

"The Glass Towers of Glimpse, of course!"

"You mean they thought the lens was a baby tower?" gasped Frothing Harris as he struggled to keep up. Castor was setting a very fast pace, but suddenly he stopped to point at the ground. Water was gargling down the asphalt road, cutting a narrow groove in the centre of the camber, and this soggy fact seemed delightful to him.

"We're on the outskirts of Venice!" he announced.

And so they were. The dunes soon vanished completely, to be replaced by magnificent buildings, and the gargling water became a wide canal full of gondolas. A far cry from Porthcawl! Castor relaxed enough to confide a terrible secret. "Glass doesn't really flow like a liquid, that's just a myth but a very persistent one," he said.

"Why exactly are we here?" asked Paddy.

"I want to prove that trolls are responsible for stealing our houses and all other empty abodes. Hopefully we'll recognise our own homes among the abducted buildings and so be able to claim them back! As you pointed out to me, trolls live under bridges, and what other city can boast so many fine bridges? It follows that the finest trolls must live here, the uppercrust trolls who are most likely to have stolen the houses. Keep your eyes open and yell when you see your property."

Frothing Harris shrugged. "Fine. But I still don't understand why trolls would actually want to steal houses!"

"Like I said before, my clothes are the clue."

Paddy shook his head. "Not much of a coherent clue to me, I'm afraid. Silk garments, very chic. Where did you get them, by the way? There's no manufacturer's label anywhere."

"Made them myself," proudly asserted Castor.

"But where did you get the material? It's extremely fine quality silk! I don't suppose it came from Wales?"

"I cut it from the Silk Road," said Castor, "which has started to fray at the edges and isn't used much, so I doubt the piece I took will be missed. I used a scimitar to make a neat incision. Probably won't be able to obtain any for you the same way, because a warlord is planning to roll the entire Silk Road up and use it for a stair carpet. He lives in the tallest pagoda in Mandalay, you see, a million levels high."

"We don't believe you," chorused Paddy and Harris.

"Why ever not?" growled Castor.

"Because the Silk Road is nowhere near Mandalay."

Castor grinned sourly. "Fair enough, I admit the deception, his pagoda is actually in Samarkand, but the rest is true. Shall we take this gondola to make our explorations even easier?"

They did so, much to the chagrin of the gondolier, who was enjoying a cappuccino in a nearby café at the time. Castor gracefully used the pole of his magnifying glass to punt them down the canals and that was how they investigated every accessible nook and corner of this magnificent city and glided under every single bridge. But all the trolls they saw looked just as innocent as the trolls back home.

"I don't see any stolen houses," remarked Paddy.

"Me neither," confessed Harris.

Castor was bewildered and he leaned on his pole and frowned deeply. Then he noticed a ship in the distance unloading cargo onto the wharf and he clapped his hands in delight. "Of course! Venice may be bursting with wonderful bridges, but where do they get their bridges from? They import them! There's a vessel depositing new bridges right now. Can you see its flag? One yellow stripe, two blue…"

"With a black trident in the middle," squinted Harris.

"The flag of Barbados!" cried Paddy.

Castor roared with laughter. "Why didn't I think of that myself? We've come to the wrong place! The most suave and fashionable trolls must live where bridges have their origin, for it's an accepted fact that every bridge comes from Bridgetown, the capital of Barbados! That's why it was given the name Bridgetown in the first instance, and that is where we'll find our stolen houses. Come on, friends!"

And he started punting with incredible speed and dexterity out to sea. Soon Venice was far behind, then it dipped over the horizon. "Too far for a gondola!" protested Paddy Deluxe.

Castor winked. "Another short cut, another parallel dimension. I saw a map of this area once. Left turn at the next wave. There we are. That tiny smudge in the distance is Barbados."

"Remarkable," conceded Frothing Harris.

"I might as well reveal," mumbled Castor, "that the handle of my pole is hollow and filled with brass tacks. *That's* how I planned to frustrate the bicycle-centaurs if we had met any."

"They can't swim, can they?" blinked Paddy.

"Nope," secretly winced Castor.

As they approached the docks of Bridgetown they saw that the streets were thronged with promenading trolls and it was immediately apparent that these trolls were different from ordinary and more familiar examples of the species. Unbelievable as it may sound to sane people, they weren't naked but dressed in clothes. And now Paddy and Harris understood the allusion their friend had made to silk.

"Makes perfect sense if you think about it," Castor said.

"Clothes woven from houses can't be sensible," protested Paddy. "I'm watching a troll with brick trousers and round windows for pockets. That one over there has a log cabin shirt and a gabled tie. His friend is wearing cement boots made from bungalows."

"Why are they doing this?" cried Harris.

"Just extend the silk analogy," continued Castor blithely.

"Do it for us, will you?" pleaded Paddy.

Castor sighed. "A silkworm spins a cocoon for itself to dwell in. After it transforms into a moth, humans come along and make clothes from its vacated home. Well, trolls have started to do the same with us. Any rock-based lifeform is bound to view the domestic human abode as a desirable source of raw materials for their textile industry. So when we aren't inside our houses, they gather them and tease them into threads from which they weave garments for every occasion."

Paddy spluttered, "You mean…?"

Castor nodded. "We are their silkworms."

They digested this, then Harris ventured, "If we return to Porthcawl it won't be easy convincing Collective Will of the truth, unless we take an item of troll fashion back with us, something I'm not sure we can manage. And as for Karl Mondaugen, he won't enjoy being upstaged. Nor will the other eminent citizens precisely be endeared to us, and they might even unleash some diabolical reprisals."

"Those are all loose ends," acknowledged Castor, "so something must be done about them, but I'm not sure what. Let's put off thinking about it until after the end of the story…"

"Very well," readily came the reply.

The intrepid trio sailed up the nearest inlet and came to rest by the side of Chamberlain Bridge. They leapt onto dry land and proceeded through National Heroes Square and up Palmetto Street, completely failing to find the famed Waterfront Café, where steel pan music can be heard live every Tuesday. Suddenly Castor stopped in his tracks. He was staring at a troll with a mixture of frustrated rage and overly strained stoicism, but the troll in question barely seemed to notice.

"Of all things, an item of casual headwear!"

"Beg your pardon?" asked Harris.

"With flaps and a peak too!" moaned Castor.

"What's the matter?" demanded Paddy, and with his eyes he followed the accusing finger. Then he licked his lips, slowly lowered his gaze and muttered to himself, "Hideous taste."

"Wherever he lays his hat, that's my home," said Castor.

ALL IN A FLAP

Castor Jenkins slid on his belly through the dunes, feeling the warm sand on his elbows as he used them to propel himself forward. Marram grass rustled as he passed; each blade was tough and sharp enough to cause him a certain amount of discomfort even through his clothing. He resembled a mutant seal stranded in the desert, desperately seeking the sea, but in fact his objective was bluer and more slippery than water. He licked his lips in anticipation as he crested the final dune.

Squinting down at the beach, he repressed a gasp of delight. Yes, there it was! An azure sentinel bird stood on a jagged rock near the wavelets of the incoming tide. Castor was aware that his heart was racing too fast but he could do nothing to calm it down. No sentinel birds had been seen in these parts for twenty years and the azure kind was the most elusive of all, practically extinct according to the textbooks. This was the apotheosis of his career as a dedicated ornithologist.

Raising his binoculars to his eyes, Castor adjusted the focus until it seemed the bird was no more than a few feet away. Then he recoiled in amazement and dropped the optical instrument. Frowning and sweating, he picked it up, blew the sand off the lenses and took a second look. Was this some sort of joke? Had one of his more mischievous colleagues made a wooden model of the bird and fixed it on the rock as a joke? But no, the sentinel bird suddenly moved. It was alive.

It was holding its own pair of binoculars to its own eyes!

* * * *

Castor fought down a rising panic. Was he going insane? Never in his life had he heard of such an occurrence. He decided it was essential to capture the bird as proof of the remarkable phenomenon. As cautiously as possible he slithered down the steep slope to the beach, and because the bird was so engrossed in its observations he believed he had a chance of catching it; he tiptoed across the soft sand towards the rock, his grasping hands reaching out to seize it from behind.

Something crunched underfoot; the shell of a dead crab. The bird flew away instantly, a reflex, its binoculars dangling from its neck on a cord. A frustrated Castor shook his fist at it. Then a wave lapped over his feet and made his shoes and socks wet and he stumbled backward. For several minutes he stood aimlessly, watching the bird shrink among the clouds; it was soon no larger than a dot. He was about to head for home with defeat weighing on his soul, but then he had an idea.

Ignoring the sensation of the glutinous water, he waded to the rock and stood in the same position as the bird. With his binoculars he studied the spot on the horizon that had intrigued the bird. The sails of a ship loomed into view. Castor could make out very few details at this range but the word 'pirates' flashed through his mind. He shook his head to clear it and looked again. No, the flag wasn't a skull and bones but a complicated symbol on a yellow diamond framed by green.

The ship was a large barquentine, an old type of clipper.

What was such an antique vessel doing off the coast of South Wales? Was somebody making a film? That was the only plausible explanation. A movie director had arranged this scenario, including a bird trained to use binoculars, and he, Castor, had wandered accidentally onto the set. Probably his presence had spoiled the filming, but that was their fault for failing to notify bystanders, not his. He waded back to shore, sat on a driftwood stump and waited for the ship to approach.

The barquentine dropped anchor a mile offshore and a longboat was lowered into the water, crewed by half a dozen men dressed in elaborate but ragged uniforms of a strange design. They rowed with efficiency to the shallows near where Castor sat. They jumped out, dragged the longboat onto the sand; and one of them, evidently the leader, planted a flag on a pole into the beach. Then they all fell to their knees and began praying, as if giving thanks for deliverance.

"You'll have to do this scene again, I'm afraid," said Castor. "It just isn't very convincing, you know."

The leader of the men turned to face him and his lips curled in a snarl. Then he sprang to his feet and advanced on Castor, drawing a sword from a scabbard at his belt. Utterly flummoxed, the birdwatcher recoiled and fell off his stump onto the ground. Then the snarling man babbled something unfriendly at him in a rough voice. It was a foreign language and Castor didn't recognise any of the words. He held up his hands in a gesture of surrender and pleaded for mercy.

Another man from the longboat ran forward. "I speak English! I even have an English surname. I am José Bandão Pepys and my grandfather came originally from a town called York. Do you know it? He taught me to speak his language as well as Portuguese. I will be your interpreter! You have made Captain Ribeiro very angry by interrupting his prayer. He has claimed this land for the Empire."

Castor blinked. "Who are you people?"

Pepys grinned. "Refugees from Brazil. We left in two ships after the Empire was abolished. We were loyal subjects, you understand, and had no desire to live in a Republic. We decided to colonise some other land but bad luck dogged our ships. Our other vessel sank, in fact, and this one was tossed about the oceans for rather longer than we had anticipated. Yes, we have been at sea a long time!"

Castor was very hazy on the subject of Brazilian history. "When did the Empire become a Republic?"

Pepys said casually, "In the Nineteenth Century. Don't worry, my friend, we aren't the ghosts of the original refugees! The men who fled took their wives with them. We are the descendants of those exiles. For more than one hundred and twenty years we have been lost on the belly of the ocean, but now at last our faith has been vindicated! Captain Ribeiro has christened this land the New Brazilian Empire and you are now subject to our decrees. Disobedience will be treated as treason."

Castor laughed. "Are you insane? You can't claim this country; it already has a government. You'll be arrested and sent to jail. We have an army equipped with modern weapons and—"

Although unable to appreciate the substance of Castor's protests, the outraged tone of his voice was enough to persuade Captain Ribeiro that action was needed to forestall further resistance. He used the hilt of his sword to knock Castor unconscious.

* * * *

When Castor awoke it was night and the Brazilians had built a vast and illegal fire among the dunes. Surely the wild flames would attract the attention of the coastguard?

His skull pounded and he sat up with some difficulty. All the other men from the barquentine had arrived in the other longboats. Captain Ribeiro leered and passed him a bottle of clear liquid and laughed as he gulped it down and began spluttering. It wasn't water as he had expected but some fiery spirit.

"Cachaça rum!" laughed Pepys as he slapped Castor on the back. Then the Captain made a short speech.

"What did he say?" croaked Castor.

"You are one of us now," explained Pepys. "You work for us. Your first job is to act as a sentry. You must keep a close watch all night and fight the urge to fall asleep. You must not shirk your duty to the New Brazilian Empire or it will be bad for you."

"What am I supposed to be watching out for?"

But Captain Ribeiro was tired of talking. He growled and rumbled and pointed at the crest of the highest dune; and Castor had no option but to leave the circle of firelight and stumble in the gloom along the paths to the steep sandy slope and climb it to the top. He reached the summit and caught his breath, then turned slowly to look in every direction. The camp of the Brazilians was a fiesta of fiery mayhem, full of drunken, singing sailors and laughing women. He sighed.

Although he could see them easily, it was unlikely they could see him with the same clarity. What was to stop him sneaking off? The town of Porthcawl was only a few miles to the west; and the village of Ogmore was even closer, just on the other side of a shallow river. There was no moon and the gleam of the sea was muted; dark clouds full of greasy rain scudded across the stars. He decided to wait five minutes and then edge slowly towards the far side of the dune.

If he slid down this, ran towards the woods to the north and managed to reach the cover of the first trees, he would surely be safe; then he could flag down passing cars on the main road that lay just beyond. A lift into Porthcawl; and after alerting the police an armed response unit could be sent out to deal with the lunatics, and within a couple of hours the absurd nightmare would probably be over. The minutes passed with excruciating slowness. He squinted at the Brazilian camp.

Nobody was looking in his direction. Gritting his teeth, he made his move, rolling and tumbling down the dune. He reached the bottom and crashed through a thorny bush, cursing the commotion he was making. A low whistle just ahead caught his attention. He looked up to see Pepys on the crest of another dune, aiming an old-fashioned rifle in his direction. The Brazilian said, "Captain Ribeiro wants you to know that an attempt to leave your post will be punished by death."

Castor sagged. It had never occurred to him that a sentry might be posted to watch over the sentry. He replied thickly, "I just need to relieve myself. I didn't plan on going anywhere."

Pepys nodded but his eyes twinkled mischievously and he didn't lower his gun for an instant. Castor was forced to pretend to urinate, his back to the lethal observer. Then he climbed resignedly back up the dune and resumed his position on the crest. He stood there silently, the ache in his legs gradually becoming almost unbearable. Still he wasn't sure what he was supposed to be looking out for. He turned to the south, the west, the north, the east; but nothing new appeared.

* * * *

The hours passed and he suddenly remembered the bird. He wondered if it was normal behaviour for members of that particular species to use binoculars on a regular basis. While he pondered this question, a breeze ruffled his hair. Then something thudded into the sand just ahead of him. Was Pepys shooting at him? But there had been no sound. He stooped to examine the object. Was it a crossbow bolt? Similar objects fell out of the sky between his dune and the sleeping camp.

The fire had died down but the embers were still bright enough for Castor to see the ensuing chaos. Figures jumped up and began tearing at themselves; others screamed or groaned. What was going on? An aerial attack of some kind, obviously. Castor gazed up and saw only clouds and a few stars. More iron missiles fell out of the sky. Was this some new kind of deadly rain? A word entered his brain, a word he had encountered once in an encyclopaedia of military history.

Flechettes. Sharp metal rods dropped from aircraft onto entrenched infantry positions. A well-aimed flechette could build enough inertia to puncture the hardest helmet; and the Brazilians wore no head protection at all. Who could be dropping them? Surely the coastguard or police had no mandate to do so? Then the clouds briefly parted and he caught sight of the beak and wings of an azure sentinel bird. More followed. They were turning to make a second bombing run.

The combined flapping of their wide wings had created the breeze that disordered his hair; now it fanned the dying fire back to life. Someone discharged a rifle vertically. Others snatched up their own guns and did the same thing. Captain Ribeiro hopped about, his trousers around his ankles, his sword in his hand. A flechette penetrated his skull and with a cough he sank to his knees, then keeled over. The storm of iron continued until every Brazilian was dead or dying.

Castor trembled, fearful for his own life, but the birds had decided to ignore him; perhaps they hadn't even noticed him on his isolated dune. The flechette that had dropped at his feet might have been an accident. He held it close to his face and saw that it resembled a long nail. Then he ran down to the Brazilian camp and stumbled among the bodies. The smell of blood nauseated him; he lurched away, remembering Pepys and hurrying back to the dune where the fellow had stood.

As he climbed up the slope, he questioned his motives. Why didn't he just return to Porthcawl? Why expose himself to more danger by going to see if Pepys was alive? He realised it was because he wanted answers to the odd questions posed by the night's events. Why had the sentinel birds attacked the Brazilians? They had gone now, but would they return? The fear of them churned thickly in Castor's blood. At the top of the dune he almost tripped over the body of Pepys.

* * * *

The Brazilian was still alive, though his injuries were serious. Leaning close, Castor softly asked about the birds. Pepys rolled his eyes and coughed blood as he tried to prop himself up on an elbow, but he failed in this endeavour because he was too weak. Yet he wished to comply with the request and began speaking softly, with considerably difficulty, teeth clenching spasmodically, muscles in his neck twitching. Castor was forced to lower his ear very close to his lips.

Pepys drew a deep shuddering breath and hissed:

"So much for the New Brazilian Empire! It lasted less than one night. But yes, I will tell you about the birds. In the winter of 1889 we set off in two ships, but almost immediately we were caught in a storm that blew us off course. Even after the storm abated we were lost for months and our supplies ran low. Finally we sighted land, but it wasn't a place where we could put ashore. The cliffs were unbroken in both directions as far as the eye could see; a towering wall of sea-battered rock, but it was no ordinary rock. It was magnetic ore, lodestone, which confuses compass readings and can even pull loose nails out of planking."

"I am unaware of such a coast," said Castor.

Pepys rasped, "There are old legends about those cliffs. The ancient geographer Ptolemy believed they fringed certain islands beyond India. The explorer Gil Eannes thought that Cape Bojador in Africa was where they might be found. Nobody knows for certain. We noted that birds had made their nests on ledges along the cliffs and because we were hungry we decided that some of us should climb up and raid the eggs. The most agile members of our crew jumped from our masts and caught hold of the cliff wall by precarious handholds. They skilfully threw the nests into the sea, where they floated near our ships."

"And you were able to fish them out?" asked Castor.

"Yes, with nets! Then the climbers jumped into the sea and we pulled them up too. We planned to sail away from that place as fast as possible, but the birds returned and went wild. At that very moment, our second ship was pulled apart by the magnetic attraction of the lodestone. It was less well made than our own ship. As the nails oozed out of the planks, the birds swooped and snatched them up. Then they flapped after us and prepared to drop them on our heads. But a sudden fog rolled across the scene and they weren't able to pinpoint us."

"That fog saved your lives!" commented Castor.

"Indeed so. Our ship managed to escape and it has been fleeing those birds ever since. They are the same species that attacked our camp just now. Blue sentinel birds, you called them. I wish to stress that neither the crew killed today, nor the birds that killed them, are the same as those present during the raiding of the nests. We are descendants of the original participants. Generations have passed on both sides. The birds never gave up the quest for vengeance and they passed it down to their subsequent hatchlings. We thought that by coming here we would finally evade them, but clearly they were already waiting for us."

Castor listened to this story with appropriate sympathy. He made soothing noises and nodded his head, but he was slightly embarrassed and felt that something else was required of him, some further response. But what? Pepys gripped his arm and opened his mouth, but no more words were audible. The telling of the story had exhausted him. Guessing only that he was supposed to reciprocate, Castor screwed up his face and searched his mind for a story of his own.

He soon found one no less remarkable than the tale of the birds, and he began telling it in the following manner:

* * * *

I watch birds on these dunes now (said Castor) but I used to watch them on Kenfig Dunes too, on the other side of the town of Porthcawl. In my mind I now divide the two different sets of dunes into 'good' and 'bad'. Kenfig Dunes are the *bad* ones. I knew they were supposed to be haunted even when I went there regularly. There was a village there long ago that was buried by the shifting sands. It has been said that on stormy nights the bells of the old church can be heard ringing at the bottom of a lake. I never heard them, so I can't confirm that.

There's also an isolated house there called Sker House. It's an accurate name, for it's rife with phantoms, the most famous being a forlorn maiden who was locked in her bedroom when her father disapproved of her lover, a wandering poet. She died of grief or malnutrition, I don't recall which, and her ghost can sometimes be seen in an upper window. There's another phantom in the shape of a monk who lives in the cellar, though I have my doubts about whether someone who has been dead for many centuries can be accurately said to 'live' anywhere at all.

Sker House doesn't play a part in what happened to me, but I thought I should mention it for the sake of local colour. Anyway, I was out late one night, kneeling on the top of a dune and watching a rare species of beach owl, when I saw a man walking near the tide line. He was coming along the beach from the direction of Porthcawl, throwing a stick for his pet as he went. His pet bounded after it each time and brought it back. Once he threw the stick into the sea and his pet splashed into the waves to retrieve it and the water at that spot turned purple.

I mean that the surf actually *glowed* with horrid phosphorescence as if the pet had somehow turned the waves radioactive. I adjusted the focus of my binoculars and studied the pet in more detail. I noted the long twisted horns, the forked tongue, the tail. Then I turned my binoculars on the man who was its master. He was dressed like a priest. I watched them walk all the way around the curve of the beach but I don't know if they came back the same way; I vacated that area as fast as my legs would take me! Back at home, I trembled under my bedsheets…

The following day I decided that I must have been imagining things. I couldn't miss the chance of observing a beach owl in its native habitat, so I went back to Kenfig Dunes after sunset. Sure enough, the owl was there, and it seemed happy to surf the waves all night on a surfboard of woven twigs, which is standard beach owl behaviour but is rarely seen in Wales. The suddenly it took fright and flapped away. The priest was back and he had a new pet with him! This pet resembled a cross between a spider and a wolf and it chased the stick thrown for it.

I was terrified. But the following night I went back and yet again the priest showed up with a new pet. In all the nights that followed he had a different monster. Always he threw sticks for them and they ran after and brought them back. Finally I couldn't bear the tension and I hurried down the dunes onto the beach after him. A current was carrying far out a stick thrown into the sea; his pet was swimming after it. I had enough time to approach him and demand an explanation. So intent was he on the game with the stick that he didn't hear me come up.

I tapped him on the shoulder and he turned calmly to regard me. Then I pointed at the monster and said, "What?"

"It's a demon," he answered.

"And the others?" I gasped.

"They are all demons," he replied casually.

I boggled. "You mean—?"

He nodded. "I am the Reverend Richards. My church in Porthcawl is overrun with demons. They are real demons from Hell. My congregation stopped coming to listen to my sermons and the bishop even threatened to expel me if I didn't do something about the problem. So I consulted some old books and learned that the best way to get rid of demons is to exercise them. That's what I'm doing now."

I absorbed this information, then I said as gently as I could, "I admire your initiative, but you've made a small mistake. The word isn't 'exercise' but *exorcise*. A slight difference."

He stroked his beard and frowned. "Oh dear! So that's why the demons keep returning to my church! I did wonder! Thanks for letting me know. I was never much good at spelling."

I wished him the best of luck and then I retreated before his pet caught the stick and brought it back to shore. As I hurried over the beach I noted that the pawprints of the demon glowed purple. I can accept that creatures glow in the dark, and in fact there are plenty of glowworms in the dunes, but the idea that their tracks can also glow is one of the strangest aspects of this case, as far as I'm concerned. Anyway, I have never returned to the dunes on that side of the town and I have no intention of ever going back. I prefer these dunes, which are safer.

* * * *

Castor finished his story and waited for Pepys to give a reaction. But the Brazilian said nothing. So he leaned forward to check if the fellow had died. As he did so, something brushed the crown of his scalp. Blood trickled down his face and at the same instant he heard an explosion. He jerked up straight again and clutched the top of his head with his hands, but the wound was only a scratch, nothing serious. Then he blinked and looked out to sea and understood.

The azure sentinel birds had taken over the barquentine. Hundreds of them were perched on all the yardarms of the masts, holding binoculars to their eyes and watching Castor. Others crowded the decks and three or four of them were clustered around a smoking cannon. They had fired a cannon at him! But it soon emerged they didn't really desire to kill him, for they never bothered reloading the antique weapon. Instead they pulled up the anchor and set sail westwards.

They were steering a course for Porthcawl. Perhaps it was high time a Welsh coastal town was invaded and taken over by birds! Or perhaps they would simply sail around rather than attacking it. Castor wondered if the ship would be intercepted by a flotilla of swimming demons coming the other way, once it rounded the cape. He sat on the sand and reached into his small knapsack for his vacuum flask. After such an eventful night he deserved a nice drink of cold beer.

HANGFIRE BUBBLER

Because he couldn't sleep, Castor got out of bed and drank a bottle of beer, but it didn't make him drowsy, so he decided to go for a midnight walk to the bottle bank and condemn his empty bottle to the recycling process. The bottle bank was a large steel container with rubber inlets and it was always fun to push bottles through the holes and listen to them smashing deep inside the metal belly. On this occasion, however, the bottle bank was full and the top had been removed, so the empty bottles tottered high above him like the bricks of an unstable glass ziggurat. He shrugged his shoulders and threw his bottle onto the pile.

But as he turned to go, two other bottles fell off and landed on the grass. He was a responsible citizen, Castor, and couldn't just leave them there, so he picked them up and threw them back. They landed in the right place but each bottle knocked off two others, so he sighed as he bent over and retrieved the four bottles, lobbing them with great accuracy onto the summit of the mound. Once again each bottle dislodged two more so that eight bottles now lay at his feet. He had no choice but to continue throwing them back, for to walk away would be to demonstrate a shocking disregard for the integrity of the environment.

This absurd charade continued and Castor felt powerless to prevent the eventual humiliation of dislodging every single bottle until the bottle bank was completely empty and he was stranded in a lake of glass vessels that would roll under his feet and send him sprawling if he attempted to escape. At this point the moon rose over the eastern hills and he was able to see that none of the bottles around him were quite empty. He reached for the nearest and held it up to the light. A blue mist swirled at the bottom, forming patterns that seemed unnatural. On impulse, Castor pulled out the cork.

The thick mist gushed from the neck and made a bulbous outline that suddenly solidified into a rotund figure with an enormous turban and eyes like miniature whirlpools. It floated above the ground unsteadily at first, then gained a sense of balance and pursed its indigo lips at Castor before speaking in a voice that resembled very distant thunder. "You're not supposed to let us out!"

"Why not?" blinked Castor.

"What's the point of depositing one genie here if you're going to set free another? Defeats the object of recycling us, I should think. You look confused. You *did* bring a genie to be recycled?"

Castor paled. "My bottle had nothing in it."

The genie sighed. "Clearly you've come to the wrong place. The ordinary bottle bank is over there. This one is reserved for bottles containing genies. An easy mistake to make, I suppose, not that anyone has made it before now, but there's a first time for everything. And so…"

Castor put his hands over his ears and shut his eyes tight, needing to disengage from reality for a few moments to regain his composure. When it was back he lowered his arms and snapped open his eyelids and met the gaze of the genie without flinching. Then he studied his surroundings more carefully. It was true that he had come to the wrong bottle bank. The correct one was beyond the bushes where the moonlight didn't reach yet, but he could just make out its dark profile among the somewhat lighter shadows.

"I didn't know that genies could be recycled," he said at last.

"It recently became possible," answered the genie.

"And all these bottles around me contain a genie, every single one?"

"With the exception of yours, obviously."

"What do you do for a living?" abruptly asked Castor.

"That's an odd question!" cried the genie.

"Is it really? I'm just curious. By the way, you smell like some sort of fruit juice. I never expected that, to be honest. Do you work in an orchard or a canning factory by any chance?"

"I'm a genie, I don't really work," pointed out the genie.

"You're broken?" gasped Castor.

"No, I mean that I don't have a profession or a career…"

"What I'm getting at," continued Castor, "is whether you grant wishes or not. I was being oblique when I asked about your job. Are you able to give me any wishes?"

The genie smirked. "I was wondering when that would come up. Of course I can. I have no choice, in fact. I suppose you want to wish for better health? You're looking a bit poorly, if you don't object to that observation."

"True," agreed Castor. "It's the frustration of my own job. I'm rather depressed at the moment, to be perfectly frank."

"What *is* your job," asked the genie politely.

"I'm a clown," answered Castor. "Let me tell you about it."

"Please don't!" begged the genie.

But that's what he did.

* * * *

From a young age (began Castor) I always wanted to be a clown. I loved the circus and desired nothing greater than to be one of those comical fellows with elongated shoes, false red noses, huge painted smiles and fake carnations that squirt water into unsuspecting faces. Unlike most normal adults, who inevitably grow out of their childhood obsessions, I never abandoned my original dream. Eventually I really did become an authentic clown.

I chose the name Hangfire Bubbler and that's how the ringmaster, Xelucha Laocoön, introduced me every night. My name had come to me in a dream and was more idiosyncratic than Coco, Mimsy, Bobo, Pogo, Sharps, Zubba, Dumpmungle or other traditional pseudonyms of that ilk. Mr Laocoön loved my act and always announced me with an especially perilous crack of his long bullwhip.

So I juggled balls and eggs, performed cartwheels and somersaults, landed flat on my face in mysterious plates of jelly, climbed rope-ladders to nowhere, was struck repeatedly on the skull by malevolent saucepans, rode on the back of a gigantic rabbit that was actually two other clowns inside a costume. I was funny and audiences always called for more and the fame went to my head or whatever other part of the anatomy is a willing host for it.

But the extreme contentment that filled me wasn't destined to last long, and maybe the name of the troupe I was with should have given me a clue, but at the time I found nothing sinister in the words LAOCOÖN'S CATASTROPHE CIRCUS and deemed my position and growing fame secure, if not inviolable. Then a new clown joined us. I saw him coming out of the ringmaster's caravan early one morning, looking very pleased with himself and exceptionally malign at the same time.

I later learned he had applied for a position, been granted an interview and so impressed Mr Laocoön that he was offered the job of warm-up clown on the spot. I was fascinated by his hideous makeup. A broad yellow smear ran from the crown of his head to his chin, overlapping the more conventional white and red paint. It turned out he wasn't a normal clown at all but one of those incredibly rare were-clowns. In other words, he was a human being or possibly a wolf by the light of day, but under the influence of the full moon he magically transformed into a clown. His name was Guttersnipe Chutney.

Alas, I soon had cause to regret setting eyes on this fellow. To maintain the form of a clown he wore a lamp strapped to his body with a stand that paralleled his spine and arched over his head, the bulb specially modified to radiate a glow identical to full moonlight. As our official warm-up clown his act consisted of bounding on before me and going through a routine that was supposed to make my own entrance easier. In fact, he achieved the opposite effect.

That vile Guttersnipe Chutney deliberately instilled a virulent strain of coulrophobia into my audience. Coulrophobia, in case you don't know, is a morbid fear of clowns and a natural development in the psychology of anyone compelled to watch *his* evil antics. By the time I entered the ring, the audience had mostly fled the environs of the circus and those few hardy souls who remained usually screamed at me or even offered threats of violence. And this went on night after night.

I complained to Guttersnipe but he merely sneered in reply, so I took my unhappiness to Xelucha Laocoön himself, but the ringmaster was equally dismissive of my grumbles and refused to take action. Then I realised they were in league against me. But why? What had poor Hangfire Bubbler done to merit such ignominious treatment? At night my dreams were full of Guttersnipe's menacing face with its weird yellow stripe. I slowly became a nervous wreck, a quivering fool.

The sabotage had its desired effect. Unable to entertain my audiences in the way I wished, prevented from being a true clown and living my dream, I had no option but to resign and leave the circus. I went without saying goodbye to anyone, in the cold hour before dawn, with my clown outfit strewn in the bushes and normal shoes on my feet. As I quietly passed the outer circle of caravans and crossed a wooden bridge over a stream into a forest, a voice called out:

"Hangfire Bubbler!"

He was lurking in the shadows and his yellow stained face gleamed softly. I stopped and waited for him to speak again. I wasn't afraid, though I couldn't guess his intentions. Did he plan to take his sabotage of my career to its ultimate limit by murdering me in cold blood? I no longer cared, to be completely truthful. The day a Bubbler is upstaged by a Chutney is the same day that everything ceases to matter very much.

At last he said, "Aren't you curious?"

"About what?" I spat.

"About why I have destroyed your life. I sought you out deliberately and applied for the job with Xelucha Laocoön simply for the chance to ruin you. I specialise in generating coulrophobia. I regard you as a stain worse than the one that covers my face and I wanted to wipe you out."

"Very well," I responded calmly. "Tell me everything."

His painted lips crinkled into a serrated smile that was surely capable of sawing through the remaining fibres of my dignity, but then he adopted a more sober expression and replied, "We are both professional clowns and thus aware of the Clown Museum in Haggerston Road, London. In fact we are *required* to be aware of it, because that's where our faces are registered."

"Of course," I said wearily.

He rubbed the yellow blot on his forehead and continued, "The Clown Museum is where those registered faces are recorded by being painted on eggs. Every accredited clown must have a unique face and those eggs enable the proprietors of the Museum to check that no face duplicates any other. I registered my own face more than two decades ago, immediately after I realised I was a were-clown. In fact it is precisely 7412 days since I presented my painted egg to the Museum and carefully added it to the trays of their collection."

My interest was finally aroused. "In that case your career as a clown precedes mine by only twenty four hours, for it is 7411 days since I added my own painted egg to the archives. Perhaps our eggs stand next to each other?"

He nodded ruefully. "I know for certain they do."

"Why so much bitterness about it?"

He grinned. "Now we get to the crux of my vendetta against you. When you added your own egg to the Museum trays you clumsily knocked it against mine. Your shell remained intact but mine cracked and the yolk poured down my registered expression, eventually drying and forming a thick yellow crust over my visage. You remained unaware of this accident and turned to depart, but a few days later I was contacted by the Museum authorities and asked to report there in person. When I saw my mutilated egg I was mortified."

I blinked at this revelation. "Clearly I must apologise to you, but I don't believe that such a minor mishap warrants so deadly a revenge."

"You fail to appreciate its full consequences," spluttered Guttersnipe Chutney, picking ineffectually at his stain with his fingernails, "because you forget that a registered clown is *never* allowed to deviate from the design submitted on his particular egg. My own egg now featured a yellow splodge and so I was forced on pain of expulsion to add an identical mark to my real face."

"Didn't you plead mitigating circumstances?"

"Certainly, but the authorities are strict and deaf to all excuses. I had no choice but to obey them. An ordinary clown would simply have used a paintbrush, but I'm a were-clown and my makeup is biological, not synthetic, so it was necessary to *grow* the stain."

The tinge of sympathy in my voice was genuine. "I see. And thus it can never be removed."

He inclined his head. "I am stuck with it for the rest of my life."

"And you hate it, I presume?"

"Very perceptive of you. It makes me look like a jaundiced cretin."

I shuffled my feet. "But you are a were-clown and can always change back into a normal human by switching off your moonlight lamp. I doubt the stain will accompany you in your transformation. Allow me to bend down and pick up this stone and I'll smash the bulb for you..."

Something appeared in his outstretched hand. "I don't want to be a man again. My destiny lies with the mightiest clowns of all time, so don't attempt to damage my lamp or I'll be forced to discharge this gyrojet pistol at your chest. I'm tempted to kill you anyway, but I'll take far more pleasure in letting you live as a failure. Goodbye, Mr Bubbler, and please have a safe journey down your imminent pit of despair, recrimination, impotence and misery…"

He waved me on with the barrel of his weapon and every trace of pity for his plight suddenly vacated my soul. I thought about rushing him and taking the full force of one of his rocket-powered bullets, to end everything there and then rather than walk away into a life of gradual descent into nullity. But I was too cowardly and I merely did as I was bid and shambled away.

I have never worked as a proper clown since, nor as anything else, and I dissipate my meagre savings on beer, for I have become an alcoholic. That's why I look so poorly and why I seem crushed by the weight of my misfortunes. I daydream about returning to the Clown Museum with a Molotov cocktail or other incendiary device and bombing that traitorous place. But I probably never will…

* * * *

"Has your story finished yet?" yawned the genie.

"No need to be so obvious about how bored you are," bristled Castor, "but yes, it has."

"Good, because it's bad form to tell your life story to a supernatural being. Cosmic etiquette and all that. It's especially rude to reminisce in front of a genie who has been deposited for recycling."

"I'm sorry," said Castor.

"You're supposed to use your three wishes and go."

"I'll remember that, but if you don't mind me asking, what exactly do genies get recycled *into*?"

"Spirits, of course," answered the genie.

Castor raised his eyebrows. "Ghosts, you mean?"

"No, like brandy or vodka or rum. Remember the fruit juice odour you detected earlier? That's our sweat. We're full of fructose and other sugars and when we die we rapidly ferment into alcohol. Hundreds of us are recycled every week."

"That's astounding," said Castor.

The genie watched him licking his greedy lips and quickly changed the subject. "Don't you want your wishes?"

"Certainly. It's high time my luck changed. I could use my wishes to get my own back on Guttersnipe Chutney but I'm sure there are more efficient ways of employing them than that. Three wishes in total, you said?"

The genie nodded. "That's the contract."

"Anything else I should be aware of before I begin? Any hidden clauses?"

The genie was impressed. "Few people have the clarity of vision to ask that question, but yes, there's a clause. Three wishes only and I get to kill you after you've had your last wish. Do you agree?"

Castor snorted. "No, I don't agree to that!"

The genie pouted. "But it really is standard procedure. Even if you don't agree to my terms I'll still kill you after your last wish. That's what genies do. I'm compelled to obey you until the last wish, then I'm free to end your life."

Castor inhaled deeply. "Very well, I agree, because I can see an easy way out of the trap. My first wish will be for more than three wishes. In fact, I hereby wish for an *unlimited number of wishes*!"

"Granted!" cried the genie, and he waved his smoky arms.

"Has it worked?" demanded Castor.

The genie bowed low. "Yes, your first wish has been granted. You now have an infinite number of wishes at your disposal. However, I must point out that it was a wasted wish, as I still intend to kill you after your third wish."

"That's unfair!" protested Castor.

"No, it's not," said the genie.

"Yes it is," persisted Castor, "because you said you would only kill me after my *last* wish, and now I have an unlimited number of wishes, so there simply isn't a last one. Infinity never ends, please remember."

"But when you agreed to my terms your third wish *was* your last…"

"Bah!" grumbled Castor.

The genie blithely examined his fingernails. "Next wish?"

"You're so mean and vicious," said Castor, "that my second wish is for you to instantly become sweet and good-natured. That way you won't *want* to kill my after my third wish and I'll be allowed to live and enjoy all the wishes that come after it. That's what I want."

"Granted!" the genie roared, and he waved his arms again.

"Really?" frowned Castor.

"Yes indeed. I've just done exactly what you asked for, but it was also a wasted wish, I'm sorry to say. You see, I was *already* sweet and good-natured. I intended to kill you with a smile on my face and that's what I still

intend. No genie is really vicious and it's not a require-
ment of any killer that he has to be mean."

"Humph!" snorted Castor.

"Your third and last wish?" prompted the genie.

Castor clenched his fists. "Very well. When I was
young and still struggling to be accepted as a professional clown, I always imagined that if I ever found a genie
I would wish for genies to stop existing, to prevent other
people from being granted wishes. That's how much of a
misanthrope I was."

"I never would have guessed," said the genie.

"And that's my third wish," continued Castor through
gritted teeth. "I want all genies to die immediately. Wherever they are."

The genie swallowed and muttered, "Granted!"

He clearly had no choice in the matter...

Castor stood in the lonely moonlight and allowed
himself to appreciate the fact he was still alive despite
having used all three wishes, but he was no better off
than when he had first approached the bottle bank and
this fact irked him. He had been offered an opportunity
to get even with his tormentors but it had slipped through
his fingers. What a loser!

Or was he? He sniffed the air gingerly. Alcohol...

The genie had died and fermented into a potent brew
that darkly stained the ground. Castor fought the urge to
get down on his hands and knees and lap the precious
juice of oblivion with his tongue. Too bestial. Then he
smiled and regarded the other bottles that surrounded
him.

They were full of dead genies, brimming with alcohol, hundreds of bottles sloshing with the fluid of forgetfulness, with a liquid escape!

Or with fuel for a daring assault on the Clown Museum...

The simple fact was that rags and matches could be obtained easily enough, and so this bottle bank had become a cache of Molotov cocktails. Castor reached into one of his pockets for his tubes of face paint. He didn't have a mirror but that didn't matter. It was time for him to adopt a new face anyway, and with the poaching of the Museum eggs in the coming inferno, how would anyone ever be able to persecute him for a mismatch?

With a lopsided grin and nostrils filled with the fumes of fermented genies, Hangfire Bubbler loped off into the night...

THE PRIVATE PIRATES CLUB

At this point, the literary agent who sold this book could restrain his impatience no longer and he said, "Although he's a fictional character that didn't exist before the author invented him, I met Castor Jenkins once. So it's time I told a story of my own. Ready?"

* * * *

My name is Thornton Excelsior and I'm highly respected in the publishing world. Some people mistakenly conclude that being a literary agent is a sedate business and that the people involved in it must have fairly bland lives. Maybe that's true for others, but my own life has been adventurous and continues to vibrate with incidents.

For instance, having recently escaped from pirates, I was invited to join a private club composed entirely of men and women who had achieved the same distinction. I went to my first meeting in an anxious frame of mind, hoping my escape would be superior to those of the other members, but prepared for disappointment. Around a rough wooden table sat a motley collection of individuals, and when I entered the room they began slamming full mugs down on the surface, applauding my arrival with spilled rum. I settled myself on a vacant chair and waited quietly to see what would develop.

The figure at the head of the table thrust his finger into the puddle that had formed on the uneven plank directly in front of him and watched the concentric ripples with a meditative smile. Lanterns swung from the ceiling on thin chains, turning all eyes into stars, ladling shadows over the lower halves of faces, an effect less mysterious than it ought to be. A brasher man might have introduced himself at this point but I preferred to err on the side of caution, inhaling the fumes deeply through flared nostrils until I could no longer smell them. Then the man with the extended finger made a little speech.

"Pirates are everywhere! Pirates are a fashion and a myth, a savagery and a custom, a colour and a doom. They are like pieces of cork in a glass of wine, spots on the sun, loose buttons on a shirt. Pirates.

"They are like notes in a song — a song about pirates.

"Pirates are like thumbs where toes should be, like needles in a camel's eye, like the words in a book that has accidentally fallen into a frying pan: can you hear the sizzle? Pirates. Like hairs on an old bar of soap..."

"With respect," I interrupted, "they aren't like that at all."

"No?" he demanded with a furious frown.

"Like none of that," I confirmed.

There was a general murmuring and the dimness of the room seemed to lessen as smiles full of rotten teeth were inversely flashed, if I may be permitted a twist of language, for a deeper darkness will lighten a lesser, when both glooms are present. And that is a maxim for you to keep, of dubious value. But the man with the extended finger remained without a smile, his frown disapproving perhaps even of itself, the very opposite of a sign of glee, however ironic, and he asked me slowly to refine my criticism of his comparisons, to prove that pirates were nothing similar to any of his examples.

"I was captured by a pirate exactly one year ago," I said, "and the experience had nothing poetic or contrived about it. On the contrary it was a grimy, dismal reality. The man who controlled the ship on which I was a prisoner was none other than Captain Salve, the second worst pirate on the first set of Seven Seas."

"Tell us the whole story," the company roared.

"Very well," I continued, filling my mug from a bottle that stood near to a platter of figs, "but talking about it doesn't help me to assimilate what happened. The therapists are wrong about that. I'm a literary agent and I was travelling to Sumatra to attend a book fair. A hundred leagues nearer than we expected, the coast of Aceh rose up on the horizon and we headed for it in all innocence. But this was a trick: Captain Salve had painted the coast on a giant floating screen and he was hiding behind it in his own heavily armed ship. I still have nightmares about how he burst through, guns blazing, smashing our poor vessel to splinters.

"I was one of the few survivors and I was plucked in a dazed condition from the water on the end of a grappling hook. I still have a scar on my shoulder. Captain Salve slapped my cheeks until they became too warm to touch and then he asked me directly 'Why shouldn't I throw you back?' and it was fortunate I blurted the following reply 'Because I'm a literary agent and might one day be in a position to sell a book of your memoirs, if they are written well enough'. After a minute of scratching his head indecisively he decided to formally accept me as part of his crew. And that's how I saved my life and went to work for the second worst rascal that ever swung a salt encrusted cutlass on a creaking deck.

"A compulsive thief was Captain Salve, a man born to always take and rarely give!

"He couldn't help himself: he was a genuine kleptomaniac. As we were near Sumatra he thought we should pay a visit to the East Pole and test my abilities at distinguishing toxic growths from beneficial. I'm sure all of you present know everything about the East Pole that ever needs to be said. It's one of the secret poles of our world, striped red and white just as you might expect and rising out of the briny deeps on the exact line of the equator at a longitude of 90°E. Just like the West, Front and Back Poles the East is a place where pirates forget their differences and meet to trade in safety.

"A sort of vast floating market is what it is.

"You could obtain almost anything you wanted there, especially if it was something with a piratical association, such as pearls, pistols, barrels of grog, slaves, earrings, pieces of eight, wooden legs, sacks of gunpowder, octants.

"Also there was plenty of food including cocoa beans, chillies, biscuits, dried beef, crispy seaweed, oysters, yoghurt, cheese and mushrooms. But some of those mushrooms were really toadstools, for that's the way it happens at the East Pole, nothing malicious but a simple mistake, and Captain Salve wanted to cook a vast risotto for all his men, he had a good side too, it was just very thin and unreflective, like a black stiletto's edge, and he cared not to poison his crew, so he asked for my advice. Maybe he thought that a literary agent knows everything on every topic. But I obliged and selected the fungi and the risotto was prepared and I was the first to sample it.

"Captain Salve watched me carefully and spotted the fact I didn't die.

"I guess I won his trust after that, at least in part, but I didn't enjoy his newfound respect for long. After the risotto was devoured he did something a bit reckless, something entirely in keeping with his awful reputation..."

* * * *

I paused for breath and clearly my pause was too long or wide, because one of the other members of the club, a man with a nose like a piece of ginger, saw an opportunity to fit the beginning of his own anecdote into it, like a foot thrust into the gap left by a door just before it closes. And once that foot is in place it is never surprising to witness the rest of the body following suit, so I poured myself more rum and nibbled at a fig and leaned back to hear the whole of his tale, and he knew more than me about the conventions of the club, for his respiration was shallow and uninterruptible during its telling.

"You describe his action — whatever it was — as *reckless*, and that word is highly evocative of the pirate who captured me, not because of his nature or lifestyle but simply because it was his surname. Captain Reckless was a rather careful sort of man, considering his chosen profession, but he was a restless and relentless experimenter. He liked to despatch his victims in new, original ways, or at least with unfeasible extensions to existing methods.

"I can positively state now that Captain Salve, with or without his risotto, was *never* the second worst pirate on the first set of Seven Seas. That title belonged to Captain Reckless. Yes, he was undoubtedly the second worst and I intend to prove it!

"Captain Reckless decided to get rid of me, one of his horribly careful decisions, by making me walk the plank, that old pirate classic. But an ordinary plank would never satisfy his innovative soul or tickle the stomach of the scientific curiosity that lurked in his brainpan like a hairy frog or maybe like a kitten covered in scales. I use the word 'scientific' in a loose sense... But I'm digressing!

"So he made me walk the longest plank in the world. That's what he did!

"Where he got such a plank from, if indeed he got it from anywhere, or where he kept it stored when not in use, were questions I asked not. I was too shaky to utter a word. I just recall being dragged from my tiny cell in the hold and pushed out on deck. The longest plank in the world jutted over the side and its far end was lost in a fine mist — or so I thought at first. Then Captain reckless muttered ruefully 'It's a shame I don't have the longest cutlass in the world to jab our prisoner down this plank' and his crew of ruffians all chortled and bared mirthfully rotten teeth.

"I took my first step along that plank and I heard the scrape of a blade being drawn from a scabbard and I assumed that Captain Reckless intended to execute me himself. A rare honour! I felt a sharp prod at the base of my spine and I increased my pace. But the further I walked, the harder and sharper became the sensation in my back. I now realised the true reason why the far end of the plank was invisible: it was obscured by the curvature of the Earth. Yes, the longest plank in the world really was that long!

"The further I walked, the lower the plank dipped, and still harder jabbed the point of that infernal sword into my flesh. As the plank bent under my weight, my journey became a descent, a mild incline at first but growing steadily steeper. I longed to reach the end and plunge into the cold sea, anything to end the pain in my spine, but still the plank went on, from one horizon to the next, and I began to fear it might circle the globe and take me back to the ship, where I would surely be forced to repeat the journey.

"Finally I could bear no more. I glanced back over my shoulder to beg Captain Reckless, or whoever it was that held the cutlass, to finish me off quickly. Imagine my dismay when I beheld no man at all but a wooden trolley mounted on wheels at the front of which the sword was fixed. There could be no pleading for mercy with this device!

"The mechanics of my doom were simple enough — as I walked along, the plank bent, and as it bent the trolley rolled faster down the increasing gradient. There was no room to stand aside and let it pass and it was too heavy to overturn into the sea. Only one course of action lay open to me: I ran as fast as I could!

"I was able to outdistance it and soon its abominable trundling became like the murmur of an empty glass rolled across a table in another room, but its progress was implacable and it was fated to always increase its speed, while I was only human and too easily fatigued. There was no doubt as to the eventual outcome of this situation...

"On the verge of giving up all hope, I was heartened by a smudge in the distance. My running legs soon resolved this vagueness into a definite shape. Land! A coastline, a port city in fact, and the plank terminated not more than a yard from the edge of a stone quay. What luck! By using a plank this long, Captain Reckless had inadvertently given me an opportunity to escape. I had only to keep running and take that final leap.

"But my legs were tiring fast and the trolley was catching up!

"It is obvious to you all what happened... After all, I am here among you, one of the oldest members of our club. I reached the end of the plank before the trolley reached me, I jumped and landed on the quay, and the plank — abruptly deprived of my weight — sprang back like a catapult, hurling the trolley in the direction of the pirate ship. I like to think it crashed onto the deck and impaled Captain Reckless through the ribs, but I know it probably didn't. Still a man is allowed his dreams!

"In the port city I climbed onto a bus when nobody was looking and hid at the back. That bus took me to another city where I found work as a dogsbody in a cat hospital and earned enough to pay my fare to yet another city, where I sold my nose — luckily I found a cheap replacement later — for a sum sufficient to keep me travelling... And thus I lived for many months, moving from one city to the next, until I finally reached my hometown. My house was waiting for me like a wife, but with a roof instead of a hat, plus my house wasn't alive, but all the same...

"I took the key from the chain around my neck, inserted it into the lock, turned once, pulled the handle and the door swung open.

"And there, waiting for me in the shadows, was — you know who!"

* * * *

We all nodded and I even clapped my hands but there was sadness in our appreciation of his story. I wondered if I ought to continue with my own tale at this point, but I was pre-empted by another member, a sweating fat man with an astoundingly unhealthy complexion. He was about fifty years of age but looked as if he had existed twice as long on a diet of nothing but beer and chips. Yet his voice was resonant and rich and I could tell he was used to relating stories. Afterwards I learned that his accent and diet were both Welsh, but at the time I assumed merely that he was overly sentimental, melancholic, verbose, impractical, unambitious and a curious blend of pompous and humble.

"At the North Star, all other directions are south! I mention this fact simply to grab your attention, but the light of that cold distant sun did shine on the lips and tongue of my lover on the night of our rescue, while we kissed.

"I shouldn't get ahead of myself like that — but it's better for me to do so than anyone else. That's my humble, and pompous, opinion!

"A few minutes ago I winced at the words *through the ribs*. I winced because they reminded me of my own incarceration aboard a pirate ship under the command of Captain Ribs. Yes, that really was his true name, and let me tell you that *he* was the second worst pirate on the first set of Seven Seas. Your own pirates were like water lilies in comparison, or like coconuts adrift on ocean currents — hairy and full of milk.

"Captain Ribs was a bony freak and a vile philosopher. He had a horrid motto, 'Life is too short for it to be long for anyone else.'

"He said that to me a dozen times. My knees knocked together!

"To stay alive I had to work for him as an official member of his crew. I was his lookout and I spent most of my time balanced precariously in the crow's nest watching out for other ships. We sailed around the island of Kurtsy so many times that it went giddy and sank very politely into the sea — which is how it earned its name — and I'm sure we visited every country in the world.

"Apart from the landlocked ones, that is. Like Hungary.

"But one day we entered a region of thick fog, so thick it could be spooned into coffee quite realistically, and I didn't do my job properly and we collided with a ship sailing the other way, another pirate vessel as it happens, and all hands were lost, and feet too, apart from those belonging to myself and a woman from the other ship, the woman who became my lover when we were finally washed up together on a deserted island. North Star, kisses with tongues.

"Our love eventually produced a baby, our son, and so we became a proper family. When I say 'eventually' I mean nine months, obviously. When I say 'obviously' I mean that it's needless to say. Needless.

"Our baby was needful, as are they all, not needless.

"I had escaped Captain Ribs but only in part... The desert island held me to its bosom in the same way a mad monkey holds a small coat. Weird simile, blame the rum, and the beer, and the chips. Anyway, years passed before we were picked up. An oil tanker did the deed, bless its commercial crudity, and its captain was a very slick fellow.

"I made a new life with my woman and child on the mainland and we lived in a cosy house and everything was fine and whenever our child cried one of us would go to its cot to see what the trouble was. One morning just after the sun had risen I heard a strange noise coming from the cot. I turned to my woman and said 'our son is saying his first words, in fact he is singing them and playing the accordion at the same time.' And what did my woman say to this? She said 'It's your turn to sort him out.'

"So I got out of bed and wrapped a dressing gown around myself and I left the bedroom and I approached the cot and I saw that it was sagging on its legs, as if it held a weight greater than any normal child, and I saw how it bulged at the sides, and I scratched my head in confusion and I approached it cautiously.

"Then I looked inside and saw — you know who!"

* * * *

Once again the entire company nodded. I felt closer to them than before and I had the feeling they finally accepted me now, regarded me as one of them, despite the fact I still hadn't finished my tale. The man with the extended finger, the evident leader of the group, grimaced as if he had swallowed an unpleasant substance, angled his head as if waiting for syrup to pour out of his left ear, and began speaking. There was regret in his eyes as he did so, but his tone was steady and elegantly sardonic.

"I can also say something striking to commence my tale. For instance: total war can elicit half-hearted cries in certain quarters... But I don't need to pepper my life with lyrical phrases, whether appropriate or not. My experience will speak for itself, even though it has no mouth. For itself, but through me.

"Knees knock together — yes, they often do. Knock hard!

"Captain Knock was the pirate who captured me and he was the second worst pirate on the first set of Seven Seas. Believe me! He wanted to be different from other pirates, more extravagant and colourful, and so he decided to own the shoulder with the biggest ever parrot sitting on it. Other pirates had ordinary parrots but Captain Knock found a parrot bigger than he was. No wonder he walked with a stoop!

"He found the parrot just off the coast of Persia — modern day Iran.

"It was a beautiful bird with orange feathers and a silver beak, but there was something not quite parroty about it, if you take my meaning, and I began to wonder if Captain Knock had made a mistake. At night it perched on the taffrail of our ship, enjoying the moonbeams. I sometimes went to visit it stealthily, but it never spoke to me, and gradually I realised that this was no parrot — it was a simurgh.

"The simurgh is a creature similar to the phoenix but completely different!

"I had heard long ago about how the simurgh is an inherently benevolent bird, and so one midnight I mounted its back and urged it to flight. Up we went, the flapping of the great wings alerting the pirates to my escape. Sleepy and bleary eyed they loaded muskets and fired, but all the bullets missed. The simurgh wanted me to survive because it had a good soul. It carried me safely away.

"It landed in a garden encircled by lofty mountains and here I lived in peace. One day, to my astonishment, it laid an egg, and we took turns sitting on it. I came closer to knowing simple happiness than ever before or since, and Captain Knock, the second worst pirate on the first set of Seven Seas, was long forgotten, but then the egg hatched while I was sitting on it. Yes, it hatched directly beneath me.

"And what came out was — you know who!"

* * * *

I made no attempt to resume my own story because I assumed everyone else would want to tell theirs first, leaving mine to be the last. But I was wrong about this and slowly all eyes around the table swivelled to focus on me. There was an air of expectation, a tainted air but an air all the same, in the same way that the air that hisses out of a punctured sausage is tainted. Well not quite like that. I also realised that apart from the three who had already spoken, the tales of the other members followed directly from my own, and then I felt guilty, although there was no reason why I should be blamed for anything. Captain Salve was the man who had caused the chaos, not me.

"You want to know what the reckless thing was?" I asked. "The reckless thing he did after that risotto at the East Pole?"

The heads all nodded and so I poured myself more rum.

"Well he was a compulsive thief, as I said before..." I began.

"And?" they whispered urgently.

I shifted uncomfortably in my chair. "And then he stole it."

"Stole what?" came the chorus.

"The pole! The East Pole! What else? He stole the pole, the actual pole, the striped length of wood at latitude 0°, longitude 90°E. He tied one end of a rope to it and connected the other end to his capstan. How we grunted as we pushed the levers. With a dreadful sucking sound out came the pole, like a healthy tooth from a tricked gum! And what then? Do you really want to know?"

"We already know, we knew all along."

I nodded and laughed. "Of course you did! The pole acted like a giant plug in an immense hole in the seabed and suddenly all the water started spiralling down into the centre of the Earth and all the pirate ships gathered at that spot began to spin round too... Well some of them were anchored with plenty of slack, some with none, others with thin ropes that snapped easily, a few weren't anchored at all, and the result was a terrible series of collisions that smashed every last vessel to splinters. What a mess!

"Fortunately for the world, some of the wreckage plugged the hole again, otherwise the oceans might have drained entirely away and the first set of Seven Seas would be nothing more than seven smelly deserts littered with pale fishbones.

"My own ship was broken and Captain Salve was probably drowned.

"His first name was Lipsy, if anyone is interested to know that. Lipsy Salve. I see that nobody here cares one way or another. That's fair enough!

"I never saw Captain Salve again, but I survived and I wasn't alone, for several other people aboard some of the other destroyed ships also survived. We clung to the East Pole as it floated across the Indian Ocean. Looking around this room I note that many of the members of the club were the men and women who shared my experience. I apologise for not recognising you earlier. During a storm the pole struck a reef and broke into many small pieces and we all went drifting off in different directions. I went south."

The man with the extended finger winked horribly. "Oh yes? And what happened next?"

Before I could answer, he withdrew his finger and I saw that it had been plugging a hole in the table. Now the puddle of spilled rum poured through it onto the floor with a grotesque slurping noise and I was brought face to face, on a more domestic scale, with what had happened on that fateful day when Captain Salve tried to steal the East Pole. But the man whose finger was no longer extended had demonstrated bad timing, because I was already past that point in my tale, and unsure of how seriously to take his gesture I almost floundered, which possibly was his intention.

"I continued south," I said, "until I stopped going that way."

"Why did you stop?" he demanded.

"I was swallowed by a whale. At least I thought it was a whale, in fact I thought it was Moby K Dick, the Paranoia Whale, but it wasn't. It wasn't anything alive. It was a false whale, a submarine disguised as a whale, with an airlock designed to work like jaws. Down I went, into the stomach, and holding aloft a lamp there stood — you know who!"

"Yes we know who! Captain Worst!"

"That's right. Captain Worst — the worst pirate on the first set of Seven Seas!"

"He waited for all of us in a similar way. He waited on the thresholds of our own homes, in the cots of our children, in the eggs of fabulous birds. There is much disagreement about who is the second worst pirate on the first set of Seven Seas, but nobody disputes who is the very worst. Captain Worst. Who else could it be?"

"What a supreme rascal he is! What an ineffable blackguard!"

"He crews his ship only with men and women who have escaped from other pirates. It's his trademark and the reason we are all together..."

Our meeting was suddenly interrupted by the tolling of an iron bell near the ceiling. I hadn't noticed it until now. At the same time, a furious stamping on the boards high above alerted the company to the fact it was time to return to work. We stood and climbed the ladder to the deck. I spied a ship on the horizon and realised we were preparing to attack it. Captain Worst is a terrible fellow but even he has his good side, allowing members of his crew to form a private club in one of the larger cabins. As I made my way to the nearest cannon I wondered aloud:

"Will any of us ever escape from Captain Worst?"

"Not worth the attempt," came the reply from behind me, and I shuddered at the sound of *that* voice. "Who knows who might pick you up next? I may be the worst pirate on the first set of Seven Seas but that says nothing about the second set of Seven Seas — Seas Eight to Fourteen. Count yourself fortunate, my friend, and remember that the worst is sometimes the best!"

I nodded briskly and loaded the cannon as quickly as I could.

3: CASTOR ON THE SEVEN PLUS SEAS

Many centuries have passed since the total number of seas on the planet was seven. Thanks to geography and inflation, the total is now closer to seventy. Some of the new seas are watery enough to satisfy the pickiest of ancient helmsmen, but others are wholly metaphoric in character, less damp than their material counterparts but equally deep or even deeper. If you care to follow Castor on those seas, and over the edge of the world, be sure to learn how to swim in ink and float on fables.

CHUCKLEBERRY GRIN

"Shall I tell a new story?" asked Castor Jenkins.

Paddy Deluxe shrugged. "I don't mind; provided it's not about the time you entered yourself in Bankcrufts, the bankrupt dogs' show, and won the first prize just by tagging your wail."

"Or about the time you hunted fossils for a living, blasting them to bits with bazookas," said Frothing Harris.

"Or about the time you ate a storm cloud and it tasted like blackcurrant jam but then it rained in your stomach for forty nights and forty days and the other foodstuffs in your gut had to construct an ark to survive but got stuck on the edge of your appetite and were forced to turn to cannibalism and be devoured for a second time."

Castor considered this. "Well, I'm willing to do negative requests. Tell me what you don't want to hear and I promise not to mention it. I have no issue with pandering to my public!"

Harris smiled. "That's good to know. For a start, I want to hear nothing at all about the time you travelled with the mad inventor Karl Mondaugen to the planet known as the Counter Earth (or Antichthon) that spins on the other side of the sun and met Lohengrin Smirka, the Duke of Laxhumbug, and taught him to play the ocarina."

Castor nodded. "Very well. I won't breathe a word about that. It would be a shame to do so anyway, as I promised Mondaugen to keep it a secret, and if the exploit became common knowledge it would necessitate a total rethink of the layout of the solar system; and intellectual overhauls of that scale are often messy and expensive. I think the inventor has scrapped the little craft that carried us there; it was badly damaged by regular knocking against the sides of the sun pipe over a period of several perilous months. I won't explain what a sun pipe is; nor will I specify that it's one hundred and eighty-six million miles long…"

"You'd better not!" growled Paddy and Harris.

Castor sipped his pint and said, "I have no intention of doing so. What do you think I am: a pledge-breaker? I can't recall exactly how I bumped into Mondaugen on that occasion, maybe I just met him in the street, but he was excited and took me to see his latest project, a submersible that he claimed could open up new trade routes with the bizarre mirror version of Earth that exists, as you pointed out, on the other side of the sun, at what I believe is often called Lagrange Point 3, where the opposing gravitational forces exerted by the Earth and the sun are cancelled out. I laughed in his face! 'There is no liquid in outer space! What you require is a spacecraft, not a midget submarine!' I told him."

"That's precisely along the lines of what we don't wish to hear," Harris said, nodding in the fashion of a sage.

"Keep going the opposite of that," added Paddy.

Castor took another sip of beer. "Very well. Then I won't admit that he shrugged in the gale of my laugh and said with twinkling eyes, 'No need to leave our atmosphere to reach the world of Antichthon, for I've found a better route: through the service ducts!' I was astonished to hear this, and naturally I asked for more details…"

"Service ducks?" frowned Harris.

"Ducts," corrected Castor.

"Please don't continue, if you would," said Paddy.

Castor wiped his lips. "He informed me with a straight face that Earth and Antichthon were connected and that this connection was necessary to prevent the planets eventually colliding; for though they occupy a stance diametrically opposite each other, like duellists skirting a bonfire, the tiny variations in the combined gravitation of all the other planets over time would nudge us out of perfect alignment and this effect would continue and the errors tend to increase rather than decrease. As we are at the same distance from the sun, and on the same plane, a collision is inevitable and the destruction of both bodies assured. But a pipe runs from the centre of our planet to the centre of the other and works as an axle, preventing any such disastrous shift of alignment."

Harris and Paddy exchanged glances and for a moment it seemed they were imagining themselves to be the two globes in question, but who was Earth and who Antichthon wasn't at all obvious; plus they weren't sitting directly opposite each other, so the analogy was patently inaccurate from the beginning. Nonetheless they stretched out a rigid arm each and joined them over the golden pint of beer standing in the middle of the table; and thus was the cosmic pipe mimicked.

Castor watched this performance with approval. He said, "Mondaugen was convinced the pipe was full of water and wide enough to easily admit his submersible. He told me the pipe's function as an axle was secondary and its primary purpose was to cool the sun and prevent that blazing body from overheating or exploding, which is logically why it's called the sun pipe. The oceans of the two worlds are constantly exchanged through this pipe, which passes directly through the heart of the sun, and so this is the true explanation of mysterious whirlpools and missing ships and strange vessels appearing from no-where, for it's a huge interplanetary circulatory system. Makes a lot of sense really."

"Especially if you're daft," Harris conceded.

Castor reached for the pint in the centre of the table; nobody else had claimed it, so he speculated it was time to make it his own. "Excuse me while I displace your sun," he said.

"That was standing there when we came in," warned Paddy.

"It might be flat," added Harris.

"Too late," lisped Castor as he took a slurp. "Now then, where was I? Ah yes, I was just keeping my mouth shut about how Mondaugen offered to take me along the sun pipe in his vehicle all the way to Antichthon for a look around. He had some crazy idea that everything, or some things at least, would be reversed there; I don't mean that black would be white, or crisps would be sweets, or any-thing along those lines; but customs, music and geogra-phy might be the inverse of what we're familiar with on Earth. I was won over by this possibility, so I agreed to accompany him. In the basement of his house he had dug a well, or maybe there had always been a well there, and the submersible was bobbing about on the top. He aided me to climb inside and followed."

"And closed the hatch with a clang?" asked Paddy.

"With a hiss," corrected Castor.

"A sibilant hiss?" wondered Harris.

Castor shook his head. "A clanging hiss," he said. He drained half the anonymous pint and continued, "Straight down we went and it grew hot inside the capsule. There were plenty of supplies in the lockers, but heat tends to reduce my appetite. I made do with a cake. At long last we came to the bottom of the well and entered a horizontal tube. This was the sun pipe. I noted that other conduits of varying diameters opened into it from sundry directions; it was an amazing plumbing job. I brushed crumbs off my fingers. Although the sun pipe was a single tube it was divided into a pair of immensely strong currents travelling in opposite directions. Why they didn't collide and blend I'll never know; probably it had something to do with eddy physics or vortices."

"Eddy physics?" Harris was intrigued.

"The lifework of Eddy Dalderbash, a colleague of Oliver Heaviside, who discovered why toast always falls jam side down. Those neglected scientists of yore! What fellows they were!" Castor sighed. "Anyhow, I didn't question Mondaugen on the phenomenon; I merely assumed this arrangement maximised the efficiency of the heat exchange mechanism and I was right about that, of course."

"Were you boiled inside?" queried Paddy.

"Yes I was. Boiled to death!" said Castor. He frowned and examined himself. "Wait a moment, I'm not a cadaver! Clearly I'm mistaken and I was boiled alive instead! So I didn't expire; neither did Mondaugen. Well, it's an easy enough mistake to make."

"I've never died either," empathised Harris.

"Nor me!" cried Paddy in innocent delight. "We ought to start a club strictly for people who are alive!"

"That's a bit elitist," sniffed Castor.

Paddy and Harris shuffled their feet under the table for a minute or so, stung by the rebuke. Then Castor continued with his tale: "The days and the weeks got together and turned into months; I never thought we would ever reach the end of the sun pipe. Because the sides of the pipe are solid and opaque, I saw nothing of outer space; and even when we passed right through the middle of the sun, the illumination inside the capsule was no brighter than before. It was quite boring, to tell the truth! When we finally reached the end of the conduit I was ready to turn back for home. But we didn't do that. Up a well we went, surfacing in a basement that was rather similar, but not identical, to Mondaugen's cellar on Earth. So we were in the Antichthon version of his house!"

"Was everything back to front?" asked Paddy.

"Yes it was. For instance, we mounted the stairs to the living room and saw that the sofa was where the arm-chairs should be; and in the fruit bowl I noticed how bananas all curved in the wrong direction. We lurched out into the streets of Porthcawl – I mean Lwachtrop – on the Counter Earth, and gazed in wonder at our environs…"

"Wait a moment! You took us to Lwachtrop in a fly-ing lighthouse and it certainly wasn't on the far side of our sun. It was a town on a planet in the constellation Gemini," said Paddy.

Castor nodded vigorously. "Precisely! And that's why Mondaugen and myself didn't stay there long, but travelled to a nation called Laxhumbug, where, as you've already pointed out, I taught the Grand Duke who ruled that country to play the ocarina. It wasn't my ocarina, by the way, but one belonging to Lohengrin Smirka himself. He was getting ready to repel an invasion by Noelopan Fleshtogether, the Emperor of Frunce, and ocarina melo-dies were a balm for his soul—"

"I'm so glad you decided not to tell us this," said Harris.

"Any of it," added Paddy.

Castor shrugged off their gratitude. "Think nothing of it. I'm a man of my word. On Antichthon I wasn't a man of my word; which over there is the same thing. We came back the same way, through the sun pipe, after a dozen adventures in the service of the Grand Duke, who not only became an ocarina virtuoso but also learned the *mbira*, which is the thumb piano, in case you didn't know. Playing them simultaneously is extremely tricky but feasible; I don't rightly know why anyone would want to play them at the same time, but it *can* be done."

"I can whistle and hum at the same time," admitted Paddy.

"He sounds like a theremin," said Harris.

"I often feel I'm levitating when I do," added Paddy.

"Like a gyroscope," said Harris.

"That's not untrue," declared Paddy.

"He's willing to demonstrate his skill," said Harris.

"Yes I am," confirmed Paddy.

Castor chose his words carefully. "I have been good enough to take to heart your resistance to hear a story about the time I visited Antichthon in the company of the mad inventor Mondaugen; because I am a considerate soul, I treated your request with respect and I held my tongue. In return I would prefer to decline your offer."

"You don't know what you're missing," said Harris.

"Thank goodness!" cried Castor.

"Why don't you tell us a story then?" demanded Paddy.

Castor tugged his nose and frowned.

"I suppose I can do that. Have you heard of a competition for dogs in debt? It's called Bankcrufts and—"

"Not that one!" shrieked Harris and Paddy.

"Very well," said Castor. "Did I ever tell you about the time I went to Lladloh and met the *Peachy Poo* in person and was turned into a human arrow and fired around the world?"

* * * *

It's surely the strangest village in Wales, though the competition is strong, and you won't locate it on any map for that reason, though exactly *who* is responsible for removing all references to it is still a mystery. Lladloh is a place where destiny goes to retire. Some years ago the traditional position of mayor was abolished by an usurper; her name's Lowri Constantine, the first *Peachy Poo*, and she still rules there. But there have been significant changes. The old way of doing utterly odd things has been replaced by a new way of doing utterly odd things.

That was her work and it can be both fairly and unfairly said that she's a revolutionary. Her most prominent skill is archery and she often shoots arrows into the hides of disobedient citizens from the window of her tall house, the former residence of the mayor. She's not really a tyrant but it's safer to act as if she is likely to have you done away with on the slightest pretext. The citizens tend to tiptoe up and down the streets; most of them appear never to leave the nameless tavern, though that's surely an illusion, for they would run out of conversation.

I was travelling in those parts for the first time last summer and down came the rain in ceaseless sheets of monsoon force, muddying all ruts on the forsaken roads, turning to mush the gnarled sheep on the anguished hills, carving meaningless scripts into the soft under parts of the toppled megaliths. But why was I tramping that desolate region of my overblown prose? I think I was on a bird watching expedition; or maybe I was going to an obscure clown festival; or maybe it had something to do with rugby in extremis. I simply don't remember.

That's one of the things that travellers never forget about that tract of dismalness in the western quarter of Wales: it seems to induce amnesia. I wonder how they manage to recall this fact? Interesting topic for endless philosophising some other time! I walked with my staff making complex ripples in the puddles each instant the point came down. At last the thick drops of sky resentment eased their intensity somewhat and I reached a stone bridge, which led me over an unpleasant hump that jarred my spine into a village of frowning buildings.

This was Lladloh. I knew of it from hearsay. I had even told stories of some of its most famous characters, such as Dennistoun Homunculus, the hideous bard of the village, a poet who wrote verses that cause the soul to curl up in a foetal position inside your ribcage. Most unpleasant! And the gravedigger Pumpkin Hewin', who by his own admission was a man who liked to call a spade a shovel and a crow a raven, and sometimes a spoon a ladle, nobody knew why. Neifion Napcyn too, a fishmonger who caught cooked trout in the crater of a volcano.

Yes, I had told tales about these characters, and more. The name of the volcano, by the way, is Mount Yandro and it's the only active, and secret, volcano in Wales. And there were the squonks, of course, not an imported breed from the hemlock forests of Pennsylvania, where they can be found posing for photographs, but the lesser known Welsh kind; a squonk won't bother crying its eyes out here because the rain dilutes the melancholy of the teardrops, watering them down to something that isn't joy but a closer analogue of it than any squonk can bear.

Am I rambling? I stopped rambling for real when I reached the village square and debated which way to go next. A new arrival in such a place must always enter the tavern first, that's a natural law of wandering, and this village had a renowned drinking hole, so my first impulse took me to the doorway of that establishment. But something went wrong. I think the spray thrown into the air by the rain confused my eyesight or judgment or luck; and I entered the wrong building. I turned the handle and the heavy door swung open with only a minor creak.

It wasn't entirely dark within; the walls glowed with phosphorescent slime and I was able to see my way without too much difficulty, but my initial reaction was one of disappointment. I was expecting a very quaint tavern interior with ploughshares on stone walls and solid chariot wheels for tables; the authentic touches that heritage societies fail to grasp when they fund sundry attempts at reconstruction. I had been looking forward to the genuine experience and instead found a peculiar maze of corridors and rooms all prepared in chaotic style.

There was absolutely no rhyme, reason or irony in the furnishings or colours. This lack of aesthetic unity created unease in my heart, but there seemed no reason to leave yet, so I pressed on. The main corridor led me to a low room full of high chairs that scraped the ceiling; beyond this was a very high room, but extremely narrow, even more constricted than the thinnest legal wardrobe; then another corridor took me to a flight of steps which I ascended. My nostrils twitched but no beer could I smell. Where were the patrons, their cribbage and scowls?

Nowhere. That was the truth of it. Couldn't see any evidence of human occupation at all, not even a spilled jar of pickles. I called out, "Hello!" in the tone of a bluff surveyor, but response came there none. I sighed. Into another room I roamed. It was free of slime and therefore darker than the others, but the window was open; I felt the breeze and heard the rain. My eyes discerned only a blur near the window, and my ears heard nothing at this stage, but one of my other senses, I don't know which, informed me I wasn't alone. Thank you, secret sense!

Despite the futility of the gesture, I bowed deeply and said, "A pint of your darkest stout, if you please!" For I still believed I was in the tavern and assumed the blur was a barman.

"I don't please," came the crisp response.

It was a female voice, sweet and deadly at the same time. My eyes had started to adjust to the murk and slowly the *Peachy Poo* herself came into focus, though at that time I didn't know it was she. Slightly disgruntled, I cleared my throat. "Cider will do."

"No, it won't. Not even to the smallest degree."

"Well, what about mead?"

"Absolutely not."

"Pale ale? Barley wine?"

"Nope. Neither."

"Don't you serve *any* drinks in this sad pub?" I blurted, and her giggle chilled the sobriety in my veins.

"I'm not a barmaid."

"Won't you summon one for me?"

"Impossible. Never."

"But why? What's wrong with you?"

"I think you have entered the wrong building. This isn't a pub but my private residence. That's why."

I was distraught to hear this; for I might have stumbled on her in the nude; and in fact *she* might have been in the nude too! I blushed deeply and thankfully my blushes were concealed by the gloom. "I beg pardon for my outrageous error, madam!"

She laughed again. "Think nothing of it. In fact I'm glad you turned up unexpectedly; you can help me with a little experiment. If you don't know already, I am Lowri Constantine, the finest archer in the human world and I have just invented a new game."

"A game that involves arrows, I suppose?"

She took a step closer and emerged from the darkest shadows and now I saw her long auburn curls, big aquamarine eyes and ironic grin and they were enchanting as well as perilous.

"That's correct. Life in Lladloh can be boring at times, because of the ceaseless rain, so I invent fresh amusements to keep me entertained. This morning I woke up with a question in my nice head. Might it be feasible to shoot seven arrows into each of the seven seas from the highest room of this building? I decided to try!"

"But the surface of the planet is curved."

"And what of that?"

"None of the seven seas are near Wales."

"I fail to grasp your point."

"When the arrow reaches the horizon it will fly off at a tangent to the ground and end up in the sky!"

She threw back her head and laughed properly this time; not a laugh of carefully rehearsed stage mockery, but an instinctive outpouring of mirth that was both malicious and inclusive. Her shoulders shook. I wondered if I ought to make a run for it, but I realised that my knees were weak, as if waterlogged from the rain, and that she would be sure to catch me on the stairs. So I remained very sessile.

"Have you never heard of gravity, fellow?" she said at last, and I was forced to admit that yes, the word rang a bell, but only if the rope holding that bell snapped, letting the brassy receptacle crash through a belfry roof onto the ground below with a mighty clang! But that's irrelevant, for she didn't care much about my answer.

She held up her arms and I saw that one delicate but strong hand held a powerful longbow while the other grasped a quiver of arrows, seven in number and feathered extravagantly. "It's an extremely thick bow and the resistance must be immense," I said.

She nodded in the affirmative and winked. "No man on this planet is forceful enough to draw this bow; and no other woman. Only myself, the *Peachy Poo* of Lladloh town has the ability to use it. I have even given it a name like the magical bows of heroic legend. I call it 'Bow-creep' but it's pointless to seek profound psychological reasons for that cognomen. Now watch what I do and learn something!"

And with a flick of her head and a subsequent lashing of her curls, she strode to the open window, selected the first arrow, nocked it to the string and pulled it back. The muscles of her arms quivered with the strain but it barely showed on her serene expression. She took aim, I can't guess how, and then released the missile; the arrow hissed like a reverse meteor over the landscape and its feathers clashed as if made of metal. She watched it until it vanished, a few seconds later.

"So this is the highest room in the building!" I gasped.

"Yes it is. Ha ha!" she chortled.

"Where have you sent that arrow?" I cried.

"It is destined for the first of the seven seas, the White Sea," she said as she nocked another slim shaft.

This one was discharged in the same manner.

"And that one is headed for the second sea, the Mauve Sea. The third will be destined for the Beige Sea."

"Are all seven seas matched with colours?" I asked, becoming acutely aware of my ignorance as to the actual names of those proverbial bodies of exotic water. She smiled gently.

"No. The fourth sea is the Wooden Sea; the fifth is the Sea of Tea; the sixth is the Tiptoe Sea; and the seventh is officially known as the Seventh Sea, which is quite logical enough."

"Yes I suppose it is," I conceded unhelpfully.

She fired all the arrows one by one. Now the quiver was empty but she didn't seem entirely satisfied. I knew what was bothering her but I didn't mention it, because I saw no obvious solution. As it happened, she soon brought up the topic on her own.

"I have no idea if any of those arrows will actually strike their targets. There's simply no way of checking."

"Couldn't you put up a reward for their retrieval?"

"That would take too long."

I shrugged. "It's too bad. Ah well!"

"But there is another way. Now you are here I see no reason why you shouldn't make yourself useful."

My voice went hoarse as I replied, "Oh yes?"

Lowri glided towards me and I felt unable to turn and flee; a tangible web of energy appeared to emanate from her eyes, wrapping around me and sticking me in place, and now I vibrated on the suddenly solid fabric of crosshatched spacetime in pulse with the oscillation of this web. With an awful howl I expelled my fear.

She said softly, "Don't be so nervous. All I plan to do is turn you into an arrow and fire you out of the window.

If I draw back the bowstring far enough you will travel further than my previous seven arrows; in fact you will circumnavigate our globe and reappear in this room, arriving through the window in the opposite wall, which I'll open in good time. You'll soar over the seven seas strictly in order and so can observe whether my seven arrows really hit their targets or not."

"That sounds like a difficult shot," I whimpered.

"My trickiest ever!" she nodded.

"And when I return I'm expected to deliver a report?"

"You have understood exactly."

"But I'm sure to be blown off course by winds or spatter myself on the slopes of an intervening mountain."

"Not so! I will calculate a safe trajectory!"

I didn't see how that would be feasible; but before I could grill her on this point, she gestured at a curious device on one of the irregular tables that cluttered the room. It was a metallic sphere bristling with wires; and on the tip of each wire was a cloud.

"That machine is a weather orrery," she said.

"No such thing!" I objected.

"Yes, there is, there truly is, and this is a fine example of one. When a normal orrery is wound up, it accurately predicts the orbits of the planets around the sun; this one predicts the movement of currents of air around the Earth. It was designed by—"

"A mad inventor named Mondaugen?" I croaked.

"Ah! You know his work?"

I sighed. "Yes I do."

"He came here on holiday last year and built it for me. I can use it to predict the direction of coming winds; then I can accurately factor these variables into my equations."

She strode to the low table and wound the device. The wires revolved individually, changing direction, and as they did so, the clouds expanded, contracted, broke up or vanished, new ones taking the place of the old. It was a marvel of ingenuity and violated some principle of indeterminacy, but I was less impressed than I should have been. Lowri carefully studied the movements of the clouds.

"I know the direction and force of every current in the atmosphere for the next few days," she told me, "and I'll aim to deposit you in the first of a series of airstreams; you'll pass from that one to another, cruising above all seven of the seven seas, avoiding lofty peaks and lethal storms, finally arriving back here next week."

"It will take that long to circle the Earth?"

"Yes, of course. Your average speed will be a little over one hundred miles an hour and our planet is a big place; you will rapidly accelerate as you leave the bow, attain your maximum velocity on the outskirts of the village and then enter a prolonged period of deceleration. If you fly any faster you'll probably combust."

I opened my mouth to beg for a postponement of her scheme. Was it really so important to know whether her arrows had reached the specified seas or not? But not a word edged out in time, for suddenly she leaped at me, cast me to the floor and trussed me up tight. My arms were strapped to my sides, my legs bound together with cord, and feathers glued to my feet. I became a human arrow!

Her implausible arms, that remained attractive despite the sheer force they were able to exert, lifted me up and nocked my soles to the string of Bowcreep; then she drew me back. She aimed at a particular point in the distance and without bidding me farewell or good luck fired me over the village. The roofs of Lladloh turned into a blur and so did the forest, hills and secret valleys beyond. My teeth chattered, but friction warmed me up and soon I desired to remove some of my clothing, but movement for me was now completely impossible.

I passed rapidly through a sequence of scudding rainclouds and thus was buffeted almost senseless by turbulence, but Lowri had clearly taken even this into account, for finally I emerged into clear sky and knew I had crossed the border into England.

Onwards I flew and the hours rushed past!

Leaving England I crossed the North Sea and might have scratched my head if my hands had been free; why wasn't this sea included in the list of seven? Denmark was the next landmass to appear; then more water until Sweden; then another body of palpitating fluid and Finland; then Karelia and the White Sea at last. I looked down. How was I expected to spot an arrow among that liquid expanse?

I noticed a rogue iceberg with something sticking out of it. Ah, so her first arrow had hit true after all! I counted this off on spare mental fingers, being presently unable to access my real ones; then I entered an opposing air current that took me south and I realised that her weather orrery hadn't deceived her, nor had she applied its predictions wrongly; for I was flying towards the Mauve Sea. Over the backbone of the Carpathians I went and the warmer sun was like a friend.

The Mauve Sea offends sensitive eyes, but I am rather fond of that hue and never wince in its presence; yet there's another quality this sea boasts that is less to my taste. It's a favourite haunt of corsairs, freebooters, sea rovers and other pirates. As I reached it and proceeded to pass over waves of curious sheen and reefs of lilac coral, I saw a pirate ship far below. The crew of this ship evidently spied me too, for the flash of several telescope lenses made a minor but intriguing daytime constellation on the inverted backdrop of pale purple. They were in the process of forcing a prisoner to walk the plank. Rearrangements to this schedule were hastily made and in a few minutes I was intercepted.

Hard to believe, but a fact nonetheless!

I don't mean they fired a cannon or harpoon at me. I was too far out of range for that. No, what happened was that the man who was certainly the captain barked orders to his henchmen and they used ropes and pulleys to pull back the extended plank like a springboard. The prisoner was given a cutlass and forced to walk to the end of the primed length of wood; then it was released. Up he flew at a rate even greater than mine and I realised he would catch me up soon enough.

In my present circumstance I was helpless and had no way to fend him off when he arrived. I was expecting to be cut up without explanation, but in fact the fellow wanted to talk before slicing me. The moment he was in earshot he shouted, "Hello there!"

I was civil enough. "Good day to you."

The fellow nodded and smiled in return but didn't introduce himself by name. "I'm a condemned captive and when I run out of momentum I'll fall into the sea and drown. And you?"

"Shot from a longbow by a girl," I said.

"Ah well! Captain Worst ordered me to be catapulted up here; he's the worst of all pirates on the seven seas and he didn't appreciate your poor manners in flying above him without doffing your hat. I know you aren't wearing one and that your hands are tied, but that's no excuse in the eyes of Captain Worst, I'm sorry to say."

"Well, it's not your fault," I reassured him.

"True. You don't mind if I take a swipe at you when I get near? It will be safer than disobeying his orders."

"What does it matter? You'll die anyway."

He shrugged. "On the face of it, your logic is sound, but it never pays to defy Captain Worst, so I'd rather not take the risk. It won't hurt much, I promise. This sword is very sharp."

I didn't bother protesting. He would have swiped at me anyway; and I had no method of evading the blow. As it happened, his strike severed my bonds but didn't scratch my flesh; then he fell away and began his descent into the mauve breakers and I don't know whether he deliberately rescued me from my coils or was simply a bad swordsman. But I was free! With a hearty laugh I flexed my numb limbs.

The pirate ship was now far behind me, but I still heard the bellows of fury as Captain Worst realised he had been bested! I'll never go anywhere near the Mauve Sea again, that's for sure. The man is unnatural! I gasped with relief when I passed over land again, despite the fact I was on course for the Beige Sea, which is a cauldron of toxic fumes. The Beige Sea is a cesspit of liquid radioactivity and other kinds of pollution and nobody can say how it came to be that way. The good news is that I was free to pinch my nostrils very tight as I crossed it.

The Wooden Sea presented a more pleasing vista, surrounded on every shore by wooden hills on the summits of which were plateaux that looked like Bedfordshire in various aspects.

Odd! But not as bizarre as the Sea of Tea, which had finally gone cold and was stewed and undrinkable; I'm glad I didn't have to dunk myself in its depths, for constitutionally I am no biscuit. The Tiptoe Sea was better, surely the most pleasant of the seas so far, and I enjoyed the soft musical notes it made as it lapped the sides of whales, sea serpents and mermaids. A great place for a leisurely cruise!

On each occasion I spotted the arrow fired by Lowri; stuck in the side of a lighthouse, tangled in seaweed or simply floating on the surface like a piece of driftwood. But as I entered the airspace of the Seventh Sea, a distant speck that seemed to be at precisely my own altitude attracted my attention and made me neglect my task. I squinted, frowned, ground my teeth, but couldn't discern what it was. Yet it rapidly grew bigger and was clearly coming straight towards me.

It wasn't an aircraft or pterodactyl, but a man!

Another man like me, rushing through the sky without wings, but with feathers on his feet. Extraordinary!

A collision was inevitable and I shut my eyes tight, bracing myself for the pain of the impact. I didn't have long to wait for that. With the sound of a titanium egg smashing a brick made of icing sugar, we banged heads and cancelled out each other's inertia.

Down we spiralled, locked in an embrace as we spun groggily through the thermals. Those vertical currents of warm air must have helped us to break our fall, or perhaps our skulls were so shocked already that another massive impact couldn't fatally impress them. Whatever the reason, a soft landing awaited us in the drink; we went under, bobbed to the surface and didn't die. Then we relaxed our mutual grip and allowed the waves to cast us onto the beach of a small island.

We lay on the sand for half an hour, recovering.

Then the stranger propped himself on an elbow, turned his gaze on me and asked for my name. "Castor," I said.

"Have you ever been a castor-way?" he punned badly.

"Yes, actually I have," I replied.

"In that case you are used to it. You are a castaway again, and so am I, and we'll have to adapt quickly if we want to survive. It's such a very tiny island! How will we collect enough drinking water to quench our thirst? Must we dine exclusively on coconuts? Shall we construct a shelter from bamboo poles and palm leaf thatch?"

"Who are you?" I asked bluntly.

He stood and bowed. "Chuckleberry Grin."

I frowned. "That's your name?"

"Well, it's not my occupation! It's not considered a peculiar cognomen, if that's what you're implying, where I come from." He rubbed his bleary eyes, stretched his limbs and yawned.

"Your accent is unusual. Where *are* you from?"

He answered without hesitating, "The Counter Earth, the world known as Antichthon that can be found on the other side of the sun. Believe it or not, I'm distantly related to Lohengrin Smirka, Grand Duke of the state of Laxhumbug. Every member of his extended family has a name connected with smiling, grinning, smirking."

"What a laugh that must be for you all!"

"It's wry, my friend; wry."

"If you are from Antichthon, what are you doing here, Mr Grin? You are a long way from home. Exile?"

"Don't be silly. I'm the official ambassador!"

I was flabbergasted by this news. "But I had no idea there was such a thing! Do you have an embassy?"

"Of course! What use is any ambassador without one of those? I have just come from there, in fact."

"And where is your embassy located, Mr Grin?"

"Call me Chuckleberry. The answer to your question is easy enough. It can be found in the Unclepodes."

"Where on Earth are they?"

He examined his fingernails with fake nonchalance. "Often on top of the Antipodes, but it's more difficult to say *which* Antipodes, for there are several. The government heads of Antichthon have established an official embassy smack in the middle of the Unclepodes; the former ambassador, Som Toyah, was recalled last month; it's a mystery, a big question mark, why that happened. Something to do with fraud, maybe. I was sent as her replacement. And so here I am!"

"Then why fly over the Seventh Sea?"

"Ah, well it's always beneficial for an ambassador to take a tour of the place he is posted to. It was felt I ought to circumnavigate this planet, the better to understand it, so I did."

"Certainly you are a man of action, not just words! Our collision has disrupted your tour; I apologise!"

He shook his head with a laugh. "Hardly your fault!"

"You were shot from a bow?"

"I was indeed. It's the best and cheapest way of going around a planet, saving money on trains and boats."

"And elephants!" I added, for I am a fan of Jules Verne, and my own circumnavigation had reminded me of his works; not only that, but being stranded on a mysterious island also helped to fill my head with thoughts of a Vernian nature. In fact I'm a member of a club devoted to honouring his character Captain Nemo, but more about that some other time, for it has absolutely no relevance here.

Chuckleberry Grin chuckled, then grinned.

He aided me to a standing position and we slapped each other's backs like old comrades. And so began our six months together as maroons. To be marooned in the Mauve Sea would have been a far greater irony and I was careful to keep that fact in mind at all times; it helped to attenuate the feelings of frustration that regularly welled up inside me. We constructed a hut, foraged for coconuts, collected rainwater, and did all the things that castaways must, if they want to live.

Every night I lit a bonfire on the beach, praying the blazing driftwood might attract a passing ship, but we were off the trade routes. No one ever came near our island. One evening, while we were sitting around the fire and sipping coconut milk beer from coconut halves, I began to reminisce about Lowri Constantine and how she had fitted me to Bowcreep with an alluring twinkle in her deadly eyes.

Chuckleberry nodded sadly. "It wasn't like that for me. I didn't have a beautiful girl to twang me aloft."

"I suppose it was the administrative staff at your embassy who fired you across the world?" I asked.

"Oh no, my staff are a bunch of useless layabouts. Most of them don't even realise they *are* my staff."

"Not them!" I cried. "Then who?"

"I fired myself. I fitted myself to my own bow and released the string myself. I'm expected to operate in neglect, you see, and that's why I was chosen, because I am self-reliant."

"You fired yourself? And left the bow behind?"

"Indeed not. It's a portable bow and I held onto it as I shot out of the embassy window. It's too valuable just to abandon. I folded it up as soon as I was aloft and stored it safely."

I jumped up. "So you have it with you now?"

He fumbled in the inner pocket of his jacket and took out a collapsible longbow. He unfolded it and nodded.

"Why the hell didn't you…" I began, but I decided to hold my tongue, for the fact he was daft didn't mean he couldn't be my saviour and thus it was more tactical not to offend him.

"A fine piece of work," he said, blinking at it.

"Can we use it to escape?"

"Of course, but only one human arrow can be nocked at a time. That's why I didn't mention it before."

I blushed, realising that I had attributed the wrong motives to him. He was actually a perfect gentleman.

Then he brightened. "But I see no reason why we can't trail you behind me. If we connect each other with a length of rope, I can shoot myself off and you'll inevitably come after."

"Let's do it now!" I roared.

"In which direction should I aim?"

"Certainly not in the direction from whence I came. I have no desire to return to the dark bosom of Lowri's hospitality. My home is Porthcawl. If I had a choice, that's where I'd like to be aimed at; but I don't know where that town is relative to this island."

"No problem. One of my duties in the embassy was to memorise maps of planet Earth. I was very good at it and I do know where Porthcawl is. I suggest we head in that direction."

"You wish to go there too? You are welcome to stay at my house. I'll enjoy introducing you to my friends."

He shook his head. "No, no, I think I'll continue my tour; but once we are over Porthcawl, I'll loosen the rope that binds us together and you can drop down on your own. Agreed? However, one day in the far future I'll pay you a friendly visit, I promise."

I nodded and we went to work, using a length of the rope that had tied my arms to attach myself to him. Then he drew back the string of the bow and nocked his feet to it, while I stood waiting. He aimed carefully and I was amazed to see that he was intending to fire us in the direction which I was already flying in prior to the collision: the same compass point from whence he had come. I pondered.

Then he released the string. Up into the sky we thrummed. The rush of the wind smoothed the creases in my brow as I continued to frown. Three days later we reached Porthcawl, and while cruising high over the town, I felt Chuckleberry loosen the knot that held us together. Down I fell while he called a hasty farewell; I landed in the sea, close enough to shore, and spluttered onto dry land. Then I went back to my house and changed into dry clothes and when I was ready I went to the pub to see my best friends, Paddy Deluxe and Frothing Harris.

I sat on the empty chair at the table next to them and begged a drink of dark beer; in return I told them all about my recent adventures. Yes, they had been worried about me; my absence was abnormally long. I shared with them the theory I had devised while flying directly behind Mr Grin. They listened and were sceptical.

"Think about it carefully!" I persisted. "Could it not be that Porthcawl is located smack on the Unclepodes;

that this town is the official embassy of Antichthon? That none of us are true Earthlings? Wouldn't this explain our maladjustment to the world?"

"It seems too far-fetched," they answered.

"If Chuckleberry Grin ever does turn up again, I'll ask him openly and he'll be sure to tell me the truth."

"Is everything on Antichthon a mirror image of things on Earth?" they wanted to know. I shook my head, for I had already asked this question of my fellow castaway and he had explained that most items were variations rather than reversals. For example, a woman is not the *opposite* of a man, and in the same way the Counter Earth was a complement to our planet, a reciprocal, a different kind of reflection. There might be another Lladloh there and another Lowri trying to hit seven other seas, but maybe she (or he) would use a catapult or cannon.

Then I frowned very deep, one of the deepest of all my frowns. "It has just occurred to me that there must be an Earth embassy on Antichthon. I wonder who the ambassador is?"

"Now you have gone beyond the frontier of our tolerance!" exclaimed my friends. "There's no space program in the world that can send manned missions to the far side of the sun."

I sighed and drained my pint, for I couldn't dispute that.

* * * *

The pub door opened and a jaunty figure entered. Jastor Cenkins, Daddy Peluxe and Hrothing Farris looked up. The newcomer held a folded bow in one hand and waved with the other. Jastor instantly jumped to his feet and cried, "He has come at last!"

"Sorry it has taken so long," said the newcomer.

Jastor introduced him to his friends. "This is Gruckleberry Chin, the official ambassador from Earth."

Daddy and Farris shook his hand politely.

"In other words, our boss," added Jastor. He finished his drink and wiped his lips with his sleeve.

"Does it always rain in this town?" asked Gruckleberry, shaking the oily droplets from his long hair.

Jastor laughed. "Yes, Lwachtrop isn't blessed with the finest climate on Antichthon. Sit down please."

The ambassador did so. Jastor sent his friends to fetch a pint for him and a packet of crisps. They grumbled but went to do his bidding. "How has life been treating you?" he asked.

Gruckleberry shrugged. "Not bad. And you?"

"Many adventures. I can't seem to stop having them. Embassy work is so light and easy that it leaves too much time for other activities. I'm not complaining, though! Shall I tell you about the time I swallowed a storm cloud, or about the time I went hunting fossils with a bazooka and bagged a set of tyrannosaur footprints?"

"No thanks," said the ambassador.

"Well then, what about the consequences of entering myself in a show for bankrupt dogs, Bankcrufts?"

"Yes, that one will do nicely. Thanks."

PENAL COLONY

Land had been sighted at last. The captain hissed a sigh of relief. His fear that the tempest had blown them into uncharted waters was unfounded. It seemed the main danger was over; but he couldn't relax just yet. The very hazardous cargo needed to be unloaded without injury before the mission was truly completed. He consulted his charts and nodded to himself. Just a few more leagues to the east there should be an oddly shaped headland. Yes, there it was. A welcome sight!

Around this headland was the entrance to a shallow bay. The southern shore of the bay had been chosen as the location of the penal colony. The captain had been instructed to liberate the convicts and leave them to their own devices. There would be no need for walls, wire, guards; the hostility of the terrain, its remoteness and in-accessibility, made this site as secure as the most sophisticated prison. The captain issued relevant orders and the vessel approached the headland.

The criminals in the hold were hardened cases. Later shipments might bring political or religious offenders, but the members of this first batch were all vicious killers. The civilised sectors of the world could no longer contain them, no longer tolerate their presence; involuntary exile was the only solution. The responsibility for facilitating this strategy was intense and the captain daily felt an immense weight on his poor spirit. But now the ordeal was coming to a conclusion.

Within hours his duty would be discharged and he would be free. Yes, free to turn the ship around and sail back to his home and family! Such a joyous moment that would be; he could hardly contain his excitement! He forced himself to remain calm, for to lose focus at this crucial stage might be a most fatal error, one he would never have the luxury of repeating. A terrible irony, to come to grief with success almost within his grasp! Best to maintain a rigid, iron self-discipline…

The headland was rounded, the bay entered. The ship dropped anchor half a league offshore. Then the officers and sailors gathered on the deck to hear the captain's orders. He stood before them and raised himself up, gazing beyond the crew at the waves that broke on the reefs and the shore itself. His face twisted into a grimace.

"It is imperative that we maintain our concentration at all times during this part of the process," he began.

The audience before him shuffled its feet.

"This is probably the most perilous moment of the entire voyage, more risky even than the recent typhoon," he continued. "I want all of you to be on your guard at every single instant. No prisoner should be accompanied by less than three sailors for a fraction of a second. This means the task of transferring them from the ship to the longboats will be quite a protracted one, but that is preferable to gambling with your lives. Operate with great caution. Be vigilant and stay alive!"

He raised a hand to dismiss them, then a thought occurred to him and he added, "Needless to say, it's not necessary to ferry *all* the convicts into the shallows. Every blue ring octopus, scorpion fish and stonefish should be deposited close to the reefs or the shore, but box jellyfish, crocodiles and sharks may be cast into deeper water; as for snakes and spiders, they must be taken onto the actual beach."

He allowed himself a wistful smile as his crew set to work. Maybe the penal colony would die out, maybe it would flourish. Who knew for sure? One day in the far future someone might wonder *why* Australia happened to have more than its fair share of venomous animals. That was assuming that the origin of the penal colony was forgotten, which wasn't beyond the bounds of feasibility. Such a futuristic questioner would probably assume it was merely an evil trick of nature.

As the captain watched the parade of funnel-web, Redback and white-tailed spiders, three varieties of taipan serpents, cone snails and irukandji jellyfish, he suppressed his mounting glee. Only when the final criminal had been marooned on the shore did he rub four of his eight legs together in satisfaction. But it was still unsafe to remain at anchor all night. Better to sail into the open ocean. Only there would he grant himself the luxury of the hammock he had spun himself.

* * * *

"And that," said Castor Jenkins as he drained his pint, "was the very last time I ever worked as a sea captain."

Paddy Deluxe and Frothing Harris blinked at him.

"It was also the very last time I was ever a spider. I haven't been one since, not for a moment," he added.

FLYING SAUCER HARMONIES

"I know what flying saucers are," announced Paddy Deluxe one evening as he slurped his pint of stout, "and they have nothing to do with surplus terrestrials from interstellar space."

"*Extra*-terrestrials," said Castor Jenkins.

Paddy began nodding. "Yes, those ones. Your average flying saucer is a hoax or misunderstood meteorological phenomenon, but a minority of reports are genuine; they refer to the saucers I'm talking about and I know what they are. I learned yesterday."

"You are willing to tell us?" asked Castor.

Paddy hadn't stopped nodding, so in effect he answered this question in the affirmative without effort. Frothing Harris shook his own head but he leaned closer anyway, to listen.

"I went to play tennis on the beach with Collective Will and I returned one of his serves with excessive force and the ball flew over his head and landed in the sea; then it floated away and we never saw it again. Because we had no spare, we decided to—"

Castor held up his hand and made a wry face. "Wait a moment, Paddy! I don't believe a word of it. You're too unfit for tennis or any physical sort of game. Look at the size of your paunch! The consumption of chips and beer doesn't count as an official sporting activity; I speak from experience and without contempt, trust me."

Paddy nodded and took another gulp of his drink. "I don't dispute what you say. Nonetheless, after the premature climax to our tennis session, we decided to skim our spare change into the waves instead. Collective Will is a highly skilled skimmer indeed; he managed to bounce one small coin nine times before it sank, whereas my best effort was six skips. When this pastime was finished, we relaxed."

Castor clapped his hands. "Your speciality!"

Paddy sighed. "Not this time. We sat on deckchairs and smoked cigars but frankly that's a pleasure more symbolic than real. After a dozen puffs we were obliged to discard them and inaugurate a coughing and wheezing tournament that ended in a draw…"

"You pitched lighted cigars onto the beach?"

"No, into the waves. By this point, the tide had risen to the edge of the Canute Threshold and lapped us."

"And how is this connected to flying saucers?" wondered Castor. "You have irritated me somewhat rather than intrigued me; the only apology I'll accept is a drink at your expense."

Paddy snorted, "You don't really want to learn anything, do you? Don't you appreciate that the events of that momentous day, whether taken in or out of sequence, led me to a cosmic revelation? Don't be so hasty in your opportunistic dismissals! For after the cessation of that coughing fit, I had a sudden inspiration; and through sheer analogy I became cognizant of an obvious, though hitherto overlooked, truth about the so-called 'aliens' that snarl our sky with shapes and lights."

"I am waiting to hear that truth," snapped Castor.

"Why! Can't you work it out for yourself? There are three major kinds of UFO and my explanation will account for them all. The spherical craft are lost balls from a fifth dimensional tennis match; the flying discs are skimmed coins; the cigar-shaped objects are gigantic discarded cigars, no more or less. Makes perfect sense."

"Why from the fifth dimension?" frowned Castor.

Paddy rolled his eyes. "It scarcely seems plausible that balls, coins or even cigars can be hurled from one solar system to another. Let's look at it from a fishy point of view. Yes, imagine how *they* felt at the time of my actions! They were going about their usual business; then abruptly, as if from nowhere, a mysterious sphere appeared; several discs and a pair of enigmatic cylinders followed. None of these objects, if the fish recovered any, were constructed of any material known to them. So what's the most basic explanation they can devise to account for their origin? Clearly they are artefacts from another ocean…"

"Whereas they actually came from a closer location, from an adjacent realm, the surface world, from the universe next door." Castor rubbed his chin and smiled. "I see your point."

* * * *

Frothing Harris could contain himself no longer. He gulped his own pint with no less fury than his friends, slammed his empty glass down on the table and began a frantic monologue:

"That's not right, none of it. I know what flying saucers really are; but I only learned the truth this morning!

"As you both already realise, Porthcawl is plagued with flying saucer sightings; I think our town is the Welsh Mecca of *saucerous* activity, so to speak, and let me say right now that coining a word may be acceptable but coining a sea isn't. Not in my view! I don't skim change, spare or not, and in fact I don't even skim stones. Skimming is wrong. Flying saucers *aren't* coins and they certainly aren't tennis balls or unsmoked cigars. Do you seek to drive me utterly insane?

"Listen carefully: the answer is straightforward.

"Last night there was another sighting of a flying saucer overhead and I believed it because I saw it with my own eyes when I rose in the early hours to fetch a glass of water back to my bedside. Flashing lights, weird flight path, eerie low drone and no sign of any human trickery. It hovered above my garden briefly, as if waiting for something, but I didn't run out in stripy pyjamas to investigate; the grass was wet and I couldn't find my slippers. So I forsook the opportunity.

"This very morning I met Sunstew Mynci in the bakery. I was buying iced buns and coincidently so was he, but to my bigger surprise he also bought a pizza with a topping of extra olives. This made me apprehensive but I wasn't sure why, so to change the subject I asked him if he had also observed the flying saucer last night?

"He nodded his head and went on to say that he had wondered about it for hours. It had hovered above many gardens, including his; then moved on. What purpose did it have? After more hours of pondering he suddenly realised! I was impressed to hear that.

"He winked and whispered, 'Yes, I know all about flying saucers, what they are and why they come here. I'm heading to the park now and if you accompany me I'll explain everything.'

"Well, this chance was too good to miss, so I followed Sunstew Mynci along a street that led to a nearby park. When we got there we gravitated to the lake and watched the ducks. I munched brutally on an iced bun and cast my spare crumbs into the ripples.

"The ducks were happy to eat the morsels I offered them, but Sunstew held my arm in a powerful grip, most unlike him, and stopped me casting more pieces. 'Watch this!' he roared.

"Like a discus thrower he span on the spot and cast his pizza as far as he could. It was still warm and the olives glittered like crystals and steam rose from the tomato paste as it soared over the water. I know little about the aerodynamic properties of Italian cuisine, but it seemed to hang in the air much longer than it should have!

"Then it dropped into the lake and sank…

"I told him that I had expected it to float, but Sunstew was too ecstatic to care about that. 'Did you see? The ducks misunderstood! They simply didn't know what to *make* of it! They didn't recognise it as food and why should they? That proves my point!'

"I quickly asked him to elaborate on this aspect.

"He said, 'Think, Harris, think! Flying saucers are scraps of food that are being thrown to us by aliens from outer space. It's obvious! Why has no one thought of this before? We throw food for ducks; the aliens throw food for us. It's a perfect analogy!'

"I didn't believe him and told him so; but I'm wondering if I should be at home right now, waiting in a garden chair with a knife and fork, rather than sitting in this pub with you two. That's the crux of it. Incidentally the type of pizza I like best is a four-cheese variety I sampled in a Hungarian restaurant in old Czechoslovakia—"

Castor Jenkins snorted, "I don't believe you."

"What! You don't concede there were any Hungarian restaurants in old Czechoslovakia? Foolhardy fellow!"

"My dear friend, you don't drink water; how then are we supposed to accept that you would ever convey a glass of the stuff to any beside that can be imagined? That's the one detail we can't swallow: the lie that you *would* swallow such a bland liquid."

Harris pouted without much grace. "Fair enough."

* * * *

Castor signalled the barman to bring three pints of stout directly over; it's not a typical Welsh custom to do that and can't be recommended, but it *is* what he did on that particular occasion.

The barman responded grumpily and demanded payment on delivery. Castor rummaged in all his pockets thoroughly, with such care that Paddy and Harris both managed to access their own money before him, despite the deliberate slowness of their own searches, and the barman went away, still grumbling but less loudly, thanks to the laws of physics and the rules of temper, which decree that distance is an important modifying factor for the register of audibility on eardrums.

Castor sipped his fresh pint just long enough to grow a thin moustache of foam and said, "The truth is, my comrades, that I've been circumspect in my reaction to your tales; but I don't feel I can hold back any longer. It wouldn't serve the sacred pursuit of knowledge to keep my secret entirely to myself. It's too crucial and vital."

"Crucial and vital to what?" asked Paddy.

"To homo sapiens," said Castor.

"But that's us, isn't it?" gasped Harris.

Castor nodded. "I'm afraid so. Let me commence my tale by denying it took place in Porthcawl. In fact it happened a dozen miles to the east, not far from Southerndown. It is a wild stretch of coastline between there and Nash Point and geologically the cliffs are bizarre. I sincerely doubt either of you have been there, because chips are not for sale, nor beer, but that's not a crippling disadvantage. Just picture to yourself a remote long beach with access at both ends but nowhere else; when the tide comes in, there's no escape and to get cut off is easy.

Even dinosaurs did so: fossils of their frantic footprints are everywhere."

"I do know the place; from postcards," said Paddy.

"Me too, same way," agreed Harris.

Castor chuckled. "Yes, and those postcards were sent by *me*; and they were posted from another world, but I don't want to get ahead of myself, so I'll simply state that I was walking that beach one day and I had got the tide times wrong. I thought drowning would be my fate, but I was briefly distracted from thoughts of glubby doom by the presence of a man sitting on a black rock; he was watching the waves wash his feet and perhaps he assumed the state of those feet would repel the waves, for they were filthy indeed. Then I saw something else."

"A ship? An old barquentine?" suggested Paddy.

"A rainbow bridge?" blurted Harris.

Castor shook his head. "No use guessing. It was something much more ordinary than those; I saw that the man was plucking a harp. The sound of his strings was odd: discordant and unique but also predictable and bland, if you can imagine such a paradox. I couldn't and still can't; and yet I was forced to listen to it. I approached him casually and cleared my throat, for I planned to ask him politely to desist.

"He turned to look at me but continued plucking with blistered fingers and said, 'Frog in the gullet, you seem to have, boyo! Should have sucked a mint, see, before you left the house.'

"I was flabbergasted by his clichéd Welsh accent and idiom and I took a step back, slipping on a mossy rock and crashing down onto my buttock cheeks. Something tinkled in my trouser pocket and I wailed, 'I hope they haven't been broken by the impact!'

"The harpist paused his din and raised his eyebrows. 'Oh yes, and what do you have in them, then? Jewels?'

"I told him not to be silly; gemstones wouldn't shatter so easily. It was a set of vacuum tubes I was carrying; and before you press me on exactly *why* I was carrying them, I'll just state that it's still a free country, to some extent, and I'm within my rights to do so; and if that reply doesn't satisfy, I'll pretend it was the birthday of Heinrich Geissler, the very first inventor of the cathode ray tube, and that I wanted to honour him by bearing them with me all day; and if that answer still doesn't convince you, I'll confess that I'm one of those men who like casting messages in bottles out to sea, yet I don't do it the standard way, with pen and paper, but with neon signs that express some insolvable riddle.

"Yes, to make the neon signs light up, I also carry waterproof batteries and a miniature transformer, also waterproof, and insulated wires and any other essential electrical component.

"That's the sort of man I am; when a tale requires it!

"Anyway, I stood up and checked the contents of my pocket and found to my relief that the vacuum tubes were still intact. Then I said to the man with the harp, 'The tide is already up around your knees and soon you will be under water. How can you just remain there and wait for death without even futilely struggling to escape?'

"He smiled wistfully and replied, 'Trying to mimic the mating call of a flying saucer, I am, for I believe they are living beasts like aerial jellyfish, and if I can attract one of them down here, I will jump on its back and end up saving my life. It's what I recommend, boyo! Help me now, why don't you? Whistle and hum at the same time while I resonate all harp strings in an eerie style. Time is running out!'

"I concurred with this latter observation and remarked that maybe time was even too short for absurd games, but he wouldn't hear of any solution to our joint dilemma other than to make the sound of a flying saucer. Five minutes of wasted effort later, the tide was up against his chest and I had prudently retreated to the very base of the towering cliffs, which the first waves had only just reached. Scratching his head, the harpist said, 'Maybe it's not the mating season after all?'

"I wanted to laugh at his naivety but it didn't seem appropriate; indeed I felt so sorry for him I decided to play along with his delusion. At least it would help to pass my final moments amusingly. I said, 'It's impossible to replicate the sound of a flying saucer with a harp and a human mouth. We need a *theremin* for an accurate match. We don't have one of those but an alternative is available. We can construct an *ondes Martenot*! Why not? I have the vacuum tubes and other electrical bits; and you have a substitute *palme*, the lyre-shaped speaker that utilises strings to develop sympathetic resonances. It's an ingenious idea!'

"To be honest he didn't seem very happy with my solution, but without a better alternative, and with the water now lapping his neck, he declined to object, so I went ahead. I constructed the frame of the instrument from driftwood, inserted the components, wired them to the harp, powered the unit up with an elasticised suspension of disbelief and pressed the *touche d'intensité* to its maximum dynamic.

"At this point I ought to explain exactly how an *ondes Martenot* works and give you some historical background about the instrument, and stress that it's capable of mimicking a *theremin* if played a certain way, but you can easily do that research yourself.

"The note that emerged from the improvised *palme* was very eerie and very loud, and it also turned out to be extremely effective, which was just as well for my new friend, for by this time the tide was at a point midway between his nose and mouth; but it didn't lure a randy flying saucer down from the sky. Oh no, not that at all!

"What happened was that a rather large section of the cliff face behind us slid open like an automatic garage door... It was brightly illuminated on the other side too, so I had no hesitation in stumbling through the gap to safety, and when I turned I saw the harpist emerging from the sea with the same idea. He crossed the threshold just in time, for the cliff suddenly closed on itself and the battering of waves on the other side was muffled, but had we merely lurched from the drowning pan into the dire? That was the contrived question on our lips.

"We explored our surroundings, just like heroes in pulp novels do, and it didn't take long to work out that we were in a wide corridor that sloped steeply into the bowels of the Earth.

"Incidentally, that's an expression I've always regarded with suspicion. If the Earth has bowels does it also have kidneys? Does it have a working appendix or just a residual one? What does it eat for supper? Where does it keep its ears? Does it have a belly button? That's the clincher for me. A planet with a navel: ramifications!

"Together we began descending the corridor.

"On the way, he told me more about himself. His name was Tin Dylan and he was a wandering bard who specialised in the old songs that no one wanted to hear;

he was travelling eastwards from Lladloh and wasn't sure of his ultimate destination; he joked it might be in continental Europe, up in the Alps somewhere, maybe the city-state of Chaud-Mellé. His exploits so far had been uniformly uncanny.

"I let him babble on for as long as he desired

"Abruptly we reached a balcony that overlooked an auditorium. That's the only word that even remotely describes the sheer vastness of the space below us. We clung to the railings and gasped. So the inside of Earth was hollow! Theorists had long speculated on the possibility; speculators had theorised on it. Hollow but not empty. Miniature worlds revolved about a tiny sun; and there were hundreds of these model planets, each the size of a small mountain. I was speechless!

"A breeze behind us ruffled the hair of our scalps; evidently the sliding door in the cliff had opened again. There was a sound like a *theremin* and a flying saucer appeared directly behind us, floating down the corridor. It reached us and cleared our heads by a few inches as it passed. The breeze dropped and I realised it was the sound of those discs that caused the door in the unbroken coastline to open.

"The saucer dropped down into the central void. I turned to Tin Dylan and blared, 'Without doubt it is headed for one of those miniature planets. This is our opportunity to hitch a ride!' He didn't understand why I was so keen to do such a thing, but after I climbed the railings and dangled down on the other side by one hand, he followed my example. Perhaps he didn't want to be left alone on the balcony.

"We let go at the same moment and plummeted just a few feet onto the convex roof of the saucer. The top of the vehicle looked smooth, but that was an illusion; and to our disgust, there was a deep depression on the top full of seawater and the convex shape was merely the shiny meniscus. So we sat in a pool of brine while the saucer floated down to one of the small globes. The saucer must have been for a dip in the Bristol Channel, which is the main sea between Wales and England, for the pool was full of local seaweed, but not the tastiest variety.

"I said to my companion, ''Never before have any human beings had a good chance to explore inner space.'

"To which he responded, 'Don't be daft, mun, psychiatrists go there all the time. And not with the benefit of a flying saucer, neither; but just with a couch, lunatic and relaxed manner.'

"I sighed, 'I don't mean metaphoric inner space, but the literal kind: the microcosmos, the mini solar-system.'

"He sneered, 'Don't care for them, boyo.'

"I didn't bother to argue with him; the water sloshed around us, and in a matter of minutes we sloshed with it, as the saucer revolved. Soon I was very giddy and sick, but before I felt the need to vomit over the rim of the disc, we had landed on firm ground.

"We eased ourselves out of the pool and slid down the saucer's side to the surface of the planet. The balcony we had previously stood on was far above us; in the sky in all other directions were other miniature worlds. I still felt dizzy and promptly sat down.

"Tin Dylan sat next to me and hugged his knees.

"Instantly some manholes in the bare rock opened and aliens came up and surrounded us. They were perfect dwarves, all of them, but one was a little more regal than his companions. He shouted, 'What the hell are you pair doing on my orb without visas?'

"I was amazed that he knew we didn't have the correct paperwork, but I decided to play for time and I said, 'We're from the topside and can't talk to you because we don't know your language, so it's pointless giving us a hard time with official bureaucracy.'

"He stamped his foot and hissed, 'That's the corniest trick in the book! I'm going to order you hurled back into space immediately. I've had a bad week and your presence doesn't help.'

"Well, that was an opening that I couldn't ignore. 'A bad week, eh? I'm sure we can be of assistance to you. My name is Castor and I'm an expert on anything; and this is Dylan and he acts as a fine contrast to me. There's no reason to deal with us too hastily.'

"The dwarf stroked his beard and responded, 'Very well. For the sake of the plot, I'll give you the benefit of the doubt. I'm King Crotchety and this is the planet Glissando. For the entire duration of my long reign, my dream has been to increase the number of notes in the indigenous octave. I hear that topside you have eight, but we have only ever had seven. Yes, that does make a mockery of the word 'octave' but an occasional dose of mock never harmed anyone, did it?'

"I nodded. 'It didn't harm the Tudors,' I said.

"The king fixed me with a fierce stare. 'The one note we are missing is Middle C. We just don't have it. So I've been dispatching flying saucers, which are actually overgrown musical notes, to the outer world in order to bring back Middle C, but so far they have only imported quantities of salt water. Soon Glissando will be deluged and rendered uninhabitable for my people: what has gone wrong?'

"I was about to speak but Tin Dylan interrupted me. 'Overgrown notes, you say? But what variety are they?'

"King Crotchety answered, 'Quavers with their stalks snapped off. We have vast forests of giant wild quavers under the crust of our little planet, for Glissando is also a hollow world, with its own miniature solar system at its core. One of those even smaller planets is my throne, in fact, and it spins me around a sun no bigger than a burning garden shed. But none of this is very relevant to our trouble.'

"I frowned and pondered his problem for almost a minute. 'I know the solution to your horrid situation; and I'll tell you, but only if you promise to spare our lives. Do you agree?'

"His little face flushed with repressed rage but finally he twiddled both his orb and sceptre as if weighing up his options and nodded. I wasted no time sharing my insights with him.

"I said plainly, 'The major problem is that *Middle C* is a homonym for *Middle Sea*, in other words for the Mediterranean, and the flying saucers are thus prone to getting confused about their exact instructions. Because they are musical notes, they can be a bit dense. They are collecting water from the Mediterranean by mistake.'

"The king was delighted with this answer. He knew it was right and he immediately issued orders to reprogram the saucers. Then he arranged for both his guests to be inundated with gifts, typical examples of Glissando arts and crafts. I got an iridium treble clef and Tin Dylan was given a new harp to replace the one that was turned into an *ondes Martenot* speaker. I was feeling cheeky so I asked the king if I might send some postcards to my friends from his planet, as proof of my adventures here. He agreed at once and I popped them in the post.

"Then King Crotchety commanded a flying saucer to carry us back to the balcony, and from there up the corridor to the main doors, which slid open at the sound of our approach.

"The saucer deposited us on the beach, but the tide had gone right out and we were perfectly safe. The doors closed again and I wondered if the king would ever regret letting us go so easily. After all, I had tricked him! The saucers weren't collecting water from the Mediterranean but from the more mundane Bristol Channel! I shared this secret with the harpist, but he simply pouted and said, 'But all the same, boyo, what if *this* sea really is the Mediterranean? It might be!'

"I stared at him in disbelief and answered, 'If that is the case, then the Gower Peninsular must be Italy; and Porthcawl is Messíni in Greece; and if you are really heading to Chaud-Mellé from here you are going in the wrong direction!' Then I guffawed.

"But he didn't take the bait and he shouldered his harp and walked off towards the east, without saying a word or looking back; and I turned to the west, back to Porthcawl and walked that way. And we never saw each other again. But I don't regret that."

* * * *

Having finished his tale, Castor moved to the task of finishing his pint; he accomplished this latter feat in the blink of an eye, or rather it would have been in that time span if any eye trained on him *had* blinked; but the orbs of Paddy and Harris were wide open.

"A miniature world inhabited by a race of dwarves?" spluttered Paddy at last, and Castor wondered at his astonishment, which was excessive for such an insignificant cosmic detail.

"Of course! It was a dwarf planet like Ceres or Eris. What other kinds of beings would you expect to find there? Giants! Be sensible please! It's an inevitable outcome of evolution."

Harris said coldly, "They aren't called dwarf planets for that reason. I suppose that gas giants are full of—"

"Hydrogen and helium whales!" nodded Castor.

Paddy shook his head. "I know for sure you lied. Your postcards were covered in chip and beer stains when they reached us, but you said there was nowhere near Southerndown to buy beer and chips, so you couldn't have posted them at that time."

Castor said nothing. Finally he shrugged.

He took a crumpled newspaper out of his pocket and began reading it while Paddy and Harris savoured their victory. Castor read the newspaper all the way through, from the front page to the back, then he put it down on the table. He yawned and his stomach rumbled. Reaching into one of his pockets he withdrew a tube.

It was made of glass and glowed like a neon sign. It said: CHIPS. Just like a sign in the average chip shop. Castor unscrewed one end and the light died. Then he tilted back his head and emptied the contents into his mouth. Straightening, he belched.

NEMO'S OMEN

"I have always enjoyed sending messages in bottles," said Castor Jenkins as he lifted his drink to his lips, "and I've been quite an innovator when it comes to the art of choosing a suitable medium and message. As well as throwing illuminated neon signs into the waves, I've often toyed with the idea of entering a bottle myself."

He gulped slowly and lowered his pint glass. "I'm now going to relate a story about the *other* inventor who lives and works in Porthcawl. He's a rival to Karl Mondaugen and some say he's no less clever and only a tiny bit dafter: I'll let you judge that for yourselves. It happened when I was a member of the local Nemo Club."

* * * *

Although Boppo Higgins was introduced to the entire membership of our society all at once, the inventor came prepared to instantly make a good impression. I remember it well. Attached to his arm was a device capable of shaking thirty hands simultaneously and he simply leaned forward and skilfully employed it for that purpose.

Some of the older members were dismayed by the whimsicality of the contraption. "I doubt *he* would have tolerated such a frivolity!" sneered Idris Gecko, jerking a thumb at the large portrait hanging on the wall directly above the fireplace.

"Merely a toy, gentlemen," conceded Boppo, detaching the automatic handshaker and laying it on the table.

But his eyes strayed to the indicated portrait and he nodded slowly. Captain Nemo returned his gaze impassively, blankly, as befits a dead man, or rather a man who has never lived. The nobility of the painted face, however, was indubitably real and inspiring. The artist who had rendered it had worked with unwavering respect, as if the subject of his study was a genuine demigod rather than a fictional character. This was secular art at its most religious.

Idris Gecko intruded into that paradox with a cough. "Toys are for children. Our society is an adult institution."

"I'm acutely aware of that fact," responded Boppo.

"Then why bring that gadget here?"

"A simple mistake. A minor error of judgement."

The other members murmured amongst themselves and I quietly bit my lower lip, for the ultimate responsibility for this encounter was mine. Membership of the Nemo Club was not a privilege to be regarded lightly and new members could only be proposed on the understanding that the member who made the proposal would be expelled if anything went wrong. I still felt confident about Boppo's abilities but it seemed I had miscalculated the present mood of the senior members, who clearly were disinclined on principle to swell the club's ranks.

The Nemo Club was in danger of allowing elitism to dominate its methodology. I ventured the observation that Boppo was not a crank but an experienced engineer, a man who made things happen, and that those things might well be great or even magnificent, as truly profound as the automatic handshaker was trivial, and that the patronage of our society would surely expand his ambitions.

"That is all very well, Mr Jenkins," sighed Idris Gecko, "but your protégé hasn't even given us a hint that he knows who Captain Nemo *was*. We advocate a set of unique ethics, we have precise political and social aspirations. Will this Boppo fellow contribute to the spirit of our institution and help it to evolve?"

"He seems just a mechanic," sniffed Caradoc Weasel.

"A sham," growled Paddy Deluxe.

"Perhaps even – an ignoramus!" sneered Frothing Harris.

This last insult was too much for Boppo. With an accusing glance at me, as if I had somehow betrayed or tricked him by bringing him here, he spoke bitterly and yet with an undertone of triumph. "Certainly I'm familiar with Captain Nemo. *20,000 Leagues Under the Sea* is one of my favourite titles. My house is full of books."

"He knows," I added uselessly.

"This is not enough. What else can he offer?" demanded Idris Gecko.

The inventor winked at the portrait, sharing a joke with the stern figure on the canvas. "I can build a fully functional replica of *his* vessel and I can do so in less than a week."

"The Nautilus?" cried Collective Will.

"The Nautilus!" echoed the other incredulous members.

"If you like," shrugged Boppo.

I disguised my own astonishment and wondered if the inventor had abruptly gone mad. His coolness was inhuman, his claim so implausible it was almost offensive. In less than a week? For an instant my faith in him faltered, then I pulled myself together and began applauding. For half a long minute my solitary clapping sounded thin and sad in the hall, but another pair of hands finally mimicked mine, then another. Caradoc was clapping now; so was Icarus Evans; and Paddy Deluxe and Frothing Harris added their own reverberations to the rhythm. At last even Idris Gecko, Collective Will and Sunstew Mynci joined in.

Boppo inclined his head slightly in a nod of appreciation.

"You will launch your vessel from the harbour at the exact same hour one week from today?" asked Idris Gecko as the applause faded, but it was a challenge rather than a question and Boppo was evidently bemused. He frowned deeply.

"As you wish. From the harbour."

"And the six most senior members of our institution will serve as her crew," specified Frothing Harris above the grumbles of the less hallowed members.

"Perfectly reasonable," returned Boppo.

"I'll also be coming along for the ride," I said quickly.

Idris Gecko raised an imperious hand to provoke a general hush. He pointed a yellow finger at Boppo's chest, as if to impale the inventor's heart on a long invisible fingernail. "If you fail to create a vehicle that can do everything the Nautilus did, in precisely the same way, the Nemo Club will exert its power and influence to hound you out of town, nor will Mr Jenkins be permitted to remain. Both of you will be exiled from Porthcawl forever. Do you understand?"

"We do," answered Boppo without consulting me.

It was decided to defer the question of the inventor's membership of the Nemo Club until after the maiden voyage of his craft. I accompanied Boppo to the door and rubbed my jaw anxiously as he set off into the night. There was no time to be lost, he explained, if the vessel was to be ready on the arranged day. He would have to live and sleep in his workshop until his version of the Nautilus was finished. As his figure diminished into the dim haze of distant streetlights, I heard him muttering ruefully, "Why the harbour?"

I returned to the hall and enjoyed the vintage brandy and soft chairs with the resignation of a man who strongly suspects they will soon no longer be available to him.

At no point during the following week did I meet Boppo Higgins. I knew better than to disturb him at work. Along the esplanade I strolled, casting my nets into the waves of high tide. I am a collector of messages in bottles as well as a sender of them, it's a hobby that serves to take my mind off my daily cares, but I discovered no new specimens over those seven fraught days. Finally the allotted time loomed and I made my way to the harbour, arriving fifteen minutes early.

Porthcawl harbour is small and quaint and dominated by the last gas-powered lighthouse in the country. Sleek and unbelievable, Boppo's submarine lay supine on the black water like a monster about to devour the brightly painted yachts that also bobbed in this liquid enclosure. Boppo himself was standing on his deck. The hatch on top of the conning tower was open. Seagulls wheeled.

"Castor!" he called as he spotted me. "Come here."

I eased myself down the rusty iron ladder bolted to the harbour wall and reached the deck. As I did so, the other passengers turned up, the senior six, Idris Gecko in the lead, though technically he had no more authority than the others. The Nemo Club was supposed to be dedicated to egalitarianism.

"Well now," said Idris. "So it was true after all!"

His tone was a complex audio wave that carried excitement, dismay, envy, admiration and irony all at the same time, but he descended to the deck and nodded

politely at Boppo. Then down came his colleagues. Caradoc Weasel snorted.

"Why have you written the words 'Nemo's Omen' on
the side?"

"It's the name of my vessel," replied Boppo.

"Not Nautilus? Why not?"

"Captain Nemo has already claimed that name. In his
honour I decided to call my own craft *Nemo's Omen*."

"But an omen is something bad, isn't it?"

"This name is merely a palindrome, it reads the same
backwards as forwards, that's all. A wordgame."

Reluctant to waste time with more idle banter, Idris
Gecko snapped, "Shouldn't we go below and commence
our great voyage?"

Boppo nodded and one at a time we entered the hatch
in the conning tower and descended into the riveted belly
of the vessel. Idris went first; followed by Caradoc; then
Paddy Deluxe, Icarus Evans, Collective Will and Frothing Harris. Then there was Castor Jenkins, who is me,
and finally the inventor himself, Boppo Higgins. We
stood together in the soft glow of ambient lighting while
Boppo secured the hatch from within. Our environment
was slightly less cramped than I had feared it might be.

"Gentlemen, I'm ready," said Boppo. "I'm not sure
why you insisted our voyage had to begin from the harbour. Departing from my own house would have spared
me the effort of conveying the vessel here."

"Of course it has to be from the harbour!" spluttered
Idris. "How else can we begin a journey twenty thousand
leagues under the sea? The word 'sea' is very important
in this case. Not that I mean to be sarcastic."

"I understand. My apologies."

"Hurry up! We're wasting time!"

"Very well. Brace yourselves, gentlemen," said Boppo.

And he pulled a smooth lever.

There was a slight shudder, a glow and a sparkle through one of the portholes, then stillness and silence. Boppo stood back and smiled. "We have arrived," he announced.

"What do you mean?" roared Idris.

"Is this some kind of joke?" bellowed Caradoc.

"Dear Boppo," I said as lightly as I could. "It seems there has been a misunderstanding. We are supposed to travel twenty thousand leagues in total, marvelling at the sights on the way and experiencing adventures, exactly as Captain Nemo did. It should be a protracted process, not an instantaneous one."

The inventor rubbed his jaw. "I see. For the sake of safety I deemed it better to cover the entire distance in less than one second. The engine is a type of matter transmitter. We have arrived now, so it's pointless to argue."

And he indicated the nearest porthole.

I went forward to it, peered out and blinked. I saw no fish.

"Stars!" I rasped. "Stars!"

"Starfish, you mean?" demanded Idris Gecko.

"Real stars!" I gurgled.

"What?" He roughly pushed me aside. "I don't believe it! The Earth is above us. We're in space! How did we get here?" He turned savagely on the inventor as his colleagues crowded the circular window. "What has happened?"

Boppo frowned. "I did what you asked. I took you where you wanted to go."

"You took us up – into space!" shrieked Idris.

"No, no! I took you *down*. Twenty thousand leagues under the sea. Naturally we passed right through the Earth on the way. The brief glow you witnessed earlier was the molten core of our planet. The sparkle was radiation from the Van Allen belts. But now we're in a stable orbit and I'm sure our altitude will remain fixed."

"Will you divulge your calculations?" I breathed.

He nodded. "Certainly. A 'league' is a somewhat archaic measurement that corresponds to three miles. So twenty thousand leagues is equivalent to sixty thousand miles. The diameter of the Earth is 7,918 miles, which means that our present altitude is 52,082 miles above the antipodes of the town of Porthcawl. We are therefore more than twice the height of the so-called Clarke Belt, the elevation of geostationary satellites. In fact we are higher than almost every other satellite that has ever been launched."

Idris collapsed onto a nearby chair. "Why?"

Boppo mistook his wail of despair for an authentic question. "Because there's little scientific, commercial or military advantage in sending satellites higher than the Clarke Belt. True, the Vela group of satellites were placed in orbits above 60,000 miles in order to monitor compliance with various nuclear test ban treaties, but they fell obsolete decades ago. Currently the only operational satellite higher than us is the Solar and Heliospheric Observatory in orbit around the First Sun-Earth Lagrange Point, the point between the sun and our own planet where there is gravitational balance between the two bodies, approximately 879,975 miles higher than we are..."

"You fool!" spat Caradoc Weasel.

"Twenty thousand leagues horizontally under the sea, not vertically!" cried Frothing Harris. "The distance is supposed to be lateral. How could you make such a stupid error? You told us it was one of your favourite books!"

Boppo looked confused. "I said it was one of my favourite *titles*. I never claimed to have read it."

He glanced at me for support.

"You haven't read it!!!" I screamed.

He pouted. "I based this vessel on the picture on the cover."

There was a long silence.

Finally Idris said, "You must take us back now."

"Yes – back home!" I cried.

Boppo arched his eyebrows, stroked the lever set into the wall, shook his head slowly. "No reverse gear."

"What did you say?"

"Exactly that. Nemo's Omen doesn't go backwards."

"So we're entombed in this metal coffin until the air runs out and we all suffocate?" demanded Paddy.

"Oh no!" laughed Boppo. "That won't happen!"

We all laughed too, nervously. "Won't it?" The desperate entreaty in our voices was tangible. "Are you sure it won't? Quite sure?"

"Absolutely," said Boppo. "We won't get the chance to suffocate. At this altitude we are above the magneto-sphere, the magnetic force field that protects the Earth from lethal doses of solar radiation. To be more precise, we are within the magnetosphere at this moment but won't be for much longer."

"Kindly elaborate," I urged.

"Well, on the side facing the sun, our planet's magnetic field extends to a height of 43,496 miles, which is

8,586 miles lower than we are. On the Earth's dark side the field extends twenty times further than that, because the solar wind doesn't compress it. The magnetosphere is an enormously stretched teardrop shape, in fact. But to return to my original point, we won't have time to asphyxiate because as we orbit the Earth we'll emerge into the full force of the sun's gamma rays. The hull of my vessel isn't adequately shielded and we'll all be baked alive."

"How could you do this to us?" I stammered.

His reply was infuriating. "A simple mistake. A minor error of judgement." Then he smiled innocently. I realised at that moment he would never be accepted as a member of our club. And my own dismissal was imminent.

As if reading my mind, Idris Gecko said, "In that case I suggest we quickly convene a meeting to correctly attribute blame."

"Good idea!" cried Boppo.

"What's wrong with you? Don't you realise who is responsible?" I hissed.

"Certainly," he replied. "The guilty party is Jules Verne, author of the book in question. He had a duty to make the meaning of his title more obvious. I suggest we ban him from future meetings!"

I rolled my eyes in exasperation and retreated to a quiet corner while the senior members of the Nemo Club voted unanimously to heap all the blame on the shoulders of the inventor and myself. I believe that two thirds of it went to Boppo and the remaining third was awarded to me. I can't be sure because I was only half listening. I had discovered a few sheets of paper and a pen lying on a desk.

All my life I have sent and collected trivial messages in bottles. Now it was time to write an important one, the very story before you. This manuscript is the message and the interior of Boppo's vessel must serve for an empty bottle. How it will ever reach a shore is beyond my conjecture but if you are reading this now, and I feel sure you must be, then clearly it did. That's a consolation.

Far away on Earth, an abandoned automatic handshaking machine has probably started clapping.

Or thumbing a nonexistent nose.

* * * *

Castor finished his tale with a sigh and drained his glass to the bottom. Then he looked around at his audience; he was amazed to discover that he had been speaking to nobody.

He sat alone at the table in the pub. The two chairs on which Paddy and Harris usually perched were both empty. Castor looked out of the grimy window at the night sky.

Among the twinkling stars, a tiny point of steady light moved without fuss through the constellations.

"Ah, now I remember! They haven't managed to get out yet!"

THE THOUSAND AND ONE PINTS

TRANSLATED FROM THE ORIGINAL THESPIAN BY RICHARD BURTON, NOT THE EXPLORER BUT THE OTHER ONE, THE DRUNKEN WELSH ACTOR.

A dreadful clattering noise woke Castor Jenkins and he climbed out of bed and went to the window and looked out. Somebody was driving a combine harvester through his garden.

It wasn't a full sized harvesting machine, of course, for his garden was rather modest in area; but it was undoubtedly real. The man who operated it was dressed in a tattered black cloak.

Castor opened the window and shook his fist.

"You've cut up all my leeks!" he shouted, but his voice wasn't audible above the din of the mighty engine.

He walked back to his bedside cabinet and picked up a vase that stood there; it was a birthday present or heirloom, he couldn't remember which, and then he returned to the window.

Taking careful aim, he lobbed the vase at the machine. It smashed into fragments against the side of the combine harvester and a few pieces of shrapnel ricocheted into the driver.

He gave a start, looked and saw Castor. He killed the engine and in the abrupt silence he craned his head up and cried, "I've come for you at last, Mr Jenkins. Sorry I'm a year late."

"I wasn't expecting you," replied Castor.

"Really? That surprises me. May I come inside for a moment? I won't delay you for long. I'm very busy."

Castor wrapped himself in a dressing gown and went down to open the back door. The hooded figure entered and offered his host a smile, but the fact he had no lips spoiled the effect.

"I know who you are, of course," said Castor.

"My fleshless skull gave me away, did it?" sighed the stranger; and his empty eye sockets seemed forlorn.

"What happened to your scythe?" asked Castor.

"Oh that!" said Mr Reaper.

"You replaced it with a combine harvester?"

"Yes, yes, naturally; we all have to move with the times. No one reaps anything with a scythe these days."

Castor considered this statement critically.

"Volunteers for certain conservation groups do; they scythe bracken. I heard about it from an acquaintance."

"Have *you* used such a tool, Mr Jenkins?"

Castor shook his head. "I don't care much for blisters."

"You don't like physical toil of any kind, do you? And that's one of the main reasons I've come for you."

Castor nodded. "I suppose I *am* out of shape."

"Too much beer, too many chips, not enough exercise. Well, I'd like to chat longer but it's not possible, my schedule's too tight, so why don't we get it over with? Step outside…"

"You want to mangle me in the blades of that contrivance? No thanks. I'll stay in one comfortable piece."

"There's really no choice for you, Mr Jenkins."

"I don't imagine there is. I've read that fable, I think Cocteau did a neat version, about a servant who met you in the garden one morning and ran to his master with the words, 'I saw Death and he gave me a threatening look. So please lend me your fastest horse so I can be in another town by nightfall'. I don't recall which town—"

"Esfahan," said Mr Reaper.

"Yes. Anyway, the servant gallops off to Esfahan and the master goes into the garden and meets Death and says, 'Why did you give my servant a threatening look this morning?' and Death says, 'It wasn't a threatening look but one of surprise, for I was amazed to see him here in your garden when I knew I was due to collect him in Esfahan tonight.' Pretty neat tale, huh? I always admired that story."

"I've heard it too many times," said Mr Reaper.

"Sure. But you did like it the first time, didn't you? The very first time you ever heard it?" pressed Castor.

Mr Reaper rasped, "Probably. But it didn't really happen in Esfahan. I don't know how that came about."

"Where did it take place then?" asked Castor.

"Bognor Regis, I think."

An awkward pause. Castor broke it by saying, "You must have known a lot of famous people in your time?"

"All of them," said Mr Reaper.

"Well, if you like tales, why don't you let me recite you a selection of my own? I could tell you about—"

Mr Reaper held up a bony hand, palm outwards.

"I don't wish to be rude, Mr Jenkins, but I'm wise to nearly every trick in the book; I have read the *Arabian Nights*, so if you were planning to do a Scheherazade then think again."

Castor shuffled his feet. "I wasn't intending to begin a story but draw it out, and then immediately start a new one, and so on, etc, as some sort of delaying tactic. Honest I wasn't!"

"I believe you, Mr Jenkins, I really do."

"Interesting case I heard about last night, though, in the pub. Might as well tell you. It's an anecdote, not a story. You know how traditional Irish dancers move their legs but not their upper bodies; and Jamaican dancers move their upper bodies but not their legs? Well now, it seems there was an Irish mother and a Jamaican father who had twins and the twins grew up, and guess what? One of them danced by moving their legs and upper body simultaneously; the other danced by failing to move at all. And that was the only way to tell them apart."

"Fascinating!" yawned Mr Reaper.

Castor sighed and looked at the floor. Then he said, "I see there's no point making things difficult."

"None at all, Mr Jenkins; none at all."

"Would you like a beer?"

"I don't have time. We must be going now."

"Fair enough. I just thought you might like to sample one of the beers in my collection. My cellar is full of quality beers from around the world. It's a collection I have built up over decades. I don't think anyone else in Wales has such a selection to hand."

"Really? Now that is interesting. But I'm afraid—"

"Thousands of bottles," added Castor.

"But how many varieties exactly?" frowned Mr Reaper.

"I only have one bottle of each."

"You are joking, surely? You don't mean that—"

"Yes. I have a single example of every beer brewed by every brewery in the entire world. I even have some from the planet Antichthon. Which reminds me: do you have jurisdiction over that world too? I've wondered about that ever since I went there."

"No, that planet is pruned by my colleague, Mrs Mirg."

"Is she also a skeleton?"

"Yes. She reads too many fashion magazines."

"They *are* a bad influence…"

"Maybe I have time to tour your cellar."

Castor ushered him to the door that led to the spiral staircase and down into a gloomy underground chamber that was cluttered with bicycle parts, washing machines, obsolete vinyl albums, ledgers full of indecipherable scribbles that might be poems.

"I don't see beer. Is this a trick?" growled Mr Reaper.

"This is just the ante-cellar. Please step under that arch and you'll enter the main cellar," insisted Castor.

Mr Reaper did as he was bid and emerged into an even gloomier room with walls covered with white web-work.

"Nitre?" asked Mr Reaper.

"Nitre," said Castor. "How long have you had that cough?"

"Cough?" Mr Reaper was bewildered.

"Come," said Castor, with decision, "we will go back; your health is precious. You are rich, respected, admired, beloved; you are happy, as once I was. You are an entity to be missed. For me it is no matter. We will go back; you will be ill—"

"No I won't. Don't be silly. Lead on!"

"These vaults," said Castor, "are extensive. The Jenkins were a great family. Do you forget my arms?"

"They're connected to your shoulders."

"Not these arms: I mean my coat of arms! Do you forget them? Glass of foaming beer sable, slurped by a pair of lips gules. And the motto? *I'll have another for the road, old son!*"

"You jest!" exclaimed Mr Reaper, recoiling a few paces. "But let us proceed to the beer stash! You don't happen to have a bottle of Abbaye des Rocs Brune, 9% ABV, near at hand, do you? I love those Belgian double-fermented warmers. Seven different malts in that one, three kinds of hops, and lots of raw spices."

Castor searched among the cobwebs, found the bottle, passed it over. Mr Reaper opened it with his bony fingers, drank it thoughtfully, nodded and grinned. "Toffee apple and prunes," he said. "Just how I remember it from holidays in Montignies-sur-Roc!"

"Good," said Castor. "It's rather a strong one."

"Yes, yes, but flavour isn't sacrificed for strength! What's that there? It looks like a bottle of Der Weisse Bock, 7.2% ABV, from Bamberg. Dark wheat beers don't come finer than that one: chocolate and pears are tangs to be found within its smooth excellence! Let me taste it! Ah, a delight on the tongue; and I don't even have a tongue, so imagine! Germanic beer is the equal of Belgian. And what's this one? Schlüssel Alt, 5%, a fine clean beer of authentic heritage. Yum!"

"I must confess there's no order to the way they are stored. It's a purely random arrangement," said Castor.

"Worry not! Worry not! What's this? Finlandia Sahti, 8%. A beer from colder climes, filtered through juniper berries. A hue like a misty morning and a flavour like arctic bananas!"

They proceeded deeper into the dank cellar.

Mr Reaper paused often, as certain labels caught his attention, and he asked for Castor to fetch that bottle for him. "This is a superb New World drink, a beer from

Denver, Colorado: Old Aged Yeti Imperial Stout, 9.5% ABV, a brew hearty enough for Sasquatch!" He drained the bottle, threw it upwards into the air with a gesticulation Castor didn't understand. Then he repeated the movement, a grotesque one. "You comprehend not? You are clearly not of the brotherhood."

Castor scratched his head and blinked. "How?"

"You are not of the alkies."

"Yes, yes," said Castor, "yes, yes. An alky!"

"Impossible! A sign!"

"It is this," answered Castor, producing a pint glass from beneath the folds of his dressing gown. It was one of those dimpled glasses with a handle that were so popular, almost ubiquitous in fact, back in the long lost 1970s. Mr Reaper took the offered glass and examined it for many moments with squinting sockets.

"You jest! Nonetheless I will drink from it."

"Yes, that's a much more civilised approach," agreed Castor. "Glance over there, if you will. Notice something odd? A beer from Africa! Hansa Urbock, 7% ABV, with a chewy malt profile. Hard to believe it originates from so hot a country as Namibia!"

Mr Reaper filled his pint glass and tasted.

"Surprisingly delicious! Do you have any other eccentric beers? Wait, I see something from Ramallah, of all places! Taybeh Golden Beer, 5% ABV, a crisp pilsner. Interesting!"

"You can't be a proper country if you don't have your own beer," said Castor. "I've always believed that."

"I recognise the quote. Who said it first?"

"Frank Zappa, the musician."

"Yes, he did. Well remembered! Look!"

He pointed a gnarled finger and Castor reached for the dusty bottle it was aimed at, opened it and filled the glass. Mr Reaper sighed with sheer delight. "Red Macgregor, 5% ABV, from Orkney. Toffee and plum and a hint of heather. Astounding! Scottish beers are grossly underrated, in my view. It slips down without fuss."

"Would you like to try a Welsh beer?" asked Castor.

"But of course! I'm unbiased!"

Castor fetched him a bottle of fruity dark ale with the strange name of Dark Side of the Moose, brewed by the Purple Moose Brewery in remote Porthmadog. Although only 4.5% ABV it had lots of bite and Mr Reaper appreciated this fact. Then he sampled another, slightly stronger Welsh beer, Ysprid y Ddraig, 5.5% ABV, from Brecon in Powys, an ale that is stored in whisky barrels for three months before bottling; during its time asleep in the barrels it absorbs a mix of flavours including vanilla, pears and cloudberries. After that, Mr Reaper stayed with the Celtic theme and drained a pint of Okells Aile Smoked Porter, 4.8% ABV, from Douglas in the Isle of Man, a pure brew that includes hints of liquorice and coffee in its dark substance. Smack those lip bones!

"You certainly know how to enjoy life," he said.

Castor bowed. "I believe I do."

"I suppose you always keep in mind that famous advice to live each day as if it's your last? Don't you?"

"Absolutely not!" cried Castor.

Mr Reaper frowned. "What do you mean?"

Castor sighed. "If I lived each day as if it was my last, I'd be a nervous wreck every hour of my existence, constantly fretting about the following morning and my oncoming death! I would spend all my time writing my will and saying goodbye to friends; and I would do this every single day without fail for the rest of my life!"

"When you put it like that... It doesn't sound so wise."

"Never live each day as if it's your last! That's the most ludicrous thing anyone ever said. Live each day as if you can live forever! That's a better suggestion! Live each day as if—"

"This really *is* your last day, though," Mr Reaper said.

Castor swallowed dryly, smiled with difficulty and guided his guest to the next beer, a bottle of Montegioco Draco, 11.5%, a strong barley wine from Piedmont in Italy. Immediately after, he took Mr Reaper to a corner where a bottle of Samichlaus stood. At 14% ABV this is one of the most potent beers in the world; brewed only on one day of the year, December 6th, and matured until the festive season of the following year. The bottle was more than a decade old. Mr Reaper drank it all down in one. Then he smiled and reached forward to shake Castor's hand. He was unsteady now and stumbled as he stepped closer.

"More beer!" he bellowed. "I want more beer!"

There's no point listing every single beer that Mr Reaper drank. In fact he drank a total of one thousand and one pints. Castor kept careful count and was finally very relieved when Mr Reaper quaffed his last drink and blinked his sockets and belched a mighty belch and embraced his host in his old skeleton arms and slurred:

"Youz my besht friend!"

Before collapsing in a heap on the damp stone floor, his bones coming apart and spilling out of his puddled cloak... For anyone who is curious, it can be reported that the beer that finally finished Mr Reaper off was the honey-coloured, hop-heavy Jihlavský Grand, 8.1% ABV, from the Czech Republic, one of the beeriest nations of all. Castor chucked with triumph, turned to leave the cellar and said:

"I have killed Death by alcohol poisoning!"

A figure materialised before him.

It was a man with long hair and a straggly beard who stood on one leg like a stork and raised a flute to his lips.

Castor frowned. "You're not his replacement?"

"No, I'm not; not at all."

"You're not a sort of meta-Death that comes to collect Death when he succumbs to his own reaping?"

"Nope. I'm Life, the opposite of Death."

"Do you have a proper name?"

"Call me Mr Tull, if you wish." The stranger studied his surroundings and noted the vinyl albums. "Living in the past!" Then he said, "I've come for you and I don't get drunk easily, so you can't trick me as neatly as you tricked naïve Mr Reaper over there."

"He didn't get drunk easily either," said Castor.

Mr Tull played a trill, lowered the flute and said, "I don't have time for chatter. My seed drill is waiting."

"Seed drill?" muttered Castor.

"Certainly. I once carried a brand new ploughshare about with me, but we must all move with the times."

"Death swapped his scythe for a combine harvester."

"A wise move; and I use a seed drill. Follow me and I'll take you to it. Too late for regrets! It was an old day yesterday but it's a new day now! I hope you won't try to be awkward?"

"If you are Life, are you going to reincarnate me?"

"No. The buck stops here."

"That's Death's job and Death has been slain."

"Yes and now I have to cover for him. I give life and what I give I'm entitled to take away, and that's how it'll work from now on. You have doubled my workload, Mr Jenkins!"

He raised the flute to his lips again and this time Castor was unable to resist the tug of the music. They both went dancing like jesters deep into the cellar, into a dark region of the underground labyrinth that Castor had never dared explore. There was no beer this way. No cobwebs. No bones. Just a wholly unsatisfactory ending.

CELEBRATION DAY

It was a perilously fine day for a celebration: the weathermen had lied again. Frothing Harris threw back the curtains and planned revenge. If only he could get his hands on one of the rascals! But how do you recognise them? What does a weatherman look like? Do they believe their own forecasts? That at least would make it easier.

He pictured a figure, oilskins and sou'wester, straining its way down the street under the hammer of the sun. He pictured his own rain, a rain of blows, as he accosted the muffled fellow outside the post office. Probably he would use his umbrella as a club. And each plum bruise raised would be proof of an absolute justice…

But no, the umbrella in question must stand idle next to the fireplace. Quite new, purchased the day before in trust, it would never be associated with the glory. A poor start to this most eagerly awaited of mornings! True, Harris hadn't relished the prospect of holding it erect for hours or flapping it at any seagull that dared disturb his nostalgia, but a needless purchase was a worse concept.

There was no stability in the world. None. He sighed and lingered over shaving and dressing and breakfast with precise motions that suggested the regular clockwork of his life was powered by an overwound spring. He bared long teeth not his own.

I should be grateful, he thought bitterly. We are old, we have been left behind, the blossom has fallen off our knotty limbs; but at least we have today. Our time has come again. Briefly, so briefly. He drained his cup of bitter chicory and stood in the hallway, buttoning his blazer in the myopic mirror affixed to the wall.

His pencil moustache had been trimmed back to nothing: it was faith alone that kept it there now, a hint of a nimbus above his lip, owl-white. Adjusting his cravat, he winked a rheumy eye at his reflection, opened his front door and stepped smartly into the day.

And rebounded off the postman...

Letters flew like chopped up words in all directions. Harris steadied himself and cried, "Fifty years ago. Today."

"What?" The postman regained his own balance and scratched a fleshy earlobe. Then he shook his head slowly, crouched down and retrieved his dropped catch, passing a small bundle to Harris, who accepted it with a magnificent, arrogant scowl.

The old lusts were flowing into his blood again. He could almost taste his youth. A high smoky rain above Simla; the snakes twisting beyond the veranda; a curry in khaki.

"Don't you remember?" He felt the muscles in his jaw rubbing against each other. "Don't you know? What we did for you, all of you, back then! Don't you care?"

The postman shrugged, shouldered his sack and walked away. Harris glowered at his back. Not enough time to fetch his catapult and stones from the attic, unfortunately!

In his attic was a tea chest stuffed full of the toys of a long life. Once a month he unlocked it and rummaged around in the gloom and carefully inspected what his bony hands brought up from its depths and wondered how the devil such stuff came into his possession. Hookah, swordstick, tigers' whiskers...

The catapult with the bag of special stones was in there too, and the stones were smooth red pebbles from the mouth of the Ganges; sticky with the oil of sins that had been washed off the devout over the entire length of the river. A fancy.

His attention was wandering again. Not good.

"Fifty years ago. Half a century. Thanks to us this town… Without us it wouldn't be… Heroes, we are."

He continued muttering as the letters fell from his hands one by one. Bills, a few promotional leaflets, one wrongly addressed postcard. Not a single message of congratulation amongst them! How could this be? It was strange, almost uncanny.

"Postal workers on strike again, I don't doubt, delaying all the most important mail, can't be any other explanation. Well, it's time to fetch Paddy, I guess. Already late."

Out on the street he flexed his limbs and winced as his joints replied with aches, a dialogue he refused to extend into a fully blown argument because there was no reasoning with the pains of decrepitude: they won every time. He proceeded down the pavement with his customary lurch, refusing to hunch his shoulders.

"Anniversary today," he informed a woman who was pushing a pram in the opposite direction. "Sure to be a big celebration on the esplanade. Fireworks and brass band. Fifty years since." And when no reply was forthcoming, he added, "Children welcome. We kept the future safe for the little ones. All for them, it was."

But the woman was gone, increasing her speed as if escaping a beggar or lunatic. Harris huffed. The ignorant lower classes: breeding like hot cakes! With no respect for their elders, for history, heritage or culture. Drug addicts, most of them, bodies crawling with unearned tattoos: none had sailed the seven seas. That din they called music, mindless pounding. Outraged I am, he told himself.

He turned the corner and still failed to observe any preparations for any street party. No flags, bunting, balloons. No row of tables covered with overlapping tablecloths so that it seemed a single immensely long trestle had been inserted into the street like a ramrod into a thin musket, the kind Afghans used, ornate, accurate. The blighters! He frowned. *Who* were the blighters? Who?

Not the Afghans, that was certain. No.

The blighters were the people who lived in this street. Ignorant asses also. Fifty years ago he and Paddy...

It occurred to Harris that an elaborate deception might be in progress. Perhaps the mayor had arranged this silence, this emptiness, this absence of excitement, in the same way that friends sometimes pretend to forget an important birthday, clustering in the house of the victim, lights off, waiting to cry "Surprise!" when the dupe enters. An explanation plausible in the extreme. And yet.

Too playful for the seriousness of the occasion.

Could the mayor, already notorious for his hatred of jokes, risk such a stunt? Surely not. "Happy celebration day! Fifty years!" called Harris to another pedestrian. "Grand occasion."

The pedestrian snorted in return, not viciously but as if in reflex to a riddle too bothersome to solve. "Ungrateful world, this one," grumbled Harris. "Not long to go, thankfully."

Further along he accosted another bystander with the words, "Yes it's me. In the flesh. Fifty years later."

But the bystander expressed no delight whatsoever.

Paddy Deluxe lived in the little house on the corner of the next street. Harris rang the antiquated doorbell, waited less than a minute. Paddy loomed in his own blazer as the door opened, elegant, almost regal, but with a faint odour of salad about him.

"Why the celery epaulettes?" blurted Harris.

Paddy answered, "The pact we made. When the fiftieth came round, we said. Symbolic of what we did."

A shadow crossed the face of Harris. "I forgot! Totally slipped my mind. You're right, old chap."

"Am I?" Paddy was now racked with doubts.

"Leave them on, please," insisted Harris, though Paddy had made no effort to remove them. "The symbol's too important. Celery. Yes! Clever of us to think of that, to make such an association with what we did, with our achievement, our act."

"I'm feeling shy now," confessed Paddy.

Harris pinched his cheek. "A shy hero: the best kind! That's true and it's a fact that won't change in the next fifty years. Fifty years! Can you credit it? So much time to pass."

"Buckets of it," agreed Paddy unhappily.

"My idea is this," said Harris as he mopped his baldness with a silk napkin. "We won't go directly to the esplanade but via the cemetery. Pay our respects to Castor first."

"But he wasn't really part of what we did," pointed out Paddy with a sour smile. "He wasn't with us all the way fifty years ago. He could have been but chose not to. He declined."

"I had forgotten that." Harris was stupefied.

"So let's not trouble ourselves about Castor. Leave his grave in peace. For some other time," suggested Paddy.

"You're right, of course you are. How stupid of me! He simply doesn't deserve to be included now."

"It was you and me," said Paddy.

"Fifty years ago, on this day, this very day. How *very* can a day be? This day must be more 'very' than any other. All other days are some or more, not very. Less very, at the most."

"Just us two. The heroes. Pair of. A credit to our town."

"Will there be statues, unveiled?"

"Of us? Today? Ought to be, even if there isn't. Statues on pedestals for what we did. Are you listening over there?"

"Dumb oafs, the lot of them. Met enough today. Did you tune the radio to the news? Anything about the anniversary, our fine celebration? How many dancing girls?"

"Curiously silent," frowned Paddy.

"Atmospheric static, I shouldn't wonder," opined Harris.

"It was an FM station. Frequency modulation, that stands for. Is less affected by disturbances in the…"

"Come on, we're wasting time," said Harris.

Off they went. The sea was visible between the shoulders of tall white houses. This was where the wealthy lived and some of them were sitting on wicker chairs on their balconies, eating rich breakfasts. Jam spreading, spoon tinkling, sugarcube plopping: it was a life of luxury up there, high on those platforms that extended like frowning brows over gardens full of tendrils and fashionable blooms.

Harris and Paddy took it in turns to shout upwards.

Chins jutted in reply, nostrils flared, eyebrows arched. Or else there was no reaction at all. Bespoke disdain, high maintenance contempt. The rich snub not as we do, vocally, but with facial angles alone. Each to his own. And there the sea, not really a sea: an estuary of the widest river in the country. A low line of cliffs on the other side, blue and hazy. Yachts and tankers interposed. Sandbanks.

"Shall we stop for a drink first?" Harris suggested.

"A little early, isn't it? The pubs aren't even open. Do you think they'll open especially for us? I *do* need lubrication. Dark beer, foaming at the corners of the mouth. Or is that rabies? Always get them mixed up. A full pint of ale for each drained hero!"

"Let's try this one. Come on, let us in!"

"Open up! Open up!"

"We used to come here with Castor, didn't we?"

"To play cards. Yes."

"Open up, you foul hibernator!"

A window rumbled, a beefy face appeared, stubbled cheeks, nose of a pig, jowls of an ox. The most basic kind of landlord, with a tongue that could drive flywheels, if necessary.

"What do you codgers want at this hour of the morning? Bugger off, you miserable alcoholic tramps!"

Harris continued to pound and kick the locked door.

"Open up! Open up!"

"Wait a moment: I'm coming down. Where did I put that cosh?" cried the landlord and his head vanished.

Harris and Paddy waited to be admitted, grinning.

Bolts slid back, a heavy key turned, the door creaked open. And there stood the landlord, twice as large as his head had led them to believe, a bottle of stout in one hand, a fist in the other, a short length of lead pipe thrust in the belt of his trousers.

"Sick and tired of nasty little men like you coming round here at all hours causing grime and nuisance."

Harris and Paddy exchanged amused glances.

"My dear chap, don't you recognise us? Must we twirl? Would do if our bones weren't sore. All the same."

The landlord snorted. "Never seen you before."

"Ha ha! You jest, surely you do. For we are heroes, the greatest within a radius of 115 miles, and today's our day, the fiftieth anniversary of what we did. That's quite clear."

"Something to do with the war?" squinted the landlord.

"War?" snapped Harris. "Certainly not! It has nothing to do with war! It was much bigger than that!"

"*Fifty* years ago, we said," added Paddy.

"What war happened fifty years ago?" demanded Harris. "And don't be clever and quote some obscure conflict in Africa. What we did was of vital importance to *this* place!"

Paddy gazed at the clutched bottle of stout. "Is that for us? Why only one bottle? Whatever happened to generosity? I remember how it used to be. Back then. If a fellow came along on a tricycle selling chestnuts and burst his front tyre and scattered his wares in a roadside ditch... Well, the people would rush from the houses, pick them up, every last nut and chest accounted for, return them. None go missing. Just an example, nothing to do with real life, my father... And we made our wine from the flowers of the fields, fruits of the forest..."

He began to sob on the shoulder of Harris, who shook him gently but hissed urgently, "Don't go getting Bradburyesque on me now, old chap. Keep your chin up. Lip stiff!"

"The upper, not the lower," mocked the landlord.

Paddy quickly regained control of himself, adjusted his tie, swallowed twice, blinked and returned a dry gaze to the bottle. "I'll ask you one last time. Is that meant for us?"

"Certainly," admitted the landlord. His thumb was over the mouth of the bottle. Now he shook his hand vigorously, removed his thumb, took care to aim the frothing spray equally at both figures, seeking out those little gaps between clothing where bare flesh might be drenched with the greatest return of shivers.

Spume everywhere. Paddy and Harris jumped.

"On the house," explained the landlord. He slammed the door, leaving the empty bottle spinning on the ground. It stopped and pointed towards the sea. The two men took its advice.

"My epaulettes are ruined!" Paddy moaned.

"And the ink is running on the backs of my hands!" Harris spluttered as he held them up to his friend.

"I don't comprehend," answered Paddy.

"You can't even make out what the pictures are supposed to be now. All that effort for nothing!"

"What *are* they supposed to be?" wondered Paddy.

"Hands. We agreed on the symbolism together, didn't we? To remind us of what we did when we did it."

"You drew hands on your hands? Wouldn't it be easier just to look at your hands as they already are?"

"Suppose it would. Doesn't matter now," sighed Harris.

"I forgot to draw hands," said Paddy.

They walked on in silence. Around the next corner was the esplanade. So far there was no commotion, no crackle of anticipation in the air. The brass band clearly hadn't started yet, nor the slap of feet of dancing girls, but soon they would. Perhaps when the heroes appeared in person. And then it would be unleashed: the tears and jelly of children, the crunching handshakes, rough but affectionate backslaps, whistle of rockets, buzz of kazoos, fawning of the mayor.

They quickened their steps, doddered faster, more efficiently, came to the turn, wheeled round. Nothing.

Not quite nothing: a few strollers, aimless. A dog. The usual esplanade business. Small waves quietly eroding a rocky beach. Wispy clouds. The gleam of the pavilion in early sun.

"I don't believe it," gasped Harris. "They can't have forgotten, it's just not possible. Beyond all reason."

"A trick, must be. Some kind of practical joke."

Harris groped forward, clutched the railings, hung his head over them, stamped his feet in turn. "Fifty years."

"An illusion, I tell you!" persisted Paddy.

"Don't be absurd. *This* is reality: the shocking neglect of tradition, the loathing of the old values, of heroes, the advent of cynicism and apathy, the end of civilisation. How could this massive and deep emptiness be a mirage? Who might construct such a travesty of a celebration day? No power on earth is cunning enough…"

"You're wrong. Mondaugen could do it."

"Karl Mondaugen, the mad inventor? Yes, why not… He has devised a machine to mask the crowds, to veil the festival. He never liked us, was always friendly with Castor. I bet Castor arranged this with him before he died. A projection of some kind. Holograms. How do we switch it off? The mayor *is* here and the people…"

"But we can't see them. Yes. The only explanation."

"All here, behind this screen, beyond the mirage. Cut the air with your arms, like this! Shred the illusion, reveal the truth! I want to be applauded and admired. Standing ovation."

"We deserve it. For what we did. Our sacrifice!"

"Let's force him to turn it off. Twist his arms, break his legs. Like we had to do once before. To that fakir. A high smoky rain above Simla. Not Simla, India, but Simla, Wales."

"I think it's spelled Cimla," said Paddy.

"I don't doubt. But now. To Mondaugen's house! Full speed ahead, full anger, full bitterness, full pride!"

"Make way for the vengeance express!"

"That's the spirit! Wine from flowers of the fields, you say! Do you mean dandelions? A diuretic, so I've been informed. Got a lady drunk once. Not on wine. On gin. Her bloomers gave me blisters. Or was it the other way around? Lost days."

"The past is another country. So is Hungary and Surinam. Have I used that joke before? If not me, someone."

"Hurry, hurry! Twist that sneak's foreign nose. I even thought poems would be written about us, dramas performed, films acted. Maybe they have been in the *real* world, behind this three dimensional screen. Fifty years today. Valorous, us!"

"Have you developed a stutter, dear boy?"

"Not yet. Is it too late, do you think? Onward! Let's ask this little girl if she wants my autograph…"

"I don't believe she does. Nor mine. To be frank."

"Shocking language from a child! When I was her age I did anything a stranger asked me to. It was expected. Same went for you, I imagine. Yes of course it did. Tradition."

"The world has gone to the dogs. The dogs have gone to the cats. The cats to the rats. A *ratastrophe*!"

"Worse. The rats have gone to the foreigners."

"Mondaugen lives here. Let's ring his bell, force our way in, make him wince! Damn hologram projectors! Smash the bleeding thing on the floor.

Get an apology from him, cash also."

"Tell me, did you get any mail this morning?"

"Not a single letter expressing gratitude or wishing good luck! What sort of a projector can do that?"

"Mondaugen's a sly devil. A genius too!"

The door swung open slowly and the desiccated face that peered out resembled a dried mango slice so accurately that Harris and Paddy licked their lips without wanting to.

"Yes, yes?" rasped the inventor. "Yes, yes? Do you want something? What business have you with me?"

Harris and Paddy barged forward, yelling and thrusting Mondaugen aside with the shoulders of unsung heroes, always harder and less well rounded than those of the sung variety. The inventor yelped, collapsed into a corner, his fall broken by a machine that made cushions and spat them out under falling men. But the impact destroyed the machine and its cushions remained unborn.

"Where is it? Your damn projector?" cried Harris.

"Projector?" croaked Mondaugen.

"For your bloody foreign holograms!" shrieked Paddy.

"I don't know what you mean... Please don't touch anything! These machines are very delicate! The product of decades of research! All of them prototypes, irreplaceable!"

"What's this?" roared Harris as he nudged one device off a table with his elbow and kicked it to bits.

"An odour amplifier! That's what it was! Helped people with weak noses to smell better. Like a hearing aid for nostrils. A bit cumbersome right now, the size of a bloodhound. In some ways it *was* a bloodhound, highly modified. Ruined now!"

"And this?" growled Paddy with a punch.

Glass tinkled, springs sprouted. "A bubble car for a tree! It's a little known fact that of all living things trees are the finest trackers, superior to bloodhounds or Apaches..."

"Bloodhounds again!" cried Harris.

"The man's obsessed!" remarked Paddy.

Mondaugen regained his feet, rubbed his bruised buttocks. "A tree can follow a fugitive's trail across an entire continent years or even centuries after he has fled, but until now they've never been able to utilise this skill. Because they can't move."

"And what are all these? Don't you ever clean?"

Mondaugen was frantic. "Don't break them! They have nothing to do with spiders. They are artificial webs designed to catch bottles of vintage wine. Have you never noticed how the best wine cellars are full of bottles covered with cobwebs?"

"Several times I've observed that," conceded Paddy.

Mondaugen stumbled forward. "Clearly vintage wines fly around like flies and blunder into the webs when nobody's looking. That's the only logical explanation. I've made the process more efficient. My synthetic cellar webs will ensure that even the poorest people can enjoy the delights of rare wine. Imagine!"

While he spoke, Harris shredded every strand with uncut fingernails on the ends of wildly waving arms.

"What's *this*?" demanded Paddy.

"A bicycle!" squealed Mondaugen. "With a hollow frame. The pedals are connected to a pump that fills the frame with compressed air when the cyclist travels on level ground. When he reaches an upward slope a valve opens and the air is released."

"And helps power the bicycle uphill?" frowned Harris.

"No, activates a device that writes begging letters to a firm of mining engineers requesting that the hill be removed with gelignite. Don't spin the wheel backwards! Too late!"

As if electrocuted by a hidden discharge, by bolts of indoor lightning, the two heroes continued to thrash and smash their way through the home of the eccentric inventor. Splinters. Shrill scream of metal against metal. Mad sparkle of scattered crystals. But the projector would not show itself, was probably hiding behind one of its own holograms, the same way the man who sells masks at a carnival wears a mask too, to make untraceable his responsibility for transformation.

Maybe not like that. Too demented to care.

The inventor fell to his knees, clutched their ankles, but in the frantic minds of Harris and Paddy he had fallen to his ankles and was clutching their knees. Debris littered the floor, litter also. Everything was a blur, except the blurs, which were in focus. Wires uncoiled like the snakes of a gorgon's hair during a bagpipe concerto. Awful carnage. Enough to make the toughest robot weep.

They reached the back door, blustered through, smashing the things of the garden, karate chopping sunflowers, uprooting cabbages, continuing to a fence that was demolished with senile headbutts until they suddenly found themselves in a back alley that took them away from that house of awful innovation and down other alleys and streets to a shady park where a bench waited to receive them.

Torn and stained, they sat slowly, more than merely fatigued. They were beyond aches and beyond disillusionment. Was the curry really in khaki or was it in beige? None of that seemed to matter now. The betrayal was total. Then Paddy mumbled:

"What exactly *did* happen fifty years ago?"

They looked at each other. "I just… I mean that my memory… I can't seem to… I don't…" he added.

Around them the world pulsed, moving one second at a time from the oblivious past to the eternal present, taking that past along with it like a gigantic suitcase stuffed full of creased items, groping towards a future it could never reach, expecting to be stopped and searched at any moment for those things no longer permitted. Tradition, respect, gratitude, dancing girls. All confiscated by fate.

"Neither do I," growled Harris.

www.ingramcontent.com/pod-product-compliance
Lightning Source LLC
Chambersburg PA
CBHW021235250626
47155CB00008B/3018